MW00935874

ZEPHYR STONE
AND THE MOON MIST GHOST

KATHRYN LOUISE WOOD

BLUE INK
PRESS

This is a work of fiction. Names, characters, places, brands, media, and incidents are either the product of the author's imagination or are used fictitiously. Any resemblance to similarly named places or to persons living or deceased is unintentional.

Published by Blue Ink Press, LLC

Copyright © 2021 by Kathryn Louise Wood

All rights reserved.
No part of this book may be reproduced in any form or by any electronic or mechanical means, including information storage and retrieval systems, without written permission from the author, except for the use of brief quotations in a book review.

ISBN: 978-1-948449-09-0
Library of Congress Control Number: 2020945674

To my husband, William Francis Ahearn,
with my deepest love and gratitude
for his patience and unwavering support of my dreams.
"It's never too late to live happily ever after."

[1]
B.G

LIFE WAS SIMPLER BEFORE THE GHOSTS SHOWED UP. IN
the B.G. (Before Ghosts) era, twelve-year-old Zephyr Stone
thought her biggest challenge would be enduring a boring,
three-day weekend at her Grandma June's house in the boonies
of southern Virginia. A house with no Wi-Fi and no cell
service, which left her pretty much stranded in the middle of a
cyber desert beside the creepy, drippy, aptly named Great
Dismal Swamp.

After goodbye hugs and see-you-Sunday kisses, Zephyr's
parents dropped her off at her grandma's house Friday morning. She spent the day helping Grandma June prepare enough
food to feed a hungry army, even though it was just going to be
the two of them and Zephyr's dog, Sam. At least her grandma
hadn't said it was to fatten her up. Zephyr was getting tired of
grown-ups reminding her of how thin she was compared to her
height. It wasn't like she didn't eat. She ate all the time!

That evening, she stuffed herself with the fruits of their
day's labor and carried the used dinner dishes to the kitchen

sink before bending down to hug her grandma goodnight. At five-foot seven, she actually stood several inches taller than Grandma June, who often described herself as vertically challenged and horizontally gifted.

"Goodnight, sweetheart," whispered her grandma, squeezing her tight then letting go and stepping back to look up into Zephyr's emerald-green eyes. "I'm so glad you and Sam came for a visit while your folks are away at their meeting in D.C."

Zephyr smiled. "Me too, Grandma."

Heading down the hall to her dad's old bedroom, Zephyr followed Sam, his beagle-belly bulging with "accidentally" dropped morsels as he trotted ahead, ready for his own good night's sleep. Closing the door behind her, Zephyr upended her travel bag onto the bed. She took quick stock of everything she'd packed and began to organize, stuffing her clothes in a drawer and placing her Nintendo Switch and stack of games on the desk. Reaching into the bag's side pocket, she pulled out a large envelope addressed with her name.

Seeing her best friend Lorie's messy scrawl on the envelope, Zephyr shook her head, her mouth curling into a sideways grin. Since Lorie's bicycle chain had broken a couple of weeks ago, she'd asked Zephyr if she could borrow her bike for the Friday-to-Monday fall break weekend while Zephyr was in "swamp prison." Zephyr had found the envelope just after sunrise earlier that morning when she'd leaned her bike against the canoe rack behind Lorie's house. Now, as she pulled out the two items Lorie had left in the envelope, Zephyr experienced the same reactions she'd had when she'd first discovered them.

She giggled again at the sheet of paper completely covered with the words "Thank you," written multiple times in every color ink imaginable. The second item, though, sent a strange, shivery, electric sensation prickling up her spine, just as it had that morning when she'd first seen it. A long, white plume with a second note from Lorie attached to the base of the quill quivered in her hand as she reread the note.

Zephyr,

A really big egret hung out on the dock at sunset last night, and when it flew away, it dropped this feather. Made me think of you, don't know why.

Lorie hadn't had any way of knowing that Zephyr had actually been awakened the night before by a silver light streaming through her white curtains. Gazing down now at her sleeping dog, she recalled how Sam's tricolored coat had gleamed metallic in the luminous glow. Her room had been so bright, she'd wondered at the time if their neighbor had put up some kind of new security light.

Zephyr had rolled out of bed and pulled her curtain aside to investigate the source of the light. Rather than finding an irritatingly bright security light mounted on her neighbor's house, she had instead seen a fat moon, gleaming in the sky directly above the canal behind her North Carolina Outer Banks home.

The moon's beams had reflected on the dark water that flowed all the way to the Albemarle Sound. And there, perched on their dock railing in the center of the moon's spotlight, had stood a snowy-white great egret. It had been strange to see it there instead of roosting in a tree for the night.

She remembered how she'd watched as the tall bird had unfurled its five-foot wingspan and had basked in the moonlight, as birds normally did in the warmth of the sun. Then, tucking in its wings and bending its long black legs, the egret had leapt into the night sky and soared in a wide circle above the canal. Zephyr had watched, mesmerized, but then had instinctively ducked as the bird's graceful arc sent it flying toward her window. Just at the last moment, though, when she had been sure it would come crashing through, the egret had pulled up and disappeared overhead like some kind of feathered, nocturnal, crop-dusting plane.

After slipping Lorie's gifts back into the envelope, Zephyr shook off the odd, tingling sensation she felt and pulled out her ponytail band, releasing her bright-red hair to fall down her back, nearly to her waist. Squinting at her reflection in the dresser mirror, she wondered if it was time to get a haircut. A summer's worth of freckles, not yet faded with the shorter autumn days, stared back at her.

Grandma calls them angel kisses. Huh. Must be a whole lot of angels assigned just to me, then.

Zephyr changed into her nightgown and fell into bed beside Sam. "I wonder how Mom and Dad are doing at their business conference," she whispered to her snoring dog. "I bet *they've* got internet. And cable. And good cell phone service." Sam did not dignify her grumbling with a response. Breathing a sigh she felt from her toes to her nose, she closed her eyes and dropped like a stone into sleep.

After what felt like only moments later, a high-pitched half moan, half wail startled Zephyr awake. She lay still, eyes wide, listening. Silence. Maybe just some super-realistic dream had woken her up, she thought, trying to make sense of it. But then...

Scratch, scratch, scratch.

[2]
THE MOON MIST

Either Grandma June had some really big mice or else it was–Zephyr rolled onto her side facing the bedroom door–yep. It was just Sam.

She sighed. "Geez, Sam, really? I knew I should have taken you out one more time before we went to bed." She pushed herself up on one elbow. "OK, keep your spots on. Let me get my shoes." As Sam thumped his tail in response on the hardwood floor, Zephyr found her sneakers and jacket and slipped them on. "OK," she whispered, zipping up her coat over her nightgown. "Now stay quiet. We don't want to wake up Grandma."

When she opened the door, Sam made a beeline for the kitchen and slurped up a few gulps of water from his bowl before trotting over to the back door. In the soft illumination of the stove's nightlight, Zephyr saw Sam's body wagging from nose to tail. Her fingers fumbled as she tried attaching the leash clamp to the ring of his collar, but his enthusiastic wriggling made it next to impossible to get a good grip.

"Hold still!" she rasped into his floppy ear. Sam sat down

on her foot as his tail whomped against the tile floor. "OK, now focus on what we're going out there for. I want to get back to sleep before the sun comes up!"

Zephyr unlocked the door and pushed it open to a world she'd never seen before. A glowing, white mist enveloped the backyard. The fog was so thick, she couldn't see where the grass ended and the forest began. She breathed the cold moisture into her lungs, feeling little separation between the inner world of her body and the outer world around her. As she turned to push the door shut, it seemed Sam could wait no longer, because he suddenly performed one of his infamous beagle bolts. Distracted by the otherworldly atmosphere, Zephyr had not been prepared for that particular canine maneuver and watched as the dog leash flew from her hand, and Sam raced away into the misty whiteout.

"Sam!" she called, her voice small and flat against the cottony air. "Come here!" she demanded as she stepped away from the comforting solidity of the house and into the swirling whiteness. Within a few footsteps, she could no longer see the house at all. "Sam! Where are you?" Following the muffled jingle of his dog tags, Zephyr strode forward, irritation warming her against the cold night. She didn't know which annoyed her more; Sam, or her own neglect in not having walked him after dinner.

"Come on, Sam! Get back—" Her foot caught on something and she sprawled face forward onto the damp ground. For a few moments she lay in stunned stillness, feeling the mist prickling her face and moisture from the ground seeping into her clothes. Pushing herself up, she staggered to her feet and brushed brown, decaying leaves from her coat and bare legs. Her hair hung damp and dark against her face. Tucking the slick, red strands behind her ears, she felt the heat of anger drain away like a receding tide, replaced by the creeping chill of anxiety.

"Please Sam, you're scaring me now."

From behind her, a rustling caught her attention and she whirled to face it. Nothing. Spinning back toward the fading tinkle of dog tags, she realized she was completely disoriented in the milky fog. A cold breeze whispered across the top of her head, raising the hairs on the back of her neck. Zephyr folded her arms, hugging them close to her body. A muffled beating of the air swept by her ear as something brushed against her cheek. Leaping sideways, she nearly fell back down into the wet carpet of leaves. *What was that? A bat? An owl?* Arching one arm over her head and stretching the other ahead of her, she inched forward.

Oh Sam, she thought miserably. *Where are you?*

Straining her ears for any sound of her dog, Zephyr continued in what she hoped was the right direction, stepping carefully across the slippery leaf bed beneath her increasingly damp sneakers. Then–*sploosh*–she sank ankle-deep into a puddle. *Ick! Just what I needed!* Pulling her foot from the sticky mud, her skin crawled as a curving ripple slithered through the water away from her.

"Ach!" she screamed. *A snake! A snake! Maybe a cottonmouth!*

Zephyr stumbled backward, bumping into a tree trunk. Grasping it for support, she worked at controlling her shallow, rapid breaths. *Passing out is not an option, Zephyr!* Using her drama teacher's calming method to ease the hyperventilation of stage fright, Zephyr closed her eyes and focused. With each inhalation, she pulled air in through her nose, filling her lungs and expanding her abdomen, then slowly exhaled through her slightly parted lips. After several shuddering breaths, she began to feel her respiration and heartbeat return to something a little closer to normal. Stepping away from the tree, she kept her eyes on the ground, hoping to avoid the nightmare contact of murky swamp water.

"Sam! Come on, boy!" Although her dog couldn't see any better than she could through the blanketing mist, she knew his sense of smell was about fifty thousand times stronger than hers and he should be able to track down her scent. *Unless this wet air interferes with that particular canine superpower...*

Zephyr clapped her hands. She thought the vibration of clapping might carry better than her voice, which was getting progressively weaker and softer as her anxiety rose, effectively clamping down her vocal cords.

Clap, clap, clap! Clap, clap, clap!

She stopped suddenly and listened. Somewhere, maybe to her right, she thought she heard a knocking, like someone hitting a stick against a hollow log.

Clack, clack, clack! Clack, clack, clack!

Then silence. With a deep intake of breath, she realized the sound was a perfect imitation of her clapping.

"Is somebody there? I can't find my dog!" She clapped again.

Clap, clap, clap!

Within a heartbeat, she heard the responding *clack, clack, clack,* but this time, the following silence was punctuated by a childlike giggle. Zephyr froze in place. Grandma's stories about cypress knees turning into dancing wood elves at midnight shot through her mind. When Zephyr had been little, the knobs of wood poking out from the mud and water surrounding the tall cypress trees were kind of scary looking to her. Some were almost as tall as her four-year-old self had been. Grandma June had tried to make her feel better by telling her a local legend about the knobs, known as knees, actually being little wood elves. She remembered now that it hadn't actually made her feel much better.

No. Cypress knees are just skinny cones of wood jutting up from the roots around cypress trees. Not stupid elves, she told herself firmly, pulling her focus back to the present.

Clack, clack, clack!

The sound grew louder and closer, although she still had no idea which direction it was coming from. Another giggle erupted at the end of the clacking. It also sounded closer, but less childlike this time—more like an adult mimicking a child. Zephyr stuck her trembling hand into her coat pocket to retrieve her cell phone but, touching the empty cloth bottom, remembered she'd left it plugged into the charger inside the house. *It probably would have been useless out here anyway.*

She heard a low, half-hearted growl rumble ahead of her. "Sam? Is that you?" *Or is that a bear?* A fresh chill washed over her. Then a familiar whine floated toward her through the mist. "Sam! It *is* you! Where are you, boy? Come! Come to me!"

Crazed giggling tittered beside her and Zephyr ran blindly forward. *Got to be some kind of weird frogs. Weird, giant, Great Dismal Swamp frogs!* Pushing away the bizarre image of wood elves or gigantic frogs, she stumbled toward the whimpering she prayed was coming from Sam.

Clack, clack, clack...clack, clack, clack. The beating stick was joined by several others, all striking in different rhythms. *Clack, clack, clackity, clackity, clack, clackity.*

More snickering voices joined the first one. Zephyr felt as if she were trapped in some kind of horrible, swampy, carnival funhouse. She pressed her palms over her ears and the outward sounds faded a little, but the pounding pulse of her heartbeat continued to hammer inside her head. Tears squeezed from Zephyr's tightly clamped eyes as she crouched down close to the boggy earth. Then, all went quiet. Not a clack, not a giggle, not a growl, jingle, or whimper. Only the whooshing rhythm of her own blood pumping through her veins.

Zephyr slid her shaking hands away from her ears and stood back up. A baying yowl bugled a few yards away. If she hadn't known better, she would have been certain some horrific swamp creature was attacking Sam. But she was flooded with relief, knowing that bloodcurdling half yodel, half bark was his normal response to something exciting, not terrifying.

"Sam!" Zephyr saw a slight disturbance in the mist ahead of her. "Sam! I'm here, boy!"

Sam continued his maniacal wailing, making it easy for Zephyr to locate him. Just as his howl dropped back to a whimper, Zephyr saw him and rushed to embrace his quivering body.

"Oh, Sam! Thank God I found you!" She hugged him close, kissing the top of his head. "Don't you ever do that again!" she cried, as tears streamed down her face, sliding onto his damp hair. "Sam?" she said, realizing he was still whimpering and not greeting her with his usual enthusiasm. "What is it, boy?" she asked and followed his unwavering gaze into the distance.

A tiny luminous point of soft green light glowed through the white mist. *What is that?* The light grew larger. Its rays, diffused in the mist, formed an outer halo around its center. Zephyr took a step backward gripping Sam's leash in both hands. He sat unmoving, solid as a rock, staring at the light. Maybe it was somebody with a flashlight. Maybe Grandma June had seen they weren't in their room and sent someone out to find them. Maybe it *was* her grandma.

"Grandma! Is that you?" Silence hung as thick as the mist around them. "Grandma? We're over here!" The light grew closer, but no one called back. Zephyr tried to pull Sam away, but the beagle wouldn't budge.

"Hello? Who's there?" Zephyr's hands shook as she reached down, grasping him by his collar and tugging. "Come on, Sam! This doesn't feel right. We need to move!" His response instead was to lie down on his stomach, head up, ears pricked forward, eyes staring at the ever-enlarging light. Then Zephyr heard a quiet sound break the stillness.

[3]
THE GHOST

IT WAS A FAMILIAR SOUND BUT IN THIS STRANGE, MISTY world, it took Zephyr a moment to remember where she'd heard it before. She closed her eyes as she knelt beside Sam, listening to the subtle *sloosh* followed by the gentle splatter of water drops. Then, it came to her. It was a memory of sound from the last time she and her dad had gone canoeing together. They'd pushed off from their dock at first light, paddling a canoe down the canal and into the quiet sunrise of Albemarle Sound. The memory calmed her a bit as she listened to the comforting, familiar sound of the water being smoothly sliced by a paddle and cascading back to its source.

Not knowing where she'd go or how to hide anyway, Zephyr decided to hold her ground as she opened her eyes and looked up, still clinging to Sam. Out of the mist, an even brighter whiteness bloomed behind the green light. Crystal water drops glittered in the light as they pattered down in a steady rhythm, a rhythm driven by the steady beat of a paddle slipping into water. But how could that be? The trees were too dense, and the water was far too shallow near Grandma's for a canoe. *No way I could have walked all the way to Lake Drummond looking for Sam. That's miles away!*

Zephyr shook her head as she saw the outline of a shimmering white canoe, followed shortly by the sight of a paddle dipping and pulling up luminous water. Gradually, two slender hands appeared, one gripping the shank of the paddle and the other pushing down from the grip. The glowing canoe slipped ever closer as the green radiance materialized into a lantern filled with light the color of frosty, green sea glass. Now she could see the hands extended from bare, slender arms that gleamed ivory in the ethereal glow.

Two more strokes brought the unearthly canoe within a few yards of Zephyr, then the paddle was pulled from the water as the boat glided several feet to a stop. Zephyr squinted. The canoe wasn't floating on a body of water at all. It was floating on a ribbon of mist. The paddle rested across the lap of a young woman wearing a snowy-white suede tunic, with long fringe hanging from the edges of her shoulders and knees. As the canoe slipped nearer, the woman's form grew a bit more solid, although the filmy air still blurred her outline as though she wasn't completely emerging from that translucent world. Peering closer, Zephyr saw that a necklace of seashells encircled the woman's swan-like neck, and white feathers peeked out from her waist-length, black hair.

Zephyr stared in disbelief. *I've got to be dreaming. This can't be happening.* The woman's large, almond-shaped eyes met her gaze. In those dark eyes, Zephyr saw a mixture of tenderness and sadness that clutched her heart and, although she was still shaken by the overall strangeness of the situation, she also felt relieved of some of the fear that had gripped her so tightly. Glancing down at Sam, she saw he was alert but calm. None of his alarm signals had been set off by this surreal vision.

The woman extended her arm forward, palm up, delicate

fingers gently curved. "Please. Can you help me?" she said, her soft voice colored by an unfamiliar accent.

Help you? I thought I was the one needing help. Zephyr swallowed hard, trying to pull words from her constricted throat. "I don't know. We're lost, ourselves."

"I am not lost," the woman said, smiling. "But," and her smile dissolved, "my child is lost from me. I have been searching for him for so very long."

"Oh wow, that's awful! How old is he?"

A frown of concentration creased her wide forehead. "I think my husband would say he is two years."

Ignoring the oddly worded response, Zephyr asked. "Is your husband out here searching too?"

The woman drew in her lips and closed her eyes. After what seemed a lifetime, she opened her eyes and spoke as a tear glistened down her cheek. "No. He has gone away. I have not seen him since before our baby was born."

The heat of sudden anger flared within Zephyr. "What? He just left you? What kind of man is that?"

The woman shook her head. "No! He is a very kind man. He only left because my father made him leave, and we did not know I was with child. You see, my husband is not like me. He is English. We were married in secret and my father threatened to harm us both when he found out. My people are of the Nansemond tribe who moved west to the Nottoway. The other Nansemond, the ones who married the English and took on their ways, live here by the great swamp."

What? What century is this? The eighteenth? She can't be talking about modern times. Zephyr looked at the woman's clothing. *Wait a minute. Could she be...could this be...* "Um, wh-when were you married? What year was it?"

The woman's face brightened. "Thomas taught me some of your ways and how to speak English. My people do not measure time in the same way as you, but he told me we were married in the year 1702."

Zephyr felt her brain imploding and all the air escaping from her lungs. She shook her head, realizing her unbelievable suspicion must be true. A ghost! She was standing face-to-face with a real, live ghost! She wrapped her arms around Sam's comforting warmth as the apparent apparition continued.

"He said we would celebrate our marriage each year on the date we were joined. Only,"—and her smile faded away once more—"I do not know when the day comes, and he is not here to tell me."

Sadness swirled around them like the mist, overshadowing the eeriness. Despite the supernatural circumstances, Zephyr found herself asking a perfectly natural question. "How did your son get lost?"

The ghostly figure sat up straighter and leaned forward. "When my little Ahanu was old enough to walk, but not yet speak many words, I took him to visit my cousin who lives with her English husband near the swamp. On the way, I grew very tired and the sun was so warm. I lay down by the great lake and closed my eyes to rest. I did not mean to, but I fell asleep, and it was not until the coolness of the setting sun that I awoke and saw that my little boy was gone." She covered her face with her hands and rocked from side to side.

Zephyr didn't know what to say to a ghost who'd been searching for her lost child for over three hundred years. "I'm so s-sorry," she stammered. That sounded pretty lame and inadequate, but she was at a loss for words. She tried to think of something, anything else, to say. "Um...my name is Zephyr. What's your name?"

The ghost lowered her hands, placing them back onto the paddle still resting in her lap. "My name is Kanti."

"That's a really pretty name. Oh, and my dog's name is Sam."

"You gave him a name? A name like a person?" Kanti smiled. "I like that," she said, the hint of sweet laughter in her voice.

"He's very good at tracking things down. We can look for Ahanu—if we ever get out of this fog."

Am I actually telling a ghost my dog can sniff out another ghost? Oh well, it's the thought that counts, they say. And maybe I'll wake up at Grandma's and realize this is all a dream. Or... wake up in a hospital because I've lost my mind.

[4]
SCAM

"Thank you, Zephyr!" said Kanti. "No one has ever really helped me before. Some said they would, but once we parted, I never saw them again." Looking down at her lap, she continued, "And, it seems, my time of seeking help is nearly gone. It is all so strange but, tonight, a woman appeared before me as though she had come from the mist itself. She told me I must be at peace by the time of the next full Beaver Moon."

Raising her eyes back to Zephyr's, she said, "If I am not, I must continue searching on my own with no help from anyone else ever again." Kanti's smooth brow creased and she shook her head. "I do not understand why this is so, but I know in my heart that it is, just as I know I only find people, like you, during nights near a full moon."

Zephyr frowned. "That's not fair! You're his mother. You should be able to get all the help you want finding him."

Kanti smiled. "You are kind, like Thomas, and I have a gift for your kindness. On the shores of the lake, there is a tree stump shaped like a great flying bird. Reach inside and you will find the coin Thomas placed there in honor of our love. I hope you can find Ahanu and bring him to me but, even if you cannot, I want you to have the coin. It is all I have to offer you."

A glowing, gray-striped head popped up from behind Kanti and Sam whimpered.

"A cat!" cried Zephyr. "You have a cat!" *A ghost cat?*

Kanti grinned and nodded. "Our people do not keep cats, like the English do, but this one leapt into my boat as I was searching for Ahanu, and he has been good company to me."

Zephyr hugged Sam closer to her. "I understand. I don't know what I'd do without my dog."

The ghost cat's white-tipped tail flicked from side to side as he placed his gray paws on the rim of the canoe. Zephyr felt Sam's muscles tensing. "It's OK, Sam. He's just a cat. Just like our neighbor's that you love to play tag with...sort of..."

An excited beagle yodel burst through the quiet stillness and Sam bolted from Zephyr's embrace straight for the spectral canoe. The cat sprang from the boat just as Sam jumped toward the phantom feline.

"No, Sam!" cried Zephyr, watching in horror as the cat's shimmering spirit flew straight into her dog's body as Sam leapt through the air and into the canoe. Suddenly, there seemed to be two Sams and no cat; one was standing solidly on the swampy ground and one was swaying in the canoe. With their soul-deep bond, Zephyr knew the real Sam was the one trying to find his balance in the otherworldly boat. Glowing now like the cat had been before, Sam shook himself as though he were trying to shake off water.

"Sam!" called Zephyr, running toward the canoe. "Come on, boy, come back!"

Kanti raised her hand, palm forward. "No, Zephyr! You must come no closer or you will not be able to return home."

"But, Sam!"

Sam stared wide-eyed through the mist at Zephyr and

whined. He placed a glimmering paw on the side of the canoe, then pulled it back. Feeling a feline-like bump against her leg, Zephyr looked down at the creature who looked like Sam, but was no longer really her dog, staring up at her. "Help me fix this," she pleaded with Kanti.

Kanti placed her hand on Sam's back, and though he still gazed at Zephyr with longing eyes, he appeared to grow calmer and his pitiful whimpering stopped. "If you can discover what has happened to my child, I will be able to return for your answer. Sam will stay with me until then, when he and Cat may be able to exchange their spirits back. Now," she said, placing the paddle blade into the billowing mist, "I must go. May all the spirits of the earth and air guide and protect you, Zephyr." She smiled softly. "I will take good care of Sam, and I know Cat is safe with you."

Tears welled in Zephyr's eyes and spilled over onto her cold cheeks. "Don't worry, Sam. I'll find out what happened to Ahanu and I'll be back for you." She wiped her hand across her eyes. "You be a good boy," she whispered, the words choking in her throat.

Sam's spirit whimpered softly as the shimmering canoe floated backward away from her. Rising unsteadily to her feet, she watched until the canoe faded and only a small green dot penetrated the mist. Then it blinked out of sight like a firefly turning off its light for the night.

She looked down at the cat trapped in her dog's body. "What do I even call you?" she asked. "Sam? Cat? Both?" Zephyr felt a ragged sigh fill her shaky body. She reached down and stroked the soft beagle head. "How about I call you *Scat,* or maybe *Scam.*" The familiar brown eyes gazed up at her with an unfamiliar inner light. "*Scam.* How about that? Scam work for you?" The black nose rubbed against her hand. "Scam, it is."

Zephyr raised her eyes and looked into the enveloping mist. "Now what?"

A beating of wings startled Zephyr and she looked up quickly just as a large, white egret flew up from behind them. As she turned around to watch it soar away, she noticed the mist dissipating with each stroke of the great wings. "Come on, Scam. Follow that bird!" The egret soared low overhead, trailing silvery moonlight in its wake. Zephyr gripped the dog leash and ran to keep up.

Within a few moments, they arrived at Grandma's back door. Zephyr looked up to see the bird circle once above them before it flew off into the night. Just as she lowered her eyes, she noticed a glistening white feather floating down. It landed softly on the ground directly in front of her. She stooped to pick it up, then gratefully opened the door into the welcoming warmth of her grandma's kitchen.

"Keep quiet," whispered Zephyr as they stepped inside.

Scam went straight for the water bowl, gulping the water so loudly that Zephyr was sure it would wake up Grandma.

Huh. He knew right where to find it. He must have some of Sam's memories.

When he finally lifted his head, water streaming from his muzzle, Zephyr tugged the leash and led him to their room. After pulling off her wet sneakers and hanging her coat over the back of a chair, Zephyr exchanged her damp nightgown for a long T-shirt and fell into bed beside an already curled-up Scam. She placed her hand on his back and felt a rhythmic rumble.

"Oh, my gosh. Are you purring?" Zephyr asked him, before shaking her head and closing her eyes. She wondered if she'd even be able to get back to sleep, but the physical and emotional exhaustion of the night's adventure plunged her into an immediate, deep slumber.

The smell of frying sausage worked its way from Zephyr's nostrils to her brain, demanding attention. Opening her eyes, she saw the bedside clock's red digits announced that the time was 9:05 a.m. She stretched her arms overhead and yawned. *Wow. That was some dream last night.* She shook her head as she sat up on the edge of the bed. Zephyr smiled when she saw Lorie's feather resting on the desk, deciding that must've been what had triggered her dream in the first place. *Hmm. I thought I'd put it back in the envelope, though.*

She felt the tiny hairs on the back of her neck prickle as she reached for the envelope that was sitting beside the lamp. She slipped her finger under the flap and peeked in. There, she saw Lorie's rainbow-colored thank-you note and...another white egret feather. She looked at the sleeping, brown and white-spotted form nestled within the blanket. The second feather could only mean one thing – she hadn't been dreaming at all.

Oh, Sam.

[5]

TELLING GRANDMA

"Everything alright, honey?" asked Grandma June, peering at Zephyr over her reading glasses as she cradled her warm tea mug in both hands. "You're mighty quiet this morning."

Zephyr looked up from her plate, its blueberry pancakes swimming in hot butter and maple syrup. Should she tell her what had happened? Would she be upset? Would she think her granddaughter was nuts? Zephyr lowered her head and swallowed a mouthful of blueberry goodness to give herself time while she decided how to respond. She glanced back up across the round kitchen table at her grandma's concerned expression.

"I'm OK. I just didn't sleep very well."

"Oh, I hope that mattress hasn't gotten too soft or lumpy. It's been a while since anyone's slept on it. And I know it's often hard to get to sleep the first night in a different place. I always have trouble the first night myself. Maybe—"

"No, Grandma. The bed's very comfortable and I got to sleep just fine. I even got back to sleep really fast, after..."

Grandma June tilted her head to one side and set her mug

23

down in the middle of the daisy design on her placemat. "After?"

Zephyr drew in her breath and gazed at the buttery sunlight filtering through the white lace curtains framing the kitchen window. Everything looked so cozy. So...normal. She exhaled her reply. "After Sam got loose outside."

Her grandma looked sharply toward the corner where he sat beside his feeding area scratching his long, floppy ears.

"What? Sam ran off last night? Before daybreak?"

Zephyr nodded. "Yeah. I should have taken him out after supper, but I didn't, so around midnight, he started crying and scratching at the door to go out. I was actually afraid he'd woken you up."

Her grandma shook her head. "No. I didn't hear a sound. You know I've lost some hearing in my right ear, and if I'm sleeping on my left side, I don't hear much at all."

"That's good. I mean...I don't mean it's good you lost your hearing, I just mean–"

Grandma June chuckled. "I know what you mean, sugar pie. It's OK. I think I lost it from too many loud rock concerts in my misspent youth. I even remember the bands at our high school dances playing so loud that, on the way home, I'd feel like I had cotton stuck in my ears."

Rock concerts? Dances? Grandma?

"Don't look so surprised. I haven't always been this old!"

Zephyr felt the flush of embarrassment flood her face.

Grandma June laughed. "No worries, sweetie. I know. It's hard to realize I haven't always been a grandma. But I have to tell you, being *your* grandma is worth every gray hair I've got," she said, tugging at a silver-streaked strand of her ginger-red hair. "Now, tell me about last night. How'd Sam get loose? I wish you'd have woken me up so I could've helped."

"Well, it all happened so fast, and I got lost in the fog almost as soon as I got outside."

Her grandma's eyes widened. "You got lost? Oh, honey, you must have been so scared!"

"At first it was kind of beautiful. I opened the kitchen door, and everything was white."

"Ahhh. The moon mist."

"Moon mist?"

"Yes. It's unusual, but when it occurs, it *is* very beautiful. The world seems to just float with a luminous glow."

"That was it! But Sam ran off into it so fast, he pulled the leash from my hand as I was closing the door. And when I stepped away from the house to call him, I couldn't tell where I was anymore. The house just disappeared."

Her grandma looked back at the dog, now nibbling his sausage-enhanced kibbles in an uncharacteristically delicate manner. Every now and then, he dropped some on his own flowered placemat by the back door and tapped it with his paw. She shook her head. "I'm so glad you found him. A moon mist only happens when there's a combination of a full moon and low-lying fog. It's the end of September, so that was a big Harvest Moon last night. The moon shines above the mist and makes it glow, but since it's not warm like the sun, the fog doesn't burn off. It can be very disorienting."

"That's for sure. And I guess your eyes—and your ears—can play tricks on you, huh?" Zephyr looked down, focusing on the purple-stained pancake crumbs lingering on her plate.

Grandma June reached across the table and cupped Zephyr's chin in her hand, gently raising it until they were eye-to-eye. Feeling tears pool in her eyes, Zephyr sniffed hard to keep them from trickling down her face.

"Did you encounter something strange while you were out looking for Sam?"

Zephyr nodded.

Grandma June placed her hand over Zephyr's. "And you're sure it wasn't a dream you had after you finally got back to bed?"

Zephyr nodded again and pushed her chair from the table. "I'll be right back." She dashed down the hall to her room, picked up Lorie's envelope and the newly acquired feather, then hurried back to the kitchen. As Zephyr entered the sunny room, Grandma June stood at the sink, rinsing off the breakfast dishes and loading them into the dishwasher. Zephyr sat back down at the table and laid out the envelope and feather on her empty placemat, feeling her rapidly beating pulse thrumming within her throat. Grandma June closed the dishwasher and turned to the teapot beside the sink. Pouring herself a fresh, hot refill, she asked Zephyr if she wanted a cup. "No thanks," murmured Zephyr, her throat suddenly almost too dry to speak. "Maybe another glass of orange juice?"

"Certainly," said her grandma, opening the refrigerator and pouring out a tall glassful. After setting the glass down on the corner of Zephyr's placemat, Grandma June took her seat across the table and lifted her mug to her lips. Wisps of steam floated in front of her grandma's face making it hard for Zephyr to read her expression.

Well, here goes. I hope she doesn't think I'm crazy. But I just don't think I can keep this to myself.

Zephyr took a long swallow of orange juice to wet her throat and help settle her nerves, and then began. "OK. So, it actually kind of got started the night before when I looked out my window at the moonlight over our canal back at home." Taking a ragged breath and focusing her eyes on her juice glass, Zephyr proceeded to tell Grandma June everything. She shivered as she recalled the creepy *clack, clack, clack* noise and the peculiar giggling. She then detailed her unearthly encounter with the ghostly woman and her cat. Zephyr ended by holding up the two feathers in the warm morning light, raising her gaze back to her grandma's eyes for the first time since she'd begun spilling out her strange tale. "And that's how I know it all really happened, that it wasn't just a dream."

Grandma June, who had remained quiet for the duration of Zephyr's story, stood and came around to her granddaughter. She bent down and pulled her into a tight embrace, smoothing down her flyaway hair and kissing the top of her head. Zephyr wasn't quite sure what to make of that response, watching with wary eyes as Grandma June released her and moved back toward her seat.

"My brave girl," her grandma murmured as she sat back down across the kitchen table.

"So...you believe me? You don't think I'm crazy?" Zephyr felt a ripple of relief easing along the edge of her nerves.

Grandma June looked down at the beagle licking his raised paw with feline fastidiousness. "Of course I believe you, and I know you aren't crazy."

"Has anything like that ever happened to you, Grandma?" asked Zephyr, allowing the full flood of relief to wash over her.

"Well, I've heard about strange things happening on a moon mist night, but I have to tell you, I've never had enough courage to go outside on such a night myself. I've peeked out my windows at it and thought I saw things moving around in the mist, but never knew if they were real or just my imagination."

"What kind of things have you heard about? What did you think you saw?" asked Zephyr, leaning forward.

Her grandmother took a sip of tea and then set down her mug, staring into its brown depths. Wrapping her hands around the cup's smooth circumference, she looked up at Zephyr, pursing her lips. "OK. I haven't talked about this to your mom or dad because I didn't want them to think I was losing my mind, living out here by myself. Your grandfather and I never told your dad the old stories when he was growing up because we thought they were just tall tales and we didn't want to frighten him."

Zephyr felt her pulse accelerating. "I won't tell them," she whispered.

Grandma June gazed out the kitchen window. "I've heard that on moon mist nights, the spirits of the dead feel at home in the filmy atmosphere. It's like our two worlds are able to come together in the mist. I've also heard about people getting lost in the white fog, never to be seen again until they return as ghosts themselves on moon mist nights."

Zephyr waited, certain there was something else she wanted to say.

Still focused on the window, Grandma June continued, "After your grandpa died, I used to pray for a moon mist night in hopes I might catch a glimpse of him. But..." she bit her lip and sighed. "I was always too afraid to go out. So I just watched from the window instead. Every now and then, I'd see a disturbance in the mist, causing it to swirl as though it were following something moving around in it. Was it your grandpa's spirit? Or a bear? Or a trespasser? I never knew for sure." A tear slipped down her cheek.

This time, it was Zephyr's turn to stand and enfold her grandma in her arms. Grandma June patted Zephyr's arm, then gently pulled away. "But you see what this means, sweetheart? There truly is something to those stories, and your experience was real. If I'd told you about them before last night, I might have thought reality and fantasy got all mixed up in your mind, and the feathers were just a coincidence. But you didn't know. You had no idea. No preconception to color your imagination. I think you actually *did* encounter a ghost. A ghost asking for your help!"

The flood of relief Zephyr had felt now turned cold as a trembling shiver crept over her.

"Here," Grandma June said, placing her warm hand on Zephyr's goose bumpy arm. "Let me pour you a cup of hot tea and we'll think about what we should do next."

Do? What could we do? How can I ever find out what happened to a boy three hundred years ago?

But just as that thought crossed her mind, she remembered Sam's whimper and Kanti's sad eyes and knew she had to do something. For whatever crazy reason, she'd been chosen to help, and her dog was being held hostage like a supernatural ransom. She watched her grandma pour boiling water into a teacup.

At least she wouldn't have to do this alone.

[6]

LIZARDS AND TURTLES AND BEARS, OH MY!

"So what do you think she meant about the Beaver Moon?" Zephyr asked.

Grandma June sat down, pushing a cup of steaming tea toward Zephyr. "Every full moon has its own name and many of the names come from Native Americans."

"Really?" Zephyr asked, spooning glistening white sugar into her cup. "We learned about the phases of the moon in school and read about lunar eclipses and super-moons, but I never knew they had animal names."

"Well," began Grandma June, sitting back in her chair, "they weren't all named after animals. Sometimes they were given names related to human activity during a particular time of year. I know September is the Harvest Moon and October is the Hunter's Moon, but I'm not sure about the rest," she said. "Can you reach that *Farmer's Almanac* behind you? It has all the moon names listed."

Zephyr twisted around in her chair and saw the old-fashioned magazine lying beside a few pieces of mail on an old, whitewashed, wooden desk. Unlike her parents, Grandma June didn't have a separate office area in her house, so the desk next to the living room entryway had always been the center of her grandparents' household business. A memory of her younger self sitting and coloring at the desk while her grandmother did her kitchen chores warmed her, calming her nerves along with the hot tea. Stretching out her arm, she grabbed the almanac and handed it across the table.

"Let's see," her grandma said, flipping through its pages. "Ah. Here it is. OK, it says the full Beaver Moon is in November and named for the time that beavers are busy preparing their dens for the winter weather ahead. This year it will occur on the twenty-fifth. That's right around Thanksgiving."

"What? Thanksgiving? But that only gives us a couple months!" Zephyr bit down on her quivering lower lip. "That's not very long to find out what I need to save Sam." Fresh tears threatened to spill from her eyes. "I have no idea where to start."

Grandma June nodded. "I think we should go to the Great Dismal Swamp Visitor Center this morning. Maybe we can find something out about the tribes who used to live here long ago." Looking down at the dog snoozing in a patch of sunlight, she said, "Tell you what. You walk—him—while I do the dishes. Will you still call him, Sam?"

Zephyr followed her grandmother's gaze. "I've decided to combine the words cat and Sam and just call him Scam."

Grandma June tittered. "Scam? Like something pretending it's something it isn't? Oh!" she said, laughing again. "I'm sorry. I know this is serious, but that's perfect. Scam!" she said. His large round eyes rolled up at her in response.

Despite everything, Zephyr felt a giggle bubble within her. "OK, Scam. Let's go for a walk," she said, reaching for his leash.

"But be sure you hold on tight," cautioned her grandma.

"His cat spirit might not like the idea of being controlled at the end of a leash."

"No problem there, we had some practice on the leash last night. I just hope enough of Sam's memory is left so he knows he's supposed to pee outside," she said, slipping on the handle loop and wrapping the leash twice around her wrist for good measure.

By the time Zephyr brought Scam back inside, Grandma June was waiting with her coat on and car keys in hand. "Ready?" she asked Zephyr once she'd unhooked Scam's leash.

"Yep! He seemed to know what to do. Scam, you stay here and guard the house," she called over her shoulder before following her grandma to the door. Turning back, she saw him jump onto the couch and curl up, tail to nose. *Fat chance of any guard duty here today.*

They'd only driven about a mile when Zephyr saw a sign pointing to the Great Dismal Swamp National Wildlife Refuge Visitor Center. Grandma June turned off Desert Road onto a narrow lane, passing a wooden entrance display with a large map of the swamp. Sunlight filtered through the tall trees, dappling the ground, and birds flitted among the branches. From there, safely inside the car in broad daylight, it didn't seem spooky at all, or even *dismal*, for that matter.

The first thing they saw when Zephyr pulled open the entry door was a huge black bear staring directly at them. For a split second, Zephyr's heart stopped, but then her common sense returned and she realized they had nothing to fear from that particular bear. Although it looked so alive it might growl at any minute, Zephyr saw it was actually the handiwork of a skilled taxidermist. Not seeing a DON'T TOUCH THE BEAR sign anywhere, she reached out with tentative fingertips and stroked its coarse, glossy hair. It was actually very beautiful. Seeing it frozen in place like that gave her a whole new perspective on what she normally thought of as a scary animal. She looked into its kind glass eyes.

Poor bear. Wonder how you ended up here. Her eyes traveled to the bear's long black claws which clung to the display log. *Still wouldn't want to meet you out in the woods, though.*

"Pretty impressive, isn't he?" her grandma asked.

"Sure is."

"Can't believe I haven't brought you here before. Never seemed to be enough time, I guess."

"And Mom isn't exactly the outdoor type."

Grandma June laughed. "That's true. I know Jimmy's glad to have a daughter who likes to go canoeing with him."

The park ranger behind the desk looked up as they approached the counter. "Hello! Welcome to the Great Dismal Swamp," she said to Zephyr. Then, seeing Grandma, she added, "Oh hey there, June! This must be your granddaughter you've told me so much about. She's definitely got your red hair. But look how tall she is!"

"Yes, this is my Zephyr," said Grandma June, smiling up at her granddaughter. "I think she must get her tall stature from Charlie's side of the family. He passed it on to our son, Jimmy, and now Jimmy's passed it on to my granddaughter." Linking her arm through Zephyr's, she continued the introductions. "Zephyr, this is Ranger Doris. We're birds of a feather, you might say. Right, Doris?"

"Yep. Your grandma and I love to scope out the birds. Especially the ducks. Did you know there are eighteen different kinds of ducks here in the swamp?"

"I didn't know there were eighteen different kinds of ducks in the whole world," said Zephyr while she scanned the room full of exhibits.

The two duck lovers chuckled and turned back to each

other. "June, did I tell you I spotted a canvasback the other day?"

"Really? Where?"

Ranger Doris pulled out a map and spread it out on the counter. While the two ladies put their heads together over the map and chatted about ducks, Zephyr investigated the wildlife displays. There were stuffed owls, ospreys, eagles, turtles, foxes, beavers, snakes, lizards, and countless more. A question occurred to her then as she ambled back over to the counter where her grandmother and the ranger were still conversing.

"Excuse me," said Zephyr. The two friends looked up from the map. "Where did you get all these animals? Did you trap them?"

Doris pushed up her glasses and shook her head. "Oh no, we'd never do that. These are all animals that died from one cause or another. Sometimes an illness, other times from an accident. Those we find that are still in good enough shape are sent to the taxidermist. It's our way of honoring them and providing education at the same time."

Zephyr nodded. "That's good to know." She peered at her grandmother and added, "I bet there's a whole lot to know about this place that might come in useful."

"Oh," said Grandma June, widening her eyes as Zephyr's meaning struck her. "Yes. Right. We were actually wondering what you might know about the people who lived here back in the early 1700s, especially in regard to the Native American population. I have to admit I know a lot more about the animals that have lived here over time than I do the people."

"Well it just so happens that we received a great resource book about the early inhabitants yesterday! Let me go in the back and find it."

"Thanks, Doris. That would be wonderful," Grandma June replied. While they waited for the park ranger to return,

Zephyr walked over to the walls covered with informative signs about the various local plants and wildlife. Grandma June trailed a few steps behind, nodding as she read to herself. "There are several new placards here I haven't seen before, Zephyr. There's always something new to learn about this place."

Soon Zephyr was drawn to an assortment of photographs and paintings on the next wall over and found herself unexpectedly absorbed in them all. The bright, colorful, and detailed images helped bring the words and names of all of the wild things to life. She finished reading a caption about the beautiful snow geese, amazed at a photo showing thousands of them covering Lake Drummond, and moved on to the next picture. Her breath froze in her chest at the image before her.

"G-Grandma?" Zephyr said, pulling the word from her tightening throat. "L-Look." She pointed her trembling finger at a painting of a glowing, white canoe being paddled by a raven-haired woman dressed all in white.

[7]

THE LADY OF THE LAKE

As ZEPHYR STARED AT THE ETHEREAL PAINTING, SHE FELT the comforting weight of Grandma's hands rest on her shoulders. "I see you've found *The Lady of the Lake*."

Zephyr nodded. "It looks a lot like what I saw," she whispered, glancing over her shoulder to be sure the ranger wasn't within listening distance. "Did you know about this?"

"Oh yes," said Grandma June, mirroring Zephyr's gaze at the painting. "But I didn't mention it because I wanted to see your reaction when you discovered it. So this is what you witnessed last night?"

"Well, kind of. The face wasn't exactly like this one, and what she wore was different. My" —she dropped her voice to an even softer whisper— "*ghost* looked like she was wearing white leather fringe instead of just a solid dress, and she didn't have a tall feather sticking up from behind her head like this one. And mine didn't have braids. Her hair hung long and loose down her back. But the canoe looks right, and there's that green light in the front."

Grandma June took her hands from Zephyr's shoulders and

stepped closer toward the display. "The legend of *The Lady of the Lake* is printed on this plaque beside the painting. You'll see both similarities and differences between what Kanti told you and this tale. Makes me wonder if they've gotten the story wrong all this time, or if there could be two such spirits wandering the swamp."

Zephyr read the printed legend. Instead of a story about a mother losing her child, it was about a pair of Native American lovers who'd been pulled apart by death on the eve of their wedding. According to the placard, local people said that, from time to time, the unfortunate ghostly maiden could be seen paddling her lamplit canoe. The thought was that she was lighting the way for her lost love to find her in the mists.

Grandma June pointed to another nearby plaque. "Back in 1803, an Irish poet named Thomas Moore visited America, including a visit to the Great Dismal Swamp. Apparently, the legend of The Lady of the Lake was already well known, even back then, and he wrote a poem about it. Here," she waved Zephyr forward. "I'll let you read it."

Zephyr stepped close to Grandma June and read the words on the sign.

A Ballad: The Lake of the Dismal Swamp
  Written at Norfolk, in Virginia
  by Thomas Moore

They made her a grave, too cold and damp
  For a soul so warm and true;
  And she's gone to the Lake of the Dismal Swamp,
  Where, all night long, by a fire-fly lamp,
  She paddles her white canoe...

The poem went on to tell the tale of the maiden's grief-stricken lover searching through the swamp for her spirit until one day he disappeared, never to be seen again. With widening eyes, Zephyr read the final verse:

> ...But oft, from the Indian hunter's camp,
>   This lover and maid so true
>   Are seen at the hour of midnight damp
>   To cross the Lake by a fire-fly lamp,
>   And paddle their white canoe!

Zephyr jumped as a loud *thunk* sounded behind them. Turning around, she saw Ranger Doris pushing up her reading glasses and thumbing through the pages of a large book she'd dropped onto the counter.

"Let's see," Doris said, running her finger along a page as Zephyr and Grandma June stepped back to the information desk. "Yes. OK. It says here that archaeologists determined that Native Americans probably first inhabited the Great Dismal Swamp around 13,000 years ago."

Zephyr looked down at the book. "That's a really long time."

"Indeed, it is," Grandma June agreed. "Does it say anything about the population around the beginning of the 1700s?"

The ranger continued to scan the page, reaching the bottom and flipping to the next one. "Seems there were a lot of different tribes. Some Chesapeake, some Chowan, some Nansemond, many related to Chief Powhatan of Pocahontas fame."

Zephyr and Grandma June exchanged eyebrow-raised glances at that comment.

"They all seemed to be from the Algonquian speaking tribes," said Doris. "It also says that as more English colonists settled nearby and brought their slaves with them, those enslaved people would sometimes run away and hide in the swamp." Turning a page, she read aloud, "Since their owners were afraid of traveling too far into a mysterious place full of snakes, bears, and wildcats, those who escaped found a safe haven in the swamp. Some even used it as part of the Underground Railroad; a resting place before they fled further north to freedom. Others settled in and made the swamp a permanent home. For a while, Native Americans and the escaped slaves—sometimes called maroons—both lived in the swamp, but eventually as more slaves entered, more Native Americans left."

Grandma June slid the book around so they could all have a sideways view of some of the accompanying historic sketches of the swamp. "Anything in there about people getting lost? Especially children. Nansemond children in the early eighteenth century?" she asked hopefully.

Ranger Doris turned to the index in the back of the voluminous book. "Nothing that specific that I can see. But..." she said after a moment, and then looked up at Grandma June with a sad expression. "You know, lots of people, including children, must have gotten lost over the years. I would assume, unless they were the children of some well-known person, they wouldn't make the history books."

Zephyr sighed.

"What exactly is it you were hoping to find out?" asked the ranger.

Grandma June nodded at Zephyr.

"Well," said Zephyr, clearing her throat, "I heard...in school...about a little Native American boy—from the Nansemond tribe, I think—who got lost back then. His father might have been an Englishman."

"Hmmm," murmured Ranger Doris thoughtfully as she

closed the book. "You know who may know something is Roger White."

Zephyr felt her pulse quicken as her hopes rose. "Do you know him, Grandma?"

Shaking her head, Grandma June turned back to the ranger. "You mean the man who just moved into the old White Farm a couple months ago?" she asked, her voice lilting up in surprise. "I haven't had a chance to meet him yet."

"Yes. Rob Marlowe pays rent to plant and harvest corn on part of the land, but Mr. White inherited the farm recently and moved down here from up in the mountains. Lives alone."

Grandma June rested her forearms on the counter and leaned forward. "So why do you think he'd know anything about local history?"

"Oh," said the ranger, pulling the book back behind the counter and adding it to a stack of books to reshelve later. "He's a historian. Taught at Radford University for a lot of years before he retired. He came by the other day and told me all kinds of things about the history of the swamp I had never heard of." She looked down at the book sitting on top of the large stack. "I think he could have written this book himself with as much as he seemed to know!"

Grandma June glanced at Zephyr with a tiny nod, then turned back to Ranger Doris. "Do you think he'd mind us stopping by?"

Zephyr crossed her fingers and sent up a wish. *Please don't say he'd mind.*

"I don't think so!"

Yes! Zephyr felt her first surge of hope since Sam had run away in the moon mist. *This could be the answer and I might get him back with me before the weekend is over!*

Ranger Doris continued, "He seemed friendly enough. He'd probably be happy to have an excuse to talk history, especially if you brought him one of your famous pies along as a welcome gift," she said, grinning at her friend.

Chuckling, Grandma June replied, "Well, I do happen to have an extra apple pie at home. Zephyr and I were going to have it with tea this afternoon, but I think she'll be willing to share it, under the circumstances. Right?" she asked, winking at her granddaughter.

"Absolutely," said Zephyr. "Sounds like a good deal to me."

"To paraphrase," said the ranger, "This way you can have your pie and eat it, too!"

[8]

THE PROFESSOR AND HIS RAGDOLL

As Grandma June eased her little red Mazda minivan around the curving Desert Road, Zephyr balanced the pie carrier on her lap. The homey aroma of apples and cinnamon seeped out from the edges of the snapped-on plastic lid, filling the car with a delicious fragrance that no cardboard air freshener dangling from a rearview mirror could ever hope to come close to. Her grandma had warmed the pie in the oven for a few minutes in order to bring out the syrupy lusciousness.

"Are you sure we need to sacrifice this pie?" Zephyr asked, her mouth watering as she imagined the filling peeking out from the patterned crust on top.

"Yes, Zephyr," Grandma June said smiling as she kept her eyes on the road. "As the old saying goes, you can catch more flies with honey than vinegar. And, besides, it's the neighborly thing to do, especially since we're actually next-door neighbors."

"Next door? But we've already passed several houses."

"Well, White Farm stretches on behind those houses. Apparently, years ago, some of the property bordering the road was sold off, but there are acres behind the backyards of those houses that still belong to the farm. Our property extends through the trees, out back a ways, and butts up against White Farm land."

A rusty, rectangular mailbox was perched up ahead on a wooden stake beside a turnoff to a dusty dirt road. Faded gray paint on a flaking, dull, red background spelled out the name, White.

"Here we go," said Grandma June, slowing down and turning the wheel sharply right to pull them off the main road.

"Look at that," said Zephyr, pointing to a No Tres-passing sign.

"Oh, I wouldn't worry about that. I suspect it's meant to keep hunters off the land and vagrants out of the house from when it was standing empty for so long." She maneuvered the car carefully along the dirt entry road, steering around the various potholes scattered along the way.

"Weren't you ever curious about this place? I mean, did you ever come down here before?"

"Yeah, I was curious. But, no, I never came down here. I've gone through our woods and seen the fields, though. There's a deer path that trails from our backyard, through the trees, and onto the farmland." Grandma June's little van joggled along the hard-packed dirt between rows of scraggly, dried cornstalks. The drive curved to the left and when Zephyr looked back, Desert Road was no longer in sight, just ghostly cornstalks in all directions. Grandma slowed the car to a stop and lowered Zephyr's window. "Listen," she murmured.

A gentle breeze blew through the fields, rattling the papery husks and stalks, creating a raspy chorus that sounded like dry voices whispering all around them.

"Kinda spooky sounding," said Zephyr.

Grandma June nodded. "Yes. But pretty cool, huh?"

"Yeah, pretty cool." Zephyr cocked her head as she looked at her grandma in wide-eyed wonder. *Rock concerts? Ghosts? Thinking spooky sounds were cool?* She was starting to see her grandmother in a whole new light. And...she liked it.

Grandma June started up the engine again, and within a few more yards, a red tin roof peeked over the autumn cornfields. As they came closer, they saw that the roof was supported by a two-story wooden house with a friendly-looking screened porch. The old house appeared to be freshly painted, with crisp, white clapboards and dark green window shutters. A black cast iron kettle full of golden chrysanthemums sat at the foot of the front steps.

"Well, this looks nice. Much better than I expected," her grandma commented. They pulled in beside a cornflower-blue Volvo station wagon with a Radford Highlanders sticker on its bumper.

"Ready?" she asked Zephyr.

"Ready."

As they walked toward the porch, the biggest cat Zephyr had ever seen burst open the screen door and ran toward them in a blur of creamy fluff. As its full weight bumped against her legs, Zephyr staggered, nearly dropping the pie.

"Watch out. That's my guard cat," a man's voice called out.

Zephyr looked up and saw a tall, thin man, dressed in faded blue jeans and a red plaid flannel shirt standing at the open door. To Zephyr's relief, a smile creased his narrow face. The thing that immediately caught her eye though was his hair—silvery gray and pulled back into a long ponytail. Anybody that old with hair that long had to be pretty cool in Zephyr's opinion.

"Well, he's very beautiful and very good at his job," said Grandma June, smiling warmly as she reached down to scratch the cat behind his ears. "I hope you don't mind my granddaughter and me stopping by uninvited with this apple pie. I've been meaning to welcome you to the neighborhood for a while now."

"Of course I don't mind. Who could mind two lovely ladies bearing such a delicious gift?" he asked with a grin as he walked down the steps. "I'm Roger White and you've already met Hamish." He gestured to the cat at their feet.

Zephyr held the pie carrier to one side to get a better look at Hamish. His body was creamy white, but his head, feet, and tail were dark brown. As though he felt her examining him, the cat looked up at her with sapphire-blue eyes and opened his mouth in a barely audible *meow*.

"Pleased to meet you," said her grandma, extending her hand. "I'm June, and this is my granddaughter Zephyr. I live a few doors down."

Mr. White pushed his rimless glasses further up his nose then smiled again as he shook Grandma June's hand. "Pleased to meet both of you. How about I take that pie off your hands, Zephyr, so you can better defend yourself against my savage cat."

Zephyr giggled as Hamish continued to weave around her legs. "He sure is friendly," she said, handing the pie to Mr. White. "I've never seen one so big before."

"Ah, yes. He's a Ragdoll cat. They're an exceptionally big breed—especially the males—but Hamish, here, is even larger than usual. This big boy tips the scales at twenty-three pounds."

Zephyr's eyes widened. "Wow. That's almost as big as my beagle."

"Oh, yes. Hamish has been known to give dogs a run for their money. Do you ladies have time to come in and share some of this pie with me?"

Grandma June turned toward Zephyr with her eyebrows

raised, as if the idea had never crossed her mind and they hadn't both been secretly hoping for an excuse to talk further. Zephyr mentally added *actress* to the growing list of her grand-ma's newly discovered qualities.

"Um, sure!" Zephyr responded. "My...dog... should be OK for a while longer."

"Then, we'd be happy to," said Grandma.

Mr. White led the way back up the porch and opened the screen door. He held it for them and gestured for them to go inside as Hamish bounded in ahead of the group. "You know, I wasn't expecting guests, especially lady guests, and I'm afraid my house is suffering from OBS."

"OBS?" asked Grandma June as she stepped through the doorway into the screened-in porch, Zephyr following quickly behind her.

"Yes. Old Bachelor Syndrome. I've still got piles of boxes stacked around from my move and the seating situation is pretty limited right now. Would you mind, too much, if we just sit out here? The sun's warmed up this side of the house nicely, I think."

Zephyr scanned the porch and saw two rocking chairs and an old-fashioned wooden swing with its chains hanging from the ceiling.

"That would be perfect," said Grandma June, moving toward one of the rocking chairs. "I'd love to sit here where I can hear the sound of the wind blowing through your cornfields."

"Oh! You like that, too? That's one of my favorite things about living out here. I'll miss that sound when Mr. Marlowe cuts it all down for the winter." He moved toward his front door as Zephyr made her way to the swing. "You two make yourselves at home and I'll be right back with some plates and forks for the pie. Hope you don't mind paper plates. Haven't located my dessert dishes yet."

"That sounds great. No need to wash dishes if you don't have to," Grandma June said with a grin while taking a seat.

"Indeed. I see you are a woman after my own heart," he commented, pushing open his freshly painted red front door.

"Well, so far so good," whispered her grandma to Zephyr once Mr. White had closed the door behind him.

"Yep. He seems pretty friendly," agreed Zephyr, settling on the wide swing.

"Yes, he does. And I really like his cat," said Grandma June, as she reached down to stroke Hamish's broad, chocolate-brown head.

"Grandma? Do you think Kanti's cat misses her?" *And does Sam miss me?*

"I'm sure he does," she said. Then, with a soft smile, as though reading Zephyr's mind, added, "Just like Sam misses you. But there are things cats and dogs understand and things they don't."

"Like?"

"Like, they know they miss their loved ones, but they don't seem to have a real sense of time. You know how excited Sam was to see you when you came home from school or when you came home after a weekend sleepover with your friends?"

"Yeah. I see what you mean. He was just as crazy about greeting me whether I was gone a few hours or a couple of days."

"Exactly," said Grandma June, leaning back in her chair. "As long as they are well cared for, I believe they are fine and look forward to their reunion with their people, or ghost, or whatever. I know you'll take good care of Scam, and from what you told me about Kanti, I'm sure she's taking good care of Sam's spirit-self."

I hope so.

The creak of the door announced Mr. White's return as he pushed it open with one elbow, balancing a tray laden with three pie slices. "Here we go," he said, placing the tray on a metal folding table standing between the two rocking chairs. "For you," he said, handing her grandma a napkin, plastic fork, and a large slice of pie on a blue and white flowered paper plate. "And, for you," he said, handing Zephyr her slice.

Settling down into the other rocker, Mr. White took a bite of the pie and moaned. "Oh my. Mrs. Smith's Pies has nothing on you. You should start your own line. I can see it now. A whole grocery store section devoted to Mrs...Mrs...?" he turned questioning eyes toward her grandma.

"Oh!" she said, and Zephyr noticed an attractive pink blush blooming over her grandmother's cheeks. "Mrs. Stone. It'd be Mrs. Stone's Pies, I suppose."

"Stone?" said Mr. White, and Zephyr thought she saw a flicker of alarm pass across his widened gray eyes.

"Yes," said her grandma. "My husband was Charlie Stone. He..." Zephyr saw her swallow and blink a couple times. Grandma June still had trouble telling people about Grandpa's death. "...he passed away about two years ago."

"Oh, I'm so sorry," said Mr. White. "And is your last name Stone too," he asked, turning to Zephyr.

"Yes, it is," she said and noticed the ghost of a frown wash over Mr. White's face before he quickly replaced it with a tight-lipped smile. Zephyr wondered at his expression.

Grandma June cleared her throat. "Mr. White, we have a confession to make."

[9]

THE WHITE FLAG OF SURRENDER

MR. WHITE RAISED ONE BUSHY EYEBROW AS HE PUT DOWN his fork. "Confession?"

Grandma June patted her lips with her napkin and set it down on her lap. "Yes. I'm afraid this isn't just a welcome-to-the-neighborhood visit."

"Well, now I am truly intrigued," he said, leaning forward.

"Zephyr and I were doing some research at the Great Dismal Swamp Visitor Center earlier today, and we found out from Ranger Doris that you are a historian."

"Yes, that's true," he said, nodding. "I was a history professor at Radford for thirty years and have just retired. But," he added, returning his attention to his pie, "I'll never retire from the study of history. It's a passion of mine."

"A true labor of love then," her grandma suggested with a smile. "And it seems you know a lot about the history of this area even though you just moved here."

Mr. White nodded as he chewed and swallowed a large mouthful of apple pie. Zephyr followed his gaze as he scanned the fields of golden-brown cornstalks surrounding his little green oasis of a front yard. Turning back to her grandma, he replied, "Sometimes people find an area more interesting if they haven't actually lived there all their lives."

"I know what you mean," said Grandma June. "We really do take our everyday places for granted."

"Indeed we do," said Mr. White, warming to the topic. "And if you throw in years of dull history lessons given by a few uninspired teachers, it's no wonder some people have no idea how interesting their own hometown really is." Mr. White turned to Zephyr as if just remembering she was still there. "What about you, Zephyr? Do you know much about the history where you live, here by the Great Dismal Swamp?"

Zephyr jumped slightly at this sudden turn of attention her way. "Me? No. But I don't live here."

Mr. White tilted his head to one side. "So you're just visiting your grandmother then?"

"Yes. I'm staying with her while my parents are at a business conference. We live on Colington Island near Kill Devil Hills."

"The Outer Banks of North Carolina!" exclaimed Mr. White, setting his plate in his lap and pointing at Zephyr. "Now that's a place with a rich history. The Wright Brothers' first airplane flight, lighthouses, legendary pirates. Even a native like yourself must be aware of it."

"Yeah," agreed Zephyr, leaning back a little from Mr. White's exuberant enthusiasm. "I guess it's maybe more obvious because it's part of the tourist business. But, yes, I see some of it every day. I pass by the Wright Brothers Memorial on my way to school. All the schools I've been to, or will go to until I graduate from high school, have the same name – First Flight. I go to First Flight Middle School right now." Zephyr paused for a moment to think back on some of her history teachers. "Actually, our teachers make history pretty interesting, but they have to spend a lot of time separating out fact from fiction."

Zephyr thought Mr. White's face was actually glowing after she finished speaking. Any hint of the frown she'd seen at the mention of their last name was now completely gone.

"That's marvelous. I'll have to take a trip out there as soon as I get things squared away here. Now, what can I do for you, ladies? Did you have any particular questions about the history of this area?"

"Yes," said Grandma June as Mr. White retrieved his plate from his lap and scooped up another forkful of pie. "Kind of like Zephyr's teachers trying to keep colorful stories from distorting the facts, we were wondering if some of the legends we've heard about the swamp may be based on things that really happened."

Mr. White swallowed and waved his plastic fork. "That's very good thinking. There's often a kernel of truth in every tall tale. The stories had to get started somewhere, and sometimes you can peel back years of embellishment to find the core of something that actually occurred."

"Do you know some of the legends? The ones that weren't completely made up?" asked Zephyr as she set down her empty plate beside her on the swing seat.

As if that were a well-known signal, Hamish jumped onto her lap, his silky body spilling over her narrow thighs.

"Hamish!" Mr. White admonished. "You didn't ask her permission. Just push him off if he's bothering you, Zephyr."

Zephyr stroked the big cat's plush chest and felt his deep rumbling purr beneath her hand. "That's OK, he can stay. He's like a great, big, living stuffed animal."

Mr. White shook his head in amusement. "He is that. But if you get tired of him, don't be afraid of shoving him down. He might act a little indignant, but he's used to me doing it."

51

"We're fine," said Zephyr, "aren't we, Hamish?" She looked up at Mr. White. "Where does his name come from?"

"Hamish? Well, as I mentioned before, I taught at Radford University. The school mascot there is a Scottish warrior, the Highlander. When I first got Hamish, I decided to give him a Scottish name. Knowing how big he'd grow and how he'd probably have his way much of the time, I decided to name him Hamish. It means 'supplanter,' one who throws his weight around and takes the place of others with force. Of course, our spelling is H-a-m-i-s-h, but in Scotland it could be spelled S-e-u-m-a-s. You see—"

"Yes!" said Grandma June with a bright smile. "Now, Mr. White, you were going to tell us about some legends you knew that might be based in truth." Zephyr threw her grandmother a grateful grin.

"Certainly. You must forgive me. I'm told I can get off course. As a matter of fact, I used to call upon a trusted student in each of my classes to hold up a small white flag when I was veering too far astray from the day's topic. They called it the White Flag of Surrender."

"Legends?" Grandma June reminded him gently.

Mr. White nodded. "Yes. Many stem from the experiences of hunters, sometimes mixing in with stories from the indigenous people who used to inhabit the swamp."

Zephyr and her grandmother exchanged a quick glance.

"And," Mr. White continued, "I think some of the stories are explanations for odd things people have seen out there. Legends often grow out of natural occurrences, sometimes even lending them religious origins.

"For instance, there's the Native American story of how Lake Drummond was formed. Did you know it's one of only two natural lakes in the whole state of Virginia? Or that its maximum depth is six feet, and only three feet deep over much of its three thousand acres? Well, ancient Native American lore says that the lake started out as the nest of a fearsome giant Firebird who abandoned it when her chicks were killed by a warrior. When she left, water flowed into the empty space and became the lake. The actual truth behind it is that the lake may have actually been formed by fire, either from the impact of a large meteor crashing into the swamp or from a great peat fire. Of course, a theory on the opposite end of the spectrum is that it was formed by a shift in the earth's continental plate as a result of the last ice age."

Grandma June broke in with a question. "What about stories of people lost in the swamp? Do you know anything about that?"

Zephyr leaned forward in her seat. *I'm sure glad Grandma is here to help steer this conversation!*

Mr. White inclined his head, emitting a soft "hmm" as he gazed at his cat. Zephyr got the distinct impression that he was deciding whether or not he wanted to answer the question. After a few moments of uncomfortable silence, he raised his head and peered into Grandma June's expectant face. "Well actually, there is one tale about a young colonist woman who wandered into the swamp one day and was accidentally shot dead by the arrow of a hunter from the Chowan tribe."

"Oh, my," murmured Grandma June, drawing her cardigan sweater closer around shoulders.

"Although," continued the professor, "why she would go into the swamp alone is beyond me. But, of course, the stuff of legend doesn't always bear up under modern scrutiny, nor does it need to, I suppose. Anyway, it is said the hunter was seeking a rare albino deer, one that many of his tribe had heard of but that few had ever seen. When he saw movement among the trees of the dense forest, he mistook the woman in her long white dress for his prey and let his arrow fly."

Even though she knew it was probably just a tall tale, Zephyr couldn't help but shudder at the thought. She knew firsthand what it was like to wander alone in the Great Dismal Swamp.

"So," whispered Grandma June, "she was struck down?"

Mr. White shrugged his narrow shoulders. "Well, the story says that the hunter, certain he'd struck the white deer, fought his way through the tangle of branches and vines but couldn't find the animal he thought he'd seen or his arrow anywhere. Some say that when the arrow pierced the woman's heart, she was transformed into the white doe the hunter had been seeking and bound away out of his sight. Legend has it that she now roams the forest forever, always disappearing if anyone draws near."

Zephyr swallowed the lump forming in her throat. "So, what part of that do you believe really happened?" She reached for Hamish's comforting warmth and scratched him behind his ears while he bore his massive head into her hand.

Mr. White swallowed his last bite of pie and set his fork and plate down on the tray. Folding his arms, he responded, "The swamp is full of tales of disappearing people and mysterious animals. I think that there probably was a young, early eighteenth or late seventeenth century woman who wandered away from her colonial village, never to be seen again. Then, when more sightings of an albino deer surfaced, it may have been wishful thinking on her loved ones' part that her spirit still lived on in the form of that rare and beautiful animal. This particular legend appears to be a case of tales from two different cultures overlapping and, over the centuries, has combined into one.

Zephyr nodded as she stroked Hamish's broad back. "So... how about the Native Americans? Do you know any stories about any of them getting lost?"

Mr. White leaned back in his chair and tented his fingers beneath his pointed chin as several more moments of silence slipped by. Zephyr sighed, lowering her chin and closing her eyes. *Come on, Mr. White! Get on with it!* At the clearing of his throat, she looked back up to see him nodding at her.

"Well let's see...there's the famous story of The Lady of the Lake. You may have read about her at the Visitor Center."

"Yes, we did," said Grandma June, rocking gently in her chair and seeming completely relaxed as the breeze blew through the rustling cornstalks and gently stirred her white-frosted red curls. "Do you have any special insights into that story?"

"Just that it seems to be one of the few things Thomas Moore found of interest or merit during his visit to America. In the introduction to his poetry book, he bemoans the fact that he had such high hopes for the young country, but—"

Where's a white flag when you need one? "Excuse me, Mr. White," said Zephyr, "but do you think that legend is based in fact, too?"

The professor gave himself a little shake as if to settle his scattering thoughts. "I think it's just another instance of someone getting lost in the swamp, and reinforced by people seeing swamp gas, which sometimes glows in the night."

Except swamp gas doesn't paddle a canoe, beg you to find her child, or take away your dog's spirit.

[10]

DOWN THE DEER PATH

GRANDMA JUNE STOPPED ROCKING AND PLACED HER hands on her knees. "We were wondering, specifically, if you knew anything about a little Native American boy who got lost when he wandered away from his mother."

Mr. White moved his hands to the arms of his rocker.

Her grandma continued, not noticing his change in posture, "It was probably close to the year 1700, and they would have been in the Lake Drummond area when he went missing." Zephyr saw the professor's knuckles turn white as he tightened his grip on the chair. "The little boy was about two years old," added Grandma June.

Deep lines etched across Mr. White's brow as red splotches bloomed on his cheekbones. Zephyr could see his chest rising and falling in quickening breaths.

Grandma June pressed on, "And probably the most important clue is that the child's mother was from the Nansemond tribe and his father was English."

At that, all the blood seemed to drain from Mr. White's face, his skin living up to his name.

"Why do you ask? Where did you hear this...story?" he asked between clenched teeth.

"Oh, nowhere in particular," said Grandma June with studied casualness. "It's just something I've heard about while living down here over the years. Can't remember who told me."

Mr. White rose from his chair and reached for her grand-mother's empty plate. "I have no idea, Mrs. Stone. There are many stories about lost people, some true, some not. But you know, I actually have a lot of work to do this afternoon, so I'm afraid I must ask you to leave now."

He turned towards Zephyr and spoke sharply, "Down, Hamish!" The cat turned his bright, unblinking eyes up toward Mr. White's stern face but didn't move a muscle. "Now!" At that Zephyr jumped and the Ragdoll cat hopped down and stalked across the porch to a far corner, curling himself into a sullen feline ball of fluff.

Grandma June stood and held her hand out to Zephyr. "We certainly understand. We didn't mean to keep you away from your work this long. Just wanted to say hello and ask what you might know from a historian's point of view."

Mr. White closed his eyes for a moment and when he opened them offered his guests a smile, although it quivered at the edges. "Of course. And I do appreciate you stopping by with your delicious pie. Another time, perhaps, we can talk longer. I'd like to hear more about life on the Outer Banks," he said, turning his twitchy smile to Zephyr.

Mr. White's sudden transformation from kindly absent-minded professor to defensive backed-into-a-corner badger mode had stunned Zephyr into silence. She nodded wordlessly and attempted a smile as she took her grandma's hand.

As they walked to their car, Mr. White called out, "Wait just a minute and I'll empty your pie carrier so you can have it back."

"Oh, no, that's alright. I won't need it any time soon. I'll just pick it up the next time I come by," said Grandma June, opening her door. She leaned in, stretching one foot inside, but then withdrew it and stood back up outside the van.

"Did you forget something?" asked Mr. White, who was still standing on his porch steps.

"Just one more question," her grandma responded, and Zephyr saw the man's shoulders tighten and rise up a notch. "In your research, I was wondering if you'd run across any small family cemeteries other than those we can see from the road? I find gravestones so interesting. They can tell you a lot about the people of the time."

He shook his head. "No. I don't know of any. Have a good afternoon, ladies. Nice to meet both of you," he said before stepping briskly inside and nearly slamming the screen door.

"Man, that got really weird, really fast," said Zephyr sliding into the passenger seat and buckling her seatbelt.

"It sure did," agreed Grandma June reaching up for her own belt. "Nice man, but definitely reacted strangely to some things."

"Yeah. Did you see his face when he found out our last name?"

"Uh huh. It was subtle and he tried to hide it, but I definitely saw something in his expression, and it definitely wasn't positive. I wish your grandpa were here so I could ask him about it. I wonder if there was some kind of family feud in the past between the Whites and the Stones?" She glanced into the rearview mirror as she carefully reversed her little minivan around Mr. White's Volvo, steering them back onto the lane that would lead them to the main road.

"And he sure got bent out of shape when you asked about the lost boy!" Zephyr said, remembering how white his knuckles had become as he'd gripped the arms of the chair.

"Yes," said Grandma June as she drove down the path between the chattering cornstalks. "Pretty odd. Too bad we didn't find out anything new. I mean new in terms of what we really came for. We learned plenty other stuff though. He sure does like to talk about history."

"I think we should bring a white flag next time. If there is a next time," Zephyr muttered, watching the stalks wave as they passed by.

Grandma June chuckled as she pulled them back onto the main road. "At least he knows he has a habit of getting off track and doesn't mind being told when he does."

As they pulled into their driveway a couple minutes later, Zephyr noticed how quiet it was. "I really miss hearing Sam bark. Usually, as soon as he heard us pull up, he'd be barking his head off." Her throat thickened as she remembered.

Grandma June reached over the center console and gently squeezed Zephyr's hand. "I know how hard this is for you. The best you can do for him, other than solving the mystery, is keep his body safe and healthy. And I'm sure the cat appreciates your kindness."

Zephyr sighed. "Yeah, you're right. I better give Scam a walk now. He probably isn't used to holding it too long."

"Good idea," said Grandma June, tucking her arm through Zephyr's as they walked up the driveway to the house. "But keep watch on the sky. The days are getting shorter and darkness creeps in even earlier near the woods."

Scam ran up to Zephyr when she opened the door, weaving himself in and out of her legs.

"Careful, Scam. You're bigger than you realize!" she said, chuckling as she struggled to keep her balance. "Come on. I'll take you for a walk." After snapping the leash to his collar, Zephyr opened the kitchen door and Scam scampered out. "Be back in a few minutes, Grandma!" she called, as the cat-beagle pulled her toward the tree line.

"Slow down, Scam! You're going to pull my arm off!" *Must be trying to find the other cat he smells on me.* When they reached the edge of the swampy forest, Scam kept his nose to the ground, shifting from side to side. "Just pee, before it gets dark."

And as if on cue, he promptly watered the base of a stringy-barked cypress tree.

"Great, now let's—" Scam yanked forward, nearly pulling the leash from Zephyr's hand. "Alright, alright. I get it. You've been locked up all day and you're feeling your new dog muscles. Just a little further then."

Scam plunged ahead, then stopped dead still beside a path leading into the woods. *This must be the deer path Grandma told me about.* Something white moved behind a curtain of gray Spanish moss hanging from a low branch. *A deer? The white deer?* Scam surged forward down the trail as Zephyr stumbled behind, straining to hold him back while skittering over the foot-tripping tree roots snaking across their path. "Scam! Slow down! I thought cats were more sedate!" *Must be Sam's dog-brain kicking in!*

The white figure danced behind a net of golden poplar leaves and Scam pulled even harder, foam slathering from his mouth as he strained against his collar. The deeper they ran, the darker it became as the tall trees closed in around them. The handle of the leash cut painfully into Zephyr's palm, but she held on tight. *No way you're getting away from me! I'm keeping Sam's body safe for his return!*

The path curved abruptly to the left and widened just as a white blur flew past. Zephyr's eyes finally landed on the mysterious shape, but it wasn't a deer after all. It was an egret. An egret flying ahead of them and out into the fading afternoon light of a rustling cornfield. Zephyr stopped suddenly at this discovery. *Oh my gosh. This must be Mr. White's land.* Even Scam seemed surprised at this sudden change in scenery and stopped in his tracks, lifting his head and sniffing the air.

The egret swooped back toward them, the lowering sun gilding the edges of its snowy feathers before it wheeled around and floated on a breeze just above the tops of the cornstalks. Scam came back to life at this and resumed pulling with all his might in the direction that the bird flew. Zephyr trotted behind him, curiosity now replacing her usual caution. What were the chances of seeing an egret in a cornfield after the one she'd encountered last night in the swamp, and the one she'd seen in the moonlight back home? An odd sensation prickled up her spine. *There's no way it can all be the same bird...is there?*

After several yards, a large clearing of mowed grass appeared amid the surrounding corn crop. The egret flew in a circle and then settled down on top of a tall picket fence a few feet away. Scam pulled Zephyr toward the great bird but, just as they reached the fence, the egret flung itself into the sky and swiftly winged out of sight. Zephyr felt her arm jerk hard as Scam bolted forward around the corner of the peeling, white fence. "Stop, Scam! You're going to hurt—" Her words stuck in her throat at what she saw.

A graveyard.

But he said he didn't know of any graveyards around here. Her thoughts were cut short by the sound of crashing cornstalks.

"Hamish!" shouted the familiar, deep voice of Mr. White. "Get back here!"

Zephyr gathered every ounce of strength she had and yanked at Scam's leash, dragging him back toward the cornfield trail that led to Grandma June's deer path. Even though the air had turned chilly with the quickly setting sun, a nervous sweat broke out across Zephyr's forehead and palms, making it even harder to keep a grip on the now slippery leash. Scam finally seemed to sense her anxiety and slowed to match her pace, staying only slightly ahead of her as they ran for the cover of the forest.

As soon as they leapt into the shade of the towering trees, it was as though someone had shut off a light switch. With no time to let her eyes adjust, Zephyr plowed forward into the darkened forest, now glad of Scam's ability to be led by his nose.

"Good boy!" she said, keeping her voice low even though they were back on her grandma's property. She didn't want to risk bringing attention to themselves.

As they ran, Zephyr's breath shortened to forced spurts. "Sc-Scam. C-can't get—my—breath," she wheezed, pulling him to a stop. She sagged against a ragged tree trunk as she gripped Scam's leash and focused on steadying her pounding heartbeat and struggling breath. Lowering her head, she inhaled as deeply as she could and closed her eyes. Scam bumped against her leg and when she opened her eyes again to look down at him, she noticed something round and gold nestled in a pile of leaves and pine needles inside of a hollow tree stump nearby.

A coin? Kanti's coin?

[11]

CLEM AND HIRAM

PEERING AT THE OBJECT, ZEPHYR SHOOK HER HEAD. *But that can't be. We're not by the lake and that stump isn't shaped like a flying bird.* She stooped down, picked it up, and examined it as she leaned back on the supportive tree. It was scuffed up, plain and flat, with a metal loop on the back. *A shank. That's what Grandma June called it when she was trying to teach me to sew. This isn't a coin. It's an old button. Probably brass.*

She whipped her head around at the sound of soft rustling behind her. *Mr. White? Hamish?*

Then, a rasping whisper, "I'm athinkin' he's gone thisaway."

Mr. White looking for his cat? Talking to himself? Whispering in a weird accent?

Zephyr froze and stood as still as the tree she leaned on and mentally willed Scam to do the same.

A second whisper, "Maybe. This swamp's full of hidey-holes."

Either he's answering himself or else...

Two men dressed in floppy, tan canvas pants and baggy shirts, with rifles resting on their shoulders, stepped onto the deer path in front of them. Zephyr felt Scam lean against her leg and looked down to see his beagle back arched up like a scared cat and his hackles standing on end. A deep growl rumbled from his throat.

Shhh, Scam!

Then the cat-beagle seemed to switch gears, lowering his spine as he bellowed a warning bark.

But the men ignored him completely. Didn't look his way. Didn't even flinch.

Zephyr pulled Scam back as she stepped away from the tree, now only a few feet away from the men. "Hush, Scam! Uh...I'm s-sorry. He's just nervous today. Not his usual friendly self," stammered Zephyr as she looked up at the men.

"Did ye bring a map?" asked the taller of the two men, brushing dingy blond hair from his eyes.

"Um, no. I-I don't have a map," Zephyr responded, confused at his question.

"Why would I bring a map, Clem?" said the other man, scratching his scruffy head.

"Cuz I didn't, Hiram!" his companion replied.

Clem slumped against the tree where Zephyr had just been leaning and slid his back down the trunk. As his bottom hit the ground, a brass button popped off his pants and sailed into the air, landing in the low notch of a broken-down cedar tree beside him. It took Zephyr a moment to realize that the deteriorating tree stood exactly where she'd just found the brass button in the hollow stump. She opened her fist and stared at the old button, wondering about the coincidence, before tucking it into her jeans pocket.

"I can't think of ever'thing, ye know," grumbled the man now sprawled on the ground.

Hiram leaned on his rifle. "Well, ye sure got that right, anyways. I'd settle fer ye rememberin' somethin' just ever now and then."

Clem looked up and turned his head until he was looking directly at Zephyr, then closed his eyes and leaned his head back against the tree trunk.

They can't see us! She realized. *What the heck is going on here?*

Zephyr held her hands out in front of her, then patted her thighs. *Well I haven't suddenly gone invisible.*

Scam inched forward and sniffed at Clem's dirty, freckled hand resting on the ground. The man never moved a muscle. Just sighed and shook his head.

"Be careful, Scam. I don't think you should get too close," she said, tugging at his leash.

With a spurt of feline stubbornness and canine strength, Scam yanked away from Zephyr and, as a result, fell against Clem's arm. No wait. He fell *into* Clem's arm. Straight through to the dirt beneath before launching himself, hair bristled and eyes wide, back to Zephyr's side.

They must be some kind of ghosts! Ghosts who can't see or hear the living. This is so weird!

"We ain't gonna get no reward if'n we don't keep lookin', ye know," said Hiram.

"Yeah, well leastways we know what we be lookin' fer," said Clem, squinting up at his partner.

"Yep. Little mixed-blood boy. 'Bout two or three. Copper skin. Blue eyes."

Zephyr sucked in a sharp breath. *Ahanu?*

"Hope the little nipper ain't been bit by a copperhead," said Hiram, ducking his head and peering on either side of the trail.

"Ye got that thing loaded an' ready fer snakes, or bears, or cougars?" asked Clem.

Hiram patted his rifle. "Yessir. Ready fer whatever come out the woods. How 'bout you?"

Clem pulled himself up to his feet and shouldered his own rifle. "Yep. Set for anything 'cept maybe them swamp spirits."

Spirits? As in ghosts? Zephyr shook her head. The irony was hanging as thick as the swampy air.

"Alrighty, Clem. Time to git movin'. Don't know exactly where we're headed, but I got a good feelin' 'bout that trail over there," he said, pointing at a tangle of vines.

"What trail?" Zephyr asked, though she was not expecting an answer. Looking down at Scam, she saw he was busily licking his fur. She glanced back up at the receding backs of the two men and heaved a sigh. "Come on. I've got to get you and Sam back in your right places, and this looks like a good lead."

Scam remained seated, his stiff-necked beagle muscles resisting her tug on the leash.

"I can't leave you here," Zephyr explained, slowly but firmly reeling him in like a big fish. "And these guys seem harmless. They can't see us or hear us. Let's just follow along for a while, or as long as this vision, or whatever it is, lasts." Zephyr looked around. "It doesn't even seem as dark as it was before. Maybe they make their own light or something."

Scam whimpered.

"Just for a little bit," urged Zephyr, pulling him behind her. "This may be my only chance. Hurry up! We don't want to lose them," she said, struggling to plow her way through the snaring undergrowth.

Zephyr heard what she could've sworn was a sigh of resignation behind her as the leash slackened and Scam crept forward to join her. Catching up with the two searchers, Zephyr heard snatches of their low conversation.

66

"The boy might've been taken by *them*, ye know," said Hiram.

Them? Them who? The Nansemond?

"We'll jest cross that bridge when we come to it," said Clem.

"Ye reckon the boy's really gonna fetch us twenty-five?"

"That's what Thomas Drake said, an' he be a man of his word," said Clem.

Zephyr felt her heart pump faster. *Thomas? Kanti's Thomas? It must be! He must have come back from England and found out he had a child and offered a reward to find him!*

"Zephyr!"

What? Who?

"Zephyr! Where are you?"

Zephyr stopped in her tracks and gave herself a shake. She spun around toward the sound of her name, then back toward Hiram and Clem. But the men were gone, as was the light they had produced, leaving Zephyr in the now suddenly dark forest.

"Zeph!" The voice called again, and this time she recognized it.

"Grandma?"

"I can barely hear you, Zephyr! Are you off the trail? Are you alright?"

The sound of Grandma June's voice led Zephyr back to the deer path. "I'm coming, Grandma!" As Zephyr sprinted through the ever-darkening gloom, she saw an even darker shape ahead. It was a log across the path that she remembered having to step over when they'd first come through the forest. When they reached it, Scam jumped smoothly over but Zephyr paused. She remembered how wide it had been and, afraid of tripping, decided to step up onto it this time rather than attempting to step over it.

As she planted her foot down though, the smooth sole of

her sneaker slid across the log's slippery bark. She lost her grip on the dog leash as she windmilled her arms, trying to regain her balance. Zephyr was able to remain upright until her ankle suddenly twisted beneath her weight as she slipped off of the log entirely. She came down hard onto the forest floor, the pain forcing her to her knees on the damp earth.

[12]
TWISTED

ZEPHYR GRABBED A NEARBY SLENDER TREE TRUNK AND hauled herself to her feet. "Scam! Where are you?" she cried, cranking her head from side to side, peering into the darkness. When she tried to step forward, pain shot up from her injured ankle. "Ouch!" *That really hurts!* A flickering white light danced across the path in front of her. *What is that? Swamp gas? Another ghost?*

"Zephyr!"

Heaving a sigh of relief at Grandma June's voice, she called back, "I'm here! I twisted my ankle! And I dropped the leash! I can't see Scam anywhere!"

Grandma June's flashlight beam grew steadier as she came closer. "I've got him! He came running towards me and I grabbed his leash. But, oh no, honey! What happened? Why were you out here in the dark? I got worried when you took so long."

"I, I didn't mean to..."

"Never mind that now," said her grandmother. "Let's just

get you inside, then you can tell me all about it. Can you walk at all?" she asked as she placed her arm around Zephyr's waist.

Carefully placing weight onto her left foot, she limped forward. "Yeah. It hurts, but I don't think it's broken. Just twisted real bad."

"OK. Just lean against me, now. I'll keep hold of Scam's leash."

Within a few minutes, they were back inside her grandma's house, and Zephyr was tucked into a cushiony recliner, a light blanket over her lap, and a bag of frozen peas resting on her hurt ankle. Scam curled himself into the corner of the couch, heaved a sigh, and went right to sleep. Over a cup of hot honeyed tea, Zephyr felt the overwhelming urge to tell her grandmother everything. But maybe it would make more sense in two parts. *Yeah, like any of this makes sense!* First she told her all that had happened, from the moment Scam pulled her down the deer path to when she'd leaned, gasping for breath, against the tree.

"Hmmm," said Grandma June, as wisps of steam floated up from her teacup. "The plot thickens, as they say. I wonder why he lied about not knowing of any other family cemeteries when he's got one on his own property?"

"Maybe he didn't know it was there," said Zephyr. "Although," she added, with a raised eyebrow, "it looked like someone had recently mowed the grass around the markers."

"Based on his reaction to my question, I bet he did know it was there and just didn't want us to know about it."

Zephyr nodded. "I think you're probably right. Wonder what he's hiding?"

Her grandma shook her head. "I don't know, but I'm afraid that's all our sleuthing for this weekend. Your mom and dad will be back tomorrow, and you need to spend the rest of the time keeping your foot elevated. I've got a crutch I can loan you to help at home. It'll be a good idea to keep your full weight off that ankle for a few days. And," Grandma June added, chuckling, "the crutch will make your injury more impressive to your friends."

"Thanks, Grandma, but there's more."

"More? What do you mean?"

Zephyr pulled the brass button from her pocket and set it on the arm of the chair. "While I was catching my breath, I found this old button on a tree stump. And then I saw how it got to be there, a really long time ago."

Her grandma gazed into Zephyr's wide eyes. "You mean you *figured out* how it got there, a really long time ago?"

Zephyr sucked in a long breath, then exhaled, puffing out her freckled cheeks. "I mean I *saw* it happen. Just like I was watching an old movie."

Alarm sparked in Grandma June's eyes.

Zephyr described her encounter with Clem and Hiram, then sat back, biting her lower lip. *Is this too much? Even for Grandma? Is she going to recommend counseling when she sees Mom and Dad tomorrow?*

Her grandmother sat silently, blinking at her granddaughter.

"Wow," she breathed, at last. "You know, I've read there are two or three different kinds of hauntings."

Zephyr shook her head. "You mean hauntings come in flavors?"

A smile tugged at the corner of Grandma June's mouth. "Yes. Let's call the one you had with Kanti strawberry. And the one you experienced today vanilla."

A wrinkle creased Zephyr's forehead.

Her grandma continued, "So a strawberry haunting is called an intelligent haunting."

"You mean because Kanti seemed intelligent and Clem and Hiram seemed, well, *not* very intelligent?"

Grandma June laughed. "No. In this case 'intelligent' means the spirit interacted with you. She could see and hear you and respond to your words and actions."

Zephyr nodded. "So was the one I had today a *stupid* haunting?"

"No." Grandma June shook her head and smiled again. "Regardless of the intelligence of the ghost, or apparent lack thereof, the vanilla type you experienced today is known as a residual haunting."

"Residual? Like the experiment we did in science class where we boiled down saltwater until there was just a white salty powder left? The residue?"

"Something like that. I'm no expert, you understand. I've just done some research. But it's said that sometimes a traumatic event can leave its energy behind in a place or in an object." Her grandma's eyes strayed to the brass button. "The spirits you see aren't there in any real sense. It truly is just like watching an old recording repeating itself over and over when the circumstances are right."

"Yeah. I figured out they couldn't see or hear us, so while it was definitely weird, it wasn't as spooky as when I met Kanti."

"Exactly. But they did lead you further into the woods, and that could have been dangerous, sweetheart," Grandma June responded as she tucked a stray lock of hair behind Zephyr's ear.

"You're right, I know. But I think they could have shown me what happened to Ahanu!"

"Possibly. But you're not going anywhere now but safely to bed. Maybe you could put that button under your pillow and dream about them, instead. But"—her grandma frowned—"I worry about you seeing the trauma that caused the residual haunting to happen in the first place."

Zephyr sighed. "Yeah, but if I know it's all strictly visual, I'll know it can't hurt me. And I'll do whatever it takes to get my Sam back." Tears welled in her eyes and Zephyr impatiently rubbed her hand across them. Grandma June knelt down by the recliner and opened her arms. Zephyr leaned into them, letting her tears flow unchecked.

At bedtime, Zephyr sat on a wheeled desk chair as her grandma rolled her down the hall to her room. "I'll help you pack up tomorrow," she said, glancing around the room at Zephyr's strewn clothes and stack of Nintendo Switch games. Zephyr followed her grandma's gaze toward the games and shook her head.

I haven't even thought about playing them. Lorie will never believe it.

[13]
BACK TO REALITY...SORT OF

DESPITE HAVING THE BUTTON BENEATH HER PILLOW, Zephyr awoke from a deep and dreamless sleep. *Just as well. Don't think I could take any more haunting experiences right now, whatever the flavor.*

While she waited for her parents to arrive, Zephyr added a countdown app to her phone. She sorted through the dozens of photos she had of Sam and chose one of her favorites as her background. Her dear beagle looked out at her with his soulful brown eyes as the digital counter below his speckled chest ticked off the time until the next Beaver Moon.

8 weeks + 4 days

In the late afternoon, Zephyr's mom and dad stopped by to pick her up. When her parents had left their business meeting in D. C., they'd set the car's built-in GPS for "Home by way of Desert Road." Now, after hugs and kisses and promises of longer visits, Zephyr watched through the car windows as the trees grew sparser and the road home grew wider with each of the ninety miles ticking by on the screen.

"So how was it?" asked her dad, making eye contact with her through the rearview mirror. "See any snakes? Run into any bears?"

After all she'd been through, snakes and bears didn't seem nearly as threatening as they had two days before. She and Grandma June had agreed it was best to keep all the strange stuff to themselves, though, or her parents might be hesitant to let her come back alone again. They'd probably think she and her grandma were both losing it. Studying the back of her dad's neatly trimmed dark auburn head and her mom's pixie-cut ash blond hair, she thought for a moment, and then chose her words with care.

"Nope. No snakes. No bears. Just...an egret."

"Oh, that's nice," her mom commented, turning in her seat to look at her with a smile. "Did you collect any more feathers to go with the one Lorie gave you?"

Zephyr's pulse quickened. Did her mom have some kind of sixth sense? "Um, yeah, actually. I did find one near the house one morning." *That wasn't a lie. Any time after midnight is a.m., so that means morning, right?*

"How did Sam do?" her father asked. "He seems quieter than usual."

Zephyr looked over at Scam, who was swaying to keep his balance on the car seat as he awkwardly tried to wash his face with his big paw. "Oh, he did good. I think he's just tired. We did a lot of walking."

"Too bad you twisted your ankle," said her mom. "I know it's better, thanks to Grandma June icing it and supporting it with an ACE bandage, but I'll write a note to get you out of gym class this week."

"Good idea," Zephyr agreed gratefully. "We're supposed to start basketball tomorrow."

Duh-duh-duh-dum—snap, snap
duh-duh-duh-dum—snap, snap
duh-duh-duh-dum—duh-duh-duh-dum
duh-duh-duh-dum—snap, snap

The Addams Family ringtone that Zephyr and Lorie had downloaded for the weeks leading up to Halloween sounded from her pocket. Pulling out her phone, she looked down at the screen, although she already knew who it was. Lorie was the only one of her friends who called her; everyone else just texted.

"Hey Lorie!"

"Hey girl! How's it going? Survive swamp prison?"

"Yep. Had a good time."

"Really?" asked Lorie, sounding doubtful. "Are you just saying that because your parents are listening?"

"No. I mean yes, they are, but it really wasn't bad at all."

"Well I know you enjoyed being with your grandma, and I know what a great cook she is, but it must've been totally boring, right?"

Boring? If she only knew. How much should I tell her? She looked at the backs of her parents' heads, knowing they were both probably straining to hear what she was saying. *Not much. Not now, anyway.*

"No. I had a good time, even without internet or cable."

"Sure you did," Lorie replied in the sarcastic tone that Zephyr knew meant she wasn't buying it. "You can tell me what it was *really* like out there later."

Zephyr sighed. "Grandma took me to the Great Dismal Swamp Visitor Center and I saw some cool stuffed animals.

The real kind, not the toy kind. I actually got to touch a huge black bear." She saw her mom's head jerk a notch to the side at that comment. "A stuffed one. But it was so lifelike it looked like it might growl at me."

"Well," said Lorie, "that's pretty impressive. What else?"

Zephyr fought the urge to spill everything out. "I learned some legends about enchanted deer and...ghosts."

"Now you're getting warmer." Zephyr could hear that she'd piqued her friend's interest with the mention of ghosts.

"How about you? How was your weekend? Do any more work on your Spider-Woman costume?" asked Zephyr, reaching down and scratching Scam behind one floppy ear.

"Yep. Almost finished. How's your Poison Ivy outfit coming?"

"Ugh," Zephyr replied. "I don't know. I have a feeling Luke Barnes is going to say I look like a long, skinny watermelon—red and green with freckles like seeds." She'd forgotten what it was like to worry about normal things for a change.

"You're going to look great! The green really matches your eyes. And why do you care what he thinks, anyway?"

Zephyr slumped back in her seat and looked glumly out the window again. "I dunno..."

"Remember when he said you looked like a bunch of carrots a couple years ago in your *Little Mermaid* costume? I think that boy's got produce issues."

"Right," muttered Zephyr. Lorie's glossy black hair and creamy caramel complexion never seemed to remind anybody of vegetables.

"Forget about that jerk," said Lorie. "I'm glad you're almost home! But gotta go now and put in a little basketball practice before we start in PE tomorrow."

"OK. But I forgot to tell you—I twisted my ankle and won't be able to participate in PE this week."

"Bummer! We need your tallness on our team! But I mean...sorry that you got hurt," her friend quickly amended.

Zephyr laughed. "Thanks. It's not too bad. I should be able to play in a few days."

"Alright. Remember to tell me later how that happened."

"Will do. See ya."

"Bye, Zeph."

Zephyr pulled the phone from her ear, clicked the screen off, and closed her eyes. She propped her pillow against the window and snuggled into it, knowing they had a bit further to go still before they would be home. *Sure am tired after such a boring weekend.* She felt herself drifting off to sleep as she heard her dad start to quietly sing *The Addams Family* theme song.

"They're creepy and they're kooky..."

Zephyr leaned on her crutch and watched the yellow bus, with its black block letters spelling out NORTH CAROLINA PUBLIC SCHOOLS-DARE COUNTY, charge up the hill like a determined groundhog. Much of the North Carolina coast was flat, but there were some areas of maritime forest growing on top of old sand dunes, and the Stone's house sat at the top of one of those rises. As the bus pulled to a squealing stop, the driver opened the door.

"Zephyr, honey, what'd you do to yourself? I swear. Give you kids a long weekend and you get into all kinds of mischief," said the driver, Mrs. Tillett. Frown lines creased her forehead, but the hint of a smile threatened to break across her plump face.

"Just stepped off a log wrong at my grandma's and twisted my ankle."

"Well, what you waitin' for, Mr. Barnes?" said Mrs. Tillett, looking over her shoulder at the tall, muscular boy sitting a few rows behind her. "Get yourself out there and help the young lady get in. Honestly. Sometimes I think y'all were raised in a barn." *Oh great. She* would *call on Luke to help me.* Zephyr steeled herself for some snarky remark about her red hair or her clumsiness.

"That's OK, I can manage," she tried, but Luke was already on his way down the bus steps. He stood awkwardly in front of her, brushing his long black hair away from his brown eyes and focusing on a point above Zephyr's shoulder. When she still didn't say anything, he quietly hooked his thumbs into his front belt loops, seeming to want to wait for her to make the first move.

"Tick tock, Mr. Barnes. We don't have all day. Do I have to spell it out for you? Take her backpack and then steady her as she climbs up," directed Mrs. Tillett. "Is chivalry a thing of the past here on Colington Island? Are southern gentlemen an endangered species?" she asked shaking her head of gray curls.

Mrs. Tillett was in one of her kids-these-days-don't-have-any-manners moods and it seemed Luke was her latest target. Zephyr almost felt sorry for him. Almost. She shrugged off her heavy pack and handed it to Luke, who took it without making any eye contact. After tossing it onto the front seat, he stepped back down and stood behind Zephyr. *This is so embarrassing! I should have taken Mom up on her offer to drive me to school.* She felt Luke's hands press lightly against her waist as she handed her crutch up to Mrs. Tillett.

"Steady now, sugar. Step up with your good foot first," Mrs. Tillett advised. "Don't let her fall, Luke."

Zephyr reached up and gripped the metal grab bars on either side of the steps. She placed her right foot on the first step and felt a twinge of pain course through her left ankle.

Luke's large hands pressed harder and his fingers curved in under her ribs as she pulled up her left foot. She was surprised to feel him actually lifting her a little as she attempted to haul herself up. Two more steps and then she was able to drop onto the seat beside her backpack.

Geez. That was more challenging than I expected. "Um, thanks, Luke," she said, looking up, but he'd already worked his way back to his seat. *He must think I'm a total klutz. I'm sure I'll hear about it, later, once we're out of Tillett Territory.* After a few more stops, Mrs. Tillett opened the door beside a driftwood sign that had tiny seashells spelling out GARCIA'S GETAWAY. Lorie's house doubled as a bed and breakfast during the summer months.

"Hey, Zeph!" sang Lorie, swinging onboard and squeezing in beside her. "How ya doin'?" She leaned down, inspecting the bandaged ankle. "Does it still hurt?"

"Not too much, unless I put all my weight on it like I had to do when I got on the bus. Mostly it just feels weak, so Grandma loaned me this nifty aluminum crutch."

"Yeah, I see," said Lorie. "Very senior citizen-y. At least it's not a walker. But, hey, if you need one of those, my great grandma has one with a basket and a horn. You could even hang little plastic jack-o'-lanterns from it."

"Very funny," Zephyr replied, rolling her eyes.

"How'd you manage the bus steps with your crutch and backpack?"

Zephyr ducked her head down before whispering, "*Luke* had to help me."

"What!"

"It wasn't *his* idea," Zephyr grumbled, raising her chin toward Mrs. Tillett.

"Oh. That makes more sense," Lorie said, nodding.

The bus rumbled down the road past the giant, stone

Wright Brothers Memorial to the First Flight school complex. They passed First Flight Elementary, followed by First Flight High, and then pulled onto the circular drive of First Flight Middle School beside a blue and white sign proclaiming, SEAHAWKS SOAR. Even though it was a chilly morning, knots of kids hung out on the covered walkway while others clustered in groups on the low stone benches.

Zephyr was grateful for Lorie's help getting off the bus and into the building. She glanced behind her as she entered and saw Luke watching her at a distance. His expression nearly made her stumble and fall. He wasn't smirking. He actually looked concerned. *Wow. Never saw that coming.*

[14]
CLUES FROM MRS. CREADLE

When the bell rang for first period, Lorie helped Zephyr navigate the halls to the gymnasium for PE. Her main job was to keep the surrounding, jostling students from bumping into Zephyr or from tripping over her crutch. When they entered the gym, Lorie headed for the girls' locker room to dress out and Zephyr hobbled over to Ms. Shoemaker.

The gym teacher, who stood several inches shorter than Zephyr, looked up as her student limped across the polished wooden floor. "I see you had a real fall *break*, Zephyr!" Ms. Shoemaker was known for her corny puns; the kids always groaned but secretly they all enjoyed them.

Zephyr handed her the note. "Luckily I didn't break it, just twisted it hard."

The teacher scanned the letter. "Well, it's too bad you're going to miss this first week of basketball. I know your team's going to miss you," she said, tilting back her head to make eye contact. "Some girls get all their height early on and I think you might be one of those. Not that your only contribution is your height, of course," Ms. Shoemaker added quickly.

Zephyr smiled a one-sided grin. "Well, I should be OK by next week, anyway."

"So," said Ms. Shoemaker, "you've got two choices. You can either sit on the bleachers and watch, or you can spend the hour in the library."

Easy choice! Zephyr loved the library and would usually spend her study hall period helping out Mrs. Creadle, the librarian. "I pick library."

"Alrighty, then," Ms. Shoemaker replied, writing a note on the outside of Zephyr's letter. "Take this to Mrs. Creadle and you can just report in there each day this week. She'll let me know if you're absent. Hope you feel better soon."

"Thanks," said Zephyr, making her way back across the glossy floor just as the first girls came out of the locker rooms. One of them, assigned to her team, made an exaggerated sad face, mouth turned down, lips poked out.

"Not fair!" she cried.

"Sorry, Meghan. Didn't do this on purpose!" Zephyr called back as she passed through the open gym doors.

Getting to the library was a lot easier with the hallways empty. A warm surge of pleasure rose up within her. Even though her ankle was uncomfortable, and she didn't mind PE, the idea of spending an extra hour each day that week in the library made her really happy. Lorie would say it made her really geeky, but she didn't care. She just loved books.

A smile broke across Mrs. Creadle's face as she read Zephyr's note. "Oh," she said, quickly backtracking as she met Zephyr's eyes. "Don't get me wrong. I'm not glad you hurt yourself, but I am glad you chose to spend your time here. I don't have too many students who'd rather spend their time in the quiet library than in the more action-packed gym, even if they're only spectators there."

"To each his own," Zephyr responded with a smile, slipping off her backpack and setting it on a nearby table.

"Do you want to read? Or study? Or help shelve books? I don't have any other students here until second period, and I have a few books that didn't get shelved yet from last week. You can scoot around on the rolling stool. Of course, don't think you have to do library work. You'll be manning the checkout desk as usual when you come back during your study hall time, right?"

Zephyr nodded. She liked shelving books because she sometimes ran across interesting ones she hadn't seen before. "Shelve."

Mrs. Creadle pushed a cart of fiction books over to the stacks where Zephyr waited, kneeling her bad leg on a low wheeled stool. "Now, if you get tired, just stop. This is a bonus for me. I wasn't expecting any extra help this week."

In the quiet of the library, Zephyr found her mind wandering back to the weekend, and after a few minutes, she transitioned to sitting on the stool with a book resting on her lap, her mind lost in thought.

"Zephyr? Are you alright?" Mrs. Creadle's voice broke into her concentration making her jump.

"Oh! Yeah, I'm fine. Sorry. I was just thinking about something."

"Well, if I can help, just let me know," the librarian replied with a warm smile.

As Mrs. Creadle turned back toward her office, Zephyr said, "Actually, maybe you could help. Over the weekend, I learned about a little Native American boy who got lost in the Great Dismal Swamp back in the early 1700s, and I'm trying to find out what happened to him."

Mrs. Creadle pursed her lips and thought for a moment. "That's going to be tricky unless he was the son of a famous chief. Native American records are pretty scant from that era other than stories written by the colonists. Do you know his name or his tribe?"

"His name was Ahanu, and I know his mother's name was Kanti. They were part of the Nansemond tribe. His father was English, though, and his name was Thomas. Maybe, Thomas Drake."

The librarian nodded. "Do you know if he got lost closer to the Virginia part or closer to the North Carolina part of the Great Dismal Swamp?"

"Grandma lives by the swamp in Virginia and that's apparently where he went missing."

Mrs. Creadle tapped her fingertips against her lips. "Hmmm...OK. This is a long shot, but it's possible you can find some help through genealogy sites. Sometimes there are personal letters or governmental papers mentioning Native Americans from that time. As an African American with nearly all my early American ancestors brought here as slaves, I have similar problems tracking down my family's past."

Zephyr's jaw nearly dropped, but she clamped it closed so as not to be rude. She'd never thought about her librarian as being the descendant of slaves. Seeing her, there, running the school library like the kindly captain of her own ship, it was strange and disturbing to think of her ancestral family having to bend to the will of slave owners.

"I tell you what," said Mrs. Creadle, placing her hands on the book cart. "I've got memberships on some ancestry websites, and since you're such a mature and responsible student, I'll log you into one of my accounts so you can do some searching on your own while you're spending time in the library this week. I'm thinking of starting a genealogy club, so this will help me, too. I'll get an idea of how to help students maneuver through all the different possible research threads."

"That sounds great! Thank you so much, Mrs. Creadle."

"My pleasure, Zephyr. I find genealogy fascinating. It's like a real live mystery story full of tantalizing clues. And you learn so much history at the same time."

Her mention of history brought Mr. White and his confusing mixture of emotions to her mind. "But how should I begin the search?"

"Has your family lived near the Great Dismal Swamp for a long time?"

"Yeah. I don't know exactly how long, but I know my Grandpa Charlie grew up there."

Mrs. Creadle nodded. "I think it's a good idea to start by searching through your own family history, then. It would help you learn the research tools and you just might find out something interesting about your family you didn't know. You may even find out the name of your first ancestor who came to America and where they came from."

Mrs. Creadle handed Zephyr her crutch. "Come on over to the computer room and we'll get started." Once Zephyr settled in front of one of the school's laptops, Mrs. Creadle leaned over and tapped in her login information. "I'll sit beside you to get you started."

The drawing of a large, many-limbed tree appeared on the screen with a WELCOME TO THE FAMILY sign hanging from one of its branches. Mrs. Creadle pointed to a section marked "Search" with lines for names, dates, places of birth and death, and known relatives. "Let's start with your grandpa. Just fill in what you know. Don't worry if it isn't exact, but the more precise information you type in, the easier it will be to narrow down the results to your own family."

Zephyr nodded as she finished filling in all the lines with as much as she could remember.

"Now comes the fun part," Mrs. Creadle said, infectious

excitement coloring her voice. "Just select submit and let the magic begin!"

Zephyr placed the cursor arrow on the submit button and clicked. Within seconds, a long list of items, each bearing the name Charles Stone, appeared on the screen. Federal census records, military draft registrations, marriage and birth records, find a grave links, death certificates, and property and probate records. Zephyr whistled. "There's so much! Where should I look first?"

"Well," began Mrs. Creadle. "Although you should always search the official records so you have an objective paper trail, you can begin by looking at what other people have already discovered."

"Other people? You mean like other people in my family doing this same research?"

"Yes, but they could be such distant relatives that you may have never heard of them. You'll find cousins, many times removed, with last names that have never turned up at your family reunions. It's amazing how far reaching family ties become over the years. Why don't you check out the Member Trees option and just see what pops up?"

Zephyr made the selection and several names appeared on the screen. She scanned the list and saw several Stones, as well as some O'Briens and Redmonds. Near the bottom of the list, one name grabbed her attention, standing out among the rest as if lit with blinking neon lights: *White*.

[15]

BIG BIRD AND COLD TAMALES

"WHITE?" BREATHED ZEPHYR.

"Does that name surprise you?" asked Mrs. Creadle, pushing up her reading glasses and leaning toward the screen.

"Y-yes. It does."

Brring

"Well, there goes the bell," said Mrs. Creadle. "Guess we'll have to tune in tomorrow to see what happens next! See? I told you genealogy could be exciting!"

That's for sure. Could this person be related to their Mr. White? It was a fairly common name. There was a chance it was just a coincidence...but then again, he'd had such a strange reaction to her own last name...

Zephyr found it hard to focus on schoolwork in her next classes. It wasn't just the mystery of the White-Stone connection, or the memory of Sam and her strange weekend, it was also all the unwanted attention she was getting from hobbling around with Grandma June's crutch. There were lots of stares and even some snickering she thought was aimed at her.

Standing head and shoulders taller than most of the other kids made her feel self-conscious enough, but add a crutch to the mix and it was impossible to blend in. And she was getting mighty tired of answering the question of the day; what happened? She'd even thought of making a sign she could hold up.

Twisted my ankle stepping off a log.
No, it's not broken.
Yes, it hurts, but not too bad.
Thanks for asking. Now please ignore me.

At lunch period, she waited outside the cafeteria doors for Lorie. Watching down the hallway, she recognized her friend's long, swinging ponytail swooping from side to side, even with other students walking in front of her. Mrs. Garcia, Lorie's mom, was always trying to get Lorie to walk more "ladylike," and to "stop stomping like a horse." Zephyr smiled, happy that Lorie was Lorie. She could walk like an orangutan as far as Zephyr was concerned.

"Hey girl," said Lorie, stopping beside her. "Are you buying or did you bring your lunch today?"

"Brought it. Grandma sent me home with some leftover ham from the weekend, so Mom made me a sandwich. And," she added with a smile, "she packed some of Grandma's home-made chocolate chip pecan cookies."

Lorie's large, coffee-colored eyes grew even larger.

"And, yes, I brought enough to share."

"Oh, thank you!" squealed Lorie. "I really could use a grandma cookie after my math class."

"That bad?" asked Zephyr, repositioning her crutch for a better grip.

"You don't even want to know." Lorie shook her head and

frowned. "Let's just say, my career as a master mathematician is in serious jeopardy."

Zephyr laughed. "How about you? Are you buying?" she asked, looking at the long string of kids snaking out of the door leading to the cafeteria serving line.

"Nope. I've got grandma-food myself today. Granny made twice as many tamales as we could eat, so I brought a couple."

"That sounds tasty. Even cold."

Lorie nodded as she walked ahead of Zephyr, clearing a path to their usual table. Dozens of eyes followed their awkward progress as they wove around tables and chairs to the far side of the room. One set of those watchful eyes belonged to Luke Barnes as he stood by a table a couple of feet away. Lorie looked back over her shoulder at Zephyr and saw her grimace.

"Hey, Barnes!" Lorie hissed as she turned to glare at him. "Take a picture. It'd last longer!"

Luke ducked his head and dropped to a crouch as he retied his shoelace.

Zephyr shook her head. Of all the strange things occurring over the last few days, Luke's behavior was, in some ways, the strangest of all. *Man. He must have been threatened with detention or something to not be throwing insults at me. I mean, right now I'm like the world's easiest target for snide remarks.*

After Lorie got them each a bottle of water, she plopped down across the table and leaned forward. "So. You never texted me last night. Tell me all about your weekend now that your parents aren't listening."

Zephyr still hadn't decided how much to tell her. Even if she did decide to tell her all the bizarre stuff, the noisy cafeteria wasn't the place to do it.

"Well, I told you about the Great Dismal Swamp Visitor Center. We also met a man who knows a lot of stories about the swamp. He told us there's a legend about how the Native

Americans believed the big lake there was created when water flooded the nest of a giant Firebird."

"Firebird? You mean like Fawkes the Phoenix from *Harry Potter*?"

"Yeah. Except this one was so big, its nest covered 3,000 acres."

"Wow. That's a big bird. Even bigger than Big Bird! Remember how much you loved Big Bird on *Sesame Street*?"

Zephyr grinned. "Yeah. I still like him. But don't tell anybody."

"Our secret. As long as you don't tell anybody I still sleep with Snooky Bear."

"Deal," said Zephyr.

Lorie glanced over at the crutch leaning against the table. "And you did what, exactly, to twist your ankle so bad? Getting hurt by just stepping off a log doesn't seem your style."

Over their lunches, Zephyr told Lorie more about the visit with Mr. White (minus their questions about the missing child), how she'd discovered a graveyard on his land, and the scary escape through the dark forest (omitting the vanilla haunting part).

"Wow. That's so weird," whispered Lorie. "I wonder why he lied to you about the graveyard?"

"I don't know. Maybe he just didn't want us poking around on his land looking for it."

"Yeah, but why? Sounds like he's hiding something. Anything else strange happen over the weekend?"

Zephyr bit her lip. "Well...there was the moon mist."

Lorie raised her eyebrows. "The what?"

Brring

Saved by the bell. Zephyr needed time to decide how much she'd tell Lorie.

"Later. Don't want to be late for English."

"OK. But don't forget to tell me later about that misty moon thing."

"Will do," said Zephyr as she and Lorie turned in opposite directions.

Zephyr dropped her backpack by the front door and fell onto the family room couch, the aluminum crutch clattering to the floor beside her. She'd never felt more exhausted in her life. Who knew limping around with a crutch was so tiring?

"How about a glass of iced tea?" asked her mom, walking into the room and eyeing the abandoned backpack and crutch.

"That sounds great," said Zephyr, closing her eyes.

A heavy weight dropped on her chest and a wet nose rubbed against her cheek. "Scam!" she said, scratching his head before pushing him away. "I missed you, too, buddy, but you don't know your own size." Zephyr rose up on her elbows and wiped the back of her hand across her face.

"Here, you go, honey," her mom said, walking back into the room, tall glass in hand.

"Thanks!"

"Did I hear you call our dog *Scam* just now?" her mom asked as she leaned down to pass Zephyr the glass of tea.

"Uh, yeah. It's a new nickname I gave him," Zephyr quickly covered, taking the chilled drink from her mom.

"Ha. Scam. Because he *scam*-pers, right?"

"Yeah, that's it," said Zephyr, exhaling her held breath.

Her mother looked down at her, tilting her head to one side. "Hard day?"

Zephyr nodded. After a swallow, she explained, "Having to use the crutch was a lot harder than I thought it would be."

"I was afraid it might be. I really think you should let me

drive you to school until you're off the crutch. I can give Lorie a ride, too, if you like."

"That sounds like a great idea." No one would have to help her onto the bus again. That was a relief. "And I'm sure Lorie would like it too."

"Settled. I'll just let the school know so the bus doesn't come this way for nothing." Her mom sat down on the easy chair that faced the couch. "Any trouble getting out of gym class?"

"Nope. Ms. Shoemaker made a joke about my fall *break* and then let me spend the period in the library."

Her mom chuckled. "That's our Ms. Shoemaker. Well I know you didn't mind having the extra library time."

"Yeah...hey, Mom? Have you ever thought about making a family tree? You know, going on genealogy sites and looking up names?"

"No. Not really. Why?" asked her mom, with a quizzical tilt of her head.

Zephyr sat up and swung her legs around, placing her left foot onto the coffee table. "Well, Mrs. Creadle is thinking about starting a genealogy club and she's using me as a kind of guinea pig this week while I'm out of gym. I looked up Grandpa Charlie's name and a whole lot of interesting stuff came up."

"Huh," said her mom, a tiny frown of concentration creasing her forehead. "Like what kind of stuff?"

"Birth and marriage records, census and military records. And if other people—Mrs. Creadle said they'd probably be distant cousins—have already done research, they'll have put their info online. We might even be able to find out the name of our ancestors who first came to America and where they came from." Zephyr smiled broadly, hoping her enthusiasm was catching.

"Well, that would be pretty cool," said her mother, slowly.

"So," Zephyr hedged, placing her hands on her knees, "I've been thinking. Since I only have this week to try out the genealogy sites while I have extra library time, I thought maybe we could sign up on one of the websites so I could do more searching at home."

Her mom puffed out her cheeks with a small shake of her head. "I've seen them advertised on TV and I get the impression they aren't cheap. Also, are you sure you have enough free time to make it worthwhile?"

Zephyr slumped back against the sofa cushions. *If I tell you what this is really about, you definitely won't want to do it. Grandma would, though, I bet!* "I'm sure I have enough spare time. Maybe I could ask Grandma June to open an account as an early Christmas present. She might like to know more about our family history too."

Her mom pushed up from her chair and took a step toward the couch. It suddenly struck Zephyr that she was taller than her own mother now. The only way her mom could look down at her was if she were standing while Zephyr sat. Her mother's stern words pulled her back to the conversation at hand. "Oh, no you don't. Your grandma would do anything for you, even if she couldn't afford it." She pulled in her lips and crossed her arms. "I tell you what. Give me a few minutes to do some research on it and I'll let you know."

"Thanks, Mom. I really appreciate it."

"You're welcome," she said as she turned to go back to her office. "But no promises, you understand."

Zephyr nodded. "I understand."

Scam leaned heavily against Zephyr's arm and thumped his tail against the sofa cushion. "You'll keep our secret, won't you, Scam? There's a good boy," she whispered as she stroked his head.

After several minutes' rest, Zephyr reached down and

grabbed the crutch, using it to help pull herself up from the couch. Just as she bent down to retrieve her backpack, her mom came back into the room.

"Well, I was right. The really good sites are pretty pricey," she announced, and Zephyr's heart sank.

[16]

CLIMBING THE FAMILY TREE

"But," her mom continued, "I found one that gives a two-week free trial with full access. We have to put in our credit card number, of course, but as long as we cancel before the trial period is up, it won't cost anything. Do you think you can find out what you want to know in two weeks?"

Zephyr thought of the deadline in her head and mentally mapped out the number of days left. "Sure! And I'll put a calendar reminder on my phone so we won't forget to cancel in time."

"No need," her mom replied with a wave of her hand, swatting away Zephyr's suggestion. "I've already signed up and put the reminder on my own phone."

Zephyr limped over and opened her arms for a hug. "Thanks! This means a lot to me."

Her mom gave her a tight squeeze, then held her at arm's length as she looked into Zephyr's eyes. "You never cease to surprise me, Zeph. Genealogy? Who'd have thought you'd get this excited over something like that."

Was there a hint of suspicion in her eyes? Did she wonder if there was more to this than Zephyr had told her?

"Well," said Zephyr, thinking fast, "I guess it's because of Mrs. Creadle. She just made it sound pretty exciting. Like being a detective."

Mom nodded and smiled. "A good teacher—or librarian— who's enthusiastic about her subject can make even the most esoteric subjects inviting to her students."

"What does *esoteric* mean?"

"It means something very unusual, only understood by a small group of people with specialized knowledge."

That sounds about right!

Her mother scooped up her backpack. "Here, I'll carry this and walk behind you up the stairs. That way if you lose your balance, I'll cushion your fall."

"Right," said Zephyr, with a crooked smile.

Zephyr's mom placed one hand on the stair railing and one on the small of Zephyr's back. The thought of Luke Barnes helping her into the bus flew back into her mind as she began hobbling up the steps.

"How'd you manage getting onto the bus? Anybody help you?"

I swear, Mom's a mind-reader!

"Um. Mrs. Tillett got somebody to take my backpack and steady me up the steps."

"Oh, good. Anybody I know?"

Lie? Can I lie about this? Darn. She's too psychic, she'd figure it out and then I'd be in trouble.

"Luke Barnes."

"Good grief. I hope he didn't make any remarks about damaged produce."

"No," said Zephyr, pulling herself up the last step. "He didn't say anything at all, actually."

"That's good. He probably didn't want to get on Mrs. Tillett's bad side...unless..."

Zephyr looked back to find her mother grinning at her suggestively. "Don't even go there, Mom. I'm sure he's just trying to keep out of detention."

"Sure," said her mom, giving her the bunny nose-twitching smile that basically said, *believe what you want, but I know better.*

Zephyr rolled her eyes as her mom stepped around her and carried the backpack to her bedroom.

"Where do you want this?" she asked.

"Just put it on the floor by my desk. Thanks, Mom."

"You're welcome," she said, turning to leave.

"Hey, Mom. Could you show me how to get onto the genealogy site before you leave?"

"Sure."

Zephyr sat down at the desk and opened her laptop. Her mom leaned over and typed in the website address. The same WELCOME TO THE FAMILY sign she'd seen on the library computer earlier that day popped up on the screen.

"This is the one with the free two-week trial. Hope it has what you want on it."

"Perfect. It's the one I was using with Mrs. Creadle."

Her mom licked her finger and flicked a quick downstroke in the air. "Score one for the Mom."

"Thanks! This is so great."

"You're welcome, honey. Here," she said, reaching for a pen and pad of paper. "I'll write down the ID and password so you can get on whenever you want. For the next two weeks, that is. And I'll let you know when dinner's ready," she said, jotting down the information, then stepping out of the room.

Zephyr quickly typed in the information about Grandpa

Charlie. *Yes!* Just like before, a long list of Charles Stone records appeared on the screen, as well as the Member Trees.

Ping!

Zephyr glanced over at her cell phone screen—a text message from Lorie.

Hang on Lorie. I'll look at your message in a minute.

Zephyr scrolled through the list of names for Member Trees until she found White. Taking a deep breath, she hovered the cursor arrow over the name for a moment before finally clicking it. A diagram appeared on the screen showing the name Charles Stone (with the note *"fifth cousin"* typed below it). It also listed Grandpa Charlie's birth and death dates and the names of his parents.

Zephyr clicked on the highlighted name of her great-grandfather, John Stone, and was disappointed to find it went no further, only giving his birth year of 1923, and repeating her great-grandmother's name. She checked several other Member Trees but never got further back in her family than 1923. *OK then. Time to start checking some of those records.* Zephyr clicked the back arrow until she returned to the records page.

Ping!

She'd forgotten about Lorie's text. Zephyr swiped the screen to reveal the two messages from her friend.

Zephyr glanced up at the computer screen with its inviting list of records. She shook her head and raised her finger to call Lorie.

"Zephyr! Dinner's ready!" Mom called up the stairs.

Scam, who had been curled up on Zephyr's bed, jumped down and trotted out the door. Sam's memory told him dinnertime for the Stone family also meant dinner for their four-legged member, who always got a little bit of "people food" stirred in with his dry kibbles. Zephyr returned to Lorie's text message instead of calling.

> Sorry! Was busy doing research.
> Have to eat dinner now.
> Will call u later!

She'd barely touched the send arrow when her phone *pinged* again.

> Ok. Glad ur not in hospital after
> falling down bus steps on the ride
> home. Or did Luke Barnes help u
> again???

Lorie had stayed after school for tennis practice, so she hadn't seen their friend, Hannah, help Zephyr get off the bus. Zephyr carried her phone with her as she made her way downstairs to the kitchen and typed back a response.

> I'm fine! LOL no, Hannah
> helped me. I'll text you after
> dinner!

Dinner, although delicious as always when her mom and dad cooked together, was a blur. Zephyr rushed through her spaghetti with meatballs and tossed salad, taking multiple bites in rapid succession.

"Hey, slow down, Zeph," urged her dad, laughing at his daughter. "You'll get a stomachache eating Mom's spicy spaghetti that fast."

Her mom frowned. "It's not *that* spicy. But really, Zephyr, what's the hurry? Do you have a lot of homework? Or is it the ancestry thing?"

"Both," said Zephyr through a full mouth, sucking up a long string of angel hair pasta.

"OK," her mom replied, slowly working through her own salad. "Just don't let the family research get in the way of your schoolwork."

"I won't," she promised before gulping down the last of her milk. "May I be excused?"

"Sure," her father said, eyeing her in amusement as he put down his forkful of spaghetti, and scooted back his chair. "Need help with the stairs?"

"Naw. I'm getting the hang of it, now. But thanks, anyway," she said pushing up from her seat and crutching her way out of the dining room.

As soon as she hobbled to her desk, Zephyr pulled out her math and science folders. The science homework involved online research, so Zephyr minimized the ancestry site, planning on setting it aside until she could get back to it. Two hours of math problems and science theories trudged by until, at last, Zephyr tucked all the homework away and reopened the ancestry website.

Now that her family had an account, at least temporarily, the sign hanging from the homepage tree announced, WELCOME *BACK* TO THE FAMILY!

Now, let's start with the oldest relative I know about so far. Zephyr went to the search box and entered her great-grandfather's information. Just as with Grandpa Charlie, a list appeared on the screen including a few Federal Census records. *Let's see what this census thing is all about.*

Zephyr selected the 1930 census and the photograph of a handwritten ledger appeared on the screen. The writing was tiny, so she zoomed in until she could read the names. There he was:

John Stone—son, age 7.

Wow. It was hard to think of her own father as a second grader, much less her great-grandfather! Tracing her finger upward, she read the names of her great-uncles and great-aunts, and then went back another generation to John's mom and dad, her great-great-grandparents:

Mary A. Stone—wife, age 42—housewife

Amos J. Stone—head of household, age 50—veterinarian

Her great-great-grandpa was a vet! And (Zephyr double checked her math on her phone's calculator) he was born way back in 1880. She sat back in her chair, impressed at the history she'd just uncovered. She tried to picture her great-great-grandfather, dressed in old-timey clothes while tending to cats and dogs, and probably horses, cows, and pigs, too. This was so cool! It was just like Mrs. Creadle had said—like a real-life detective story, discovering things about people who were part of her DNA.

But how about that name the ghost guys on Grandma's deer path talked about, Thomas Drake? Nothing here refers to him. Our family history is really interesting, but I don't see it connecting to Ahanu's father.

Zephyr returned to the search page and typed in "Thomas Drake, 1702." But where? What was the name of the nearest town? Opening another browser window, Zephyr pulled up a mapping site and typed in "The Great Dismal Swamp, Virginia." She scanned the map. *OK. So, the nearest town looks like Suffolk.*

Moving back to the ancestry page, Zephyr added "Suffolk, Virginia" to her Thomas Drake information and clicked submit. Within seconds, a list of Drakes popped up. Scanning down the list, she was disappointed to see that there weren't any Thomas Drakes listed with City of Suffolk references prior to the 1800s. As a matter of fact, there weren't *any* Drakes listed in Suffolk in the 1700s at all.

Hmmm. Maybe that's because Suffolk wasn't around till the nineteenth century? Let me just open another window and search Suffolk's history...

Zephyr jumped as Scam's wet nose reached up and brushed her elbow. "Scam! I didn't know you were there. How long you been up here, boy?" she asked as she scratched behind his ears. She glanced at her digital desk clock; 9:45 p.m. *What? You're kidding me! How'd it get so late so fast?*

"Lorie! I forgot to call her back!" Zephyr picked up the phone but then quickly set it back down. It was too late, even for a text. Both their parents had strict rules about no calls or messages after nine o'clock on school nights. *Man, she probably thinks I totally dissed her.*

Zephyr closed the laptop and proceeded to get ready for bed. It had been a long day; she was tired, both in body and brain. Luckily, since she was injured, her dad had taken over her usual dog walking duty. This left her one less thing to do before she could climb into her comfy bed and join Scam who was already asleep, curled up at the foot. Zephyr sighed as she opened the phone to set her wake-up alarm and saw there was another text from Lorie. One she hadn't even heard come in.

The time stamp read 8:38 p.m. She swiped the screen and read the text.

> **Did u forget me? AGAIN???**

Lorie was *mad.*

[17]

A REALLY WEIRD PROBLEM

ZEPHYR WOKE FROM A FITFUL SLEEP FULL OF STRESSFUL dreams. She'd spent the night pushing her way through tangling vines and spiderwebs, following the sound of Sam's pitiful crying. She rolled to her side and looked at the clock—as she had every two hours since she went to bed with Lorie's agitated text message on her mind—6:45 a.m. *Ugh.* She may as well get up. Stretching over her snoring cat-beagle, she turned on the lamp and turned off her phone's alarm setting. Zephyr gave Scam a gentle pat on his head, happy to see he had worked his way up in the night to cuddle next to her. *Glad he feels at home with me.* Scam opened one eye, huffed his disapproval, and then buried his face deeper into the comforter.

"I don't blame you a bit. I'd go back to sleep, too, if I could." Looking at his curled-up comfort, Zephyr's eyes filled with tears. *Oh, Sam. I hope you're OK. Please don't be afraid. I'm coming back for you. I promise!*

After brushing her teeth and rinsing the sleep from her eyes, Zephyr sunk back down on the bed. What should she say to Lorie? Heaving a sigh, she typed out a text.

105

> Sorry I didn't get back to u!
> Tons of homework

Well that sounds pretty lame and isn't totally true. Zephyr deleted the message and started again.

> Really sorry I didn't call. Will
> explain later.

I will? What will I say? My genealogy research is more important than you? Lorie gets her feelings hurt so easy...

Zephyr looked at the dozing Scam. "What do you think, Scam? Should I tell her everything? Will she think I've lost my mind? Will she think I made it all up as an excuse for not calling her back?"

Zephyr stared at her last entry for a moment, made her decision, and deleted it. She started a new text once more. *OK. She's my best friend. And, after all, Grandma believed me.* Zephyr put her face down at Scam's level. "And you'll back me up, right, buddy?"

> Sorry, my bad... lot on my
> mind. Some weird stuff
> happened over the weekend.

> I didn't get a chance to fill u in
> all the way at lunch yesterday.

> Will tell u in person. Want a
> ride to school today?

Zephyr pressed send and waited. Two minutes later, the

"Read" alert showed up on the screen just below her text. That was usually followed by an immediate response from Lorie. But not this time. Fifteen minutes crept by, still nothing. Zephyr decided she'd better go ahead and get dressed so she wouldn't be late. She could afford to take a little more time since her mom was driving her, but not a whole lot longer. Pulling on her clothes, she glanced down at the quiet phone screen every few minutes. *She's giving me a taste of my own medicine.* Then, finally, at half past seven, as Zephyr was tying her shoes, *ping!* She snatched her phone from the desk and swiped the screen.

OK

OK? She accepted my apology? She'd ride to school with me? Zephyr quickly texted back.

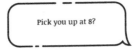

Pick you up at 8?

This time, Lorie texted back immediately.

OK

That's more like it. Zephyr sent her a thumbs up emoji and slipped the phone into her jeans pocket. When they pulled into the Garcia's driveway twenty minutes later, Zephyr peered out from the backseat behind her mother to see Lorie sitting on the wooden bench on her house's wide porch. Seeing their car,

Lorie stood and ducked her head inside the front door. A moment later, a smiling Mrs. Garcia, dressed in a black running suit, walked to the driver's side of the car. Lorie followed and Zephyr strained to read her expression. It was pretty blank but that didn't mean a whole lot. Lorie wasn't a morning person.

"Good morning, Meredith!" Mrs. Garcia called, leaning down by the car window. "This is so nice of you."

"Good to see you, Maria," Zephyr's mom replied, matching Mrs. Garcia's warm smile. "It's no trouble at all. You're right on the way. And even if you weren't, we'd want to give Lorie a ride."

"Well, I know she loves Zephyr's company and appreciates not having to ride that crowded school bus. I'm sorry Zephyr hurt herself, though," she said, peeking into the back seat.

"Thanks, Mrs. Garcia. It's not too bad," Zephyr said, leaning up toward her as Lorie opened the back passenger door across from Zephyr and slid in beside her.

"I'll pick the girls up at three thirty," her mom told Mrs. Garcia as she put the car into reverse.

"Great! Thanks again, Meredith. Have a good day, girls!"

They waved goodbye as the car pulled back onto the main road. Lowering her arm, Zephyr felt Lorie's gaze and turned to face her.

"Well?" said Lorie, both eyebrows raised above wide eyes. "What was so weird it made you forget to call me back yesterday?"

Zephyr saw her mom tilt her head and look back at her in the rearview mirror. Zephyr sunk lower in the seat and mimed a wide-eyed shushing face as she grabbed a pen and notebook out of her backpack.

"Oh, it was just a really weird math problem I had trouble figuring out," Zephyr covered as she scrawled a quick note. "This one," she said, pushing the notebook into Lorie's hand.

Lorie's lips moved as she silently read: *Can't tell u in front of Mom.*

Lorie's raised eyebrows elevated even closer to her hairline. "Oh, I see," she said, louder than necessary. "A *really* weird problem."

"Yeah," said Zephyr, glancing at the mirror. "Maybe you could come home with me this afternoon and we can work on it together."

Lorie gave an exaggerated wink and nod. "OK. That sounds like a good plan. I'll just text Mom and let her know. I'm sure it'd be fine with her."

"Better text her now, before we get to school and have to put our phones in our lockers for the day," said Zephyr.

"Right," said Lorie, sliding her phone out of her pocket.

They pulled into First Flight's circular drive a few cars behind their own bus. As they waited their turn to get closer to the entrance, they watched the kids from their bus get off and pile inside the building or gravitate into clusters along the walkway. A flutter of anticipation surprised Zephyr as she waited to see if Luke Barnes was at school that day. She released a breath she hadn't known she was holding as she saw him finally emerge with a couple of his friends. When the last students had left the bus, they watched as Mrs. Tillett closed the door. However, even though the bus ahead of hers pulled away, number 48 remained in place.

"Mrs. Tillett must be asleep at the wheel," Lorie grumbled. "Come on, lady! I have to go to the restroom before class starts!"

"You could get out here," Zephyr offered.

"No way. I'm your bodyguard, remember? And besides the restroom, I've got to be sure Ms. Grimstead's latest Social Studies notes are in my locker. I'm having trouble deciding which explorer to choose for our big Age of Exploration report.

Who did you choose? Knowing you, it's probably already written."

"Oh my gosh! I forgot all about it! I meant to work on it last night but—" Zephyr glanced up at the rearview mirror and briefly met her mother's gaze before she ducked her head back down to Lorie.

"Hey, welcome to my world," Lorie said smiling, then craned her neck toward the front windshield and glared at their bus. "Get it in gear, Mrs. Tillett!"

"She's probably filling out some paperwork," observed Zephyr's mom, tapping the steering wheel.

"Whatever," muttered Lorie as both girls stared at the bus, willing it to move.

"Finally," breathed Zephyr as number 48 rumbled away.

When they got closer to the entrance, Zephyr's mom stopped the car and announced, "All ashore that's going ashore! I'll see you girls after school. Have a good day!"

"Thanks, Mom," Zephyr replied opening her door.

"Thanks a lot, Mrs. Stone!" Lorie chimed in, hustling around the back of the car to help her friend get out. Zephyr's ankle felt much stronger than the day before, and she found that she didn't have to lean as heavily on her crutch.

Maybe I can get rid of this thing by tomorrow!

From the corner of her eye, she saw Luke heading for the entry door as Lorie walked ahead, elbows out, clearing the way. When they reached the entrance, Luke stepped ahead and held it open for them.

"Step aside, Barnes," said Lorie, "I got this." She turned back toward Zephyr and rolled her eyes. Zephyr felt blushing heat rise to her face as Luke threw her a glance before walking inside. He never released the door, however, as he studied the ceiling, waiting for Lorie to take the door from him. As Zephyr shuffled in, Lorie murmured loudly, "Bet he was going to trip you!"

Zephyr shrugged her shoulders. Somehow, she didn't think that had been his plan at all. *Am I annoyed? Flattered? I have no idea.*

[18]
SPILL

WHEN THE BELL RANG FOR THE FIRST CLASS, ZEPHYR headed straight for the library. As soon as she sat down at a computer, she saw Mrs. Creadle walking over to her smiling.

"Good morning, Zephyr! Ready to delve back into the past and start climbing your family tree?"

"Yep. As a matter of fact, my mom signed us up for a free two-week trial on the same ancestry site you and I looked at yesterday and I was able to explore it a little bit last night."

"Outstanding!" beamed Mrs. Creadle. "What did you learn? I believe you were surprised to find the name White listed with a Member Tree, right?"

Zephyr nodded as the librarian signed into her account. "I clicked on it and got as far as my great-grandfather, John Stone. Then I looked him up on a 1930 census record."

"I am so impressed, Miss Stone! You are a natural at this. You know, there's a teacher workday coming up in a few weeks, and since I'm all caught up with my own work, I thought it would be fun to go and investigate the genealogy records at the Library of Virginia in Richmond. Since so many people in this part of North Carolina are descendants of early English settlers who first landed in Jamestown, Virginia, I think it could be a treasure trove of information. I'd like to invite you and a few other students and make a field trip of it. What do you think? I completely understand if you don't want to give up a day off, though."

"That sounds great. I'm sure my parents would let me go."

"Wonderful! I'll just run it by administration and secure one of the school vans and a driver and get the permission forms all sorted. I'm sure I'll get the OK. For now, though," said Mrs. Creadle, smiling, "why don't you open the page to the latest information you found last night and we'll go from there."

For the next forty-five minutes, Zephyr tracked down various leads that the librarian had suggested to her before she went back to her own desk, including something called Probate. Probate displayed the wills that people wrote, and thereby told who they left money and other property to within their family. She found her great-great-grandpa Amos's name listed on an 1898 will (thank goodness she could read cursive writing!) in which his father, Elijah, left him sixty acres of land on Desert Road.

Desert Road! So the Great Dismal Swamp land has been in the family at least as far back as the 1800s. Could they have lived there a hundred years before that, in the 1700s? Zephyr's pulse quickened. *Could her family have lived there when Kanti lost her child?*

"How's it going, Zephyr?" asked Mrs. Creadle, walking back over to check on her.

"Really well. I've gotten back pretty far with my family. But I was hoping you could help me with that other name I mentioned yesterday—Thomas Drake."

Brring!

"Not today, it sounds like."

Heck.

"OK. *Spill*," urged Lorie, tapping her toe as she stood in Zephyr's room after school, that afternoon. "What happened at your grandma's that made you totally ignore your best friend?" she asked as she reached into the bag of salt and vinegar potato chips on Zephyr's desk. Zephyr popped a chip into her own mouth, then walked to her door, looked up and down the hallway, and closed it with a soft *click*.

"Wow. This must be really good," Lorie commented, grabbing the potato chip bag and sinking cross-legged on Zephyr's bed.

Zephyr sat down beside her, leaning on a pillow propped against the wall. "OK, so it's like this. I haven't told Mom and Dad because I don't want them to think I'm going nuts. They wouldn't believe me, anyway, and they'd just write it off as one of the phases they claim I'm going through every other week. Even worse, I'm afraid they'd blame Grandma June, somehow, and think she was entering some kind of early dementia like my Great-Aunt Margie did."

Lorie stuffed three chips into her mouth at one time and nodded encouragement.

"So I told you there was a moon mist. That's when a full moon shines through a thick fog and turns everything white. Apparently, it's something you see at the swamp sometimes. Well, around midnight Friday night, Sam got loose from me when I had to take him outside to pee, and one of those moon mists had settled in around Grandma's house. It was so thick that I couldn't even see where I was going, but I kept listening for Sam and tried to head in the direction I thought he went."

"Did your grandma go out with you to find him?" Lorie asked.

"No," replied Zephyr, shaking her head. "I didn't want to wake her up, and besides, as soon as I ran after Sam, I got lost in the mist. I would've had no idea how to find the house."

"Whoa. That must have been scary," Lorie whispered, her eyes wide. "So, you don't want to tell your parents you got lost in the fog because they'll blame your grandma?"

"No. That's not it. It's because of something that happened to me out in the moon mist. Something Grandma believes happened, but something that I know Mom and Dad wouldn't."

"Right," said Lorie, wiping her greasy fingers on her jeans. "So what *did* happen out in the misty moon thing?"

"Well, I finally found Sam."

"Yeah, I figured, since he's up here nosing around for potato chip crumbs," she said, her mouth curling into a one-sided grin as they both looked down at the dog scrounging for crumbs.

"But after I found him, I saw..." Zephyr slowly reached into the bag and took another chip.

"You saw...?"

"I saw a ghost."

"A ghost," said Lorie, pulling in one side of her mouth, a dimple forming in her cheek.

"Yeah. A ghost. *Really*," Zephyr added, seeing her friend's skeptical expression.

"Soooo what did this ghost look like?" Lorie asked, crossing her arms.

"It was the ghost of a Native American woman. She was dressed in white and was paddling a white canoe with a lantern that had a glowing, green light in the front of her boat."

Lorie focused squinting eyes on Zephyr. "Okaaay. And

115

then what happened? Did you wake up and realize it was just a dream?"

"No! It wasn't a dream. The ghost asked me to help her find her lost child. A little boy who wandered off while she was napping by the lake." Zephyr cleared her throat. "Three hundred years ago."

"Three hundred years ago? Boy, she's been paddling around a long time. Then what happened in the dre—mist?"

"We went back home and got back in bed."

"So, how'd you get back to your grandma's if you couldn't see anything then?" asked Lorie, taking the potato chip bag from between them and holding it in her lap.

"Well, there was this great big egret—"

"You mean, like that great big Firebird?"

Zephyr sighed. "No. Not like the Firebird *legend*. A real egret. After the ghost left, it flew overhead and the mist cleared behind it until we were able to find the house again."

"I seeee," said Lorie slowly.

Zephyr got up and opened her desk drawer, pulling out the envelope containing Lorie's thank-you note and the two egret feathers. "Here's the feather you gave me," said Zephyr, pulling out the long white plume. "And here is the feather that the moon mist egret dropped in front of me just as we got back to the house. It's how I knew for sure that it *hadn't* all been a dream when I woke up the next morning."

Lorie took the two feathers and inspected them in the late afternoon light streaming through the window. Creasing her forehead, she handed them back to Zephyr.

"I think you better tell me everything. Start from the beginning and don't leave anything out."

"Alright," Zephyr agreed. "But we're going to need another bag of chips."

[19]

SEE YOU LATER, ALLIGATOR

THIRTY MINUTES AND A FULL BAG OF SOUR CREAM AND chive potato chips later, Zephyr finished her account from the time she'd seen the egret out her bedroom window Thursday night, to her run through the forest away from the White graveyard and the "vanilla" haunting she'd witnessed on Saturday. Slumping back against her pillow, she waited for Lorie's reaction. Zephyr watched as Lorie scooted off the bed and began pacing the room as she thought it all over.

"And here I thought you were going to be bored out of your gourd all weekend at your grandma's!" She squinted at Scam who was meticulously licking between each of his toes. "So what does all this have to do with your ancestry research and not calling me back last night?"

Zephyr pulled her pillow out from behind her back and hugged it against her middle. "When I asked Mrs. Creadle how to find out about Native American children lost in the Great Dismal Swamp, she said there might be some clues in letters and stories people found when they researched their family history." She glanced over at her desk to a framed photograph of Grandma June and Grandpa Charlie hugging her between them when she was eight years old. "And since I have family who have lived in the swamp area for a long time, she said I should start with my own relatives. That's when I went on her computer and saw that one of the site members, whose last name was White, had information on my dad's side of the family."

"White? You mean like that guy who lied about his graveyard?"

"Exactly. So I talked Mom into signing us onto an ancestry site here at home last night so that I could go ahead and look into it without having to wait until I got back to the library. After I finished all my homework, I went back on it and kept running into cool info about our family. I tried to dig up stuff on Thomas Drake, too, but kept hitting dead ends. Anyway, I totally lost track of time until I realized it was too late to call you!"

"So how does this ancestry thing work, anyway?" Lorie asked leaning forward, hand on one hip.

"Here, I'll show you. It's amazing." She crawled off of her bed, scratching Scam on the way to the desk.

"If you say so. But your definition of amazing is a little different than mine..."

Zephyr moved her desk chair closer to her laptop and opened the Family Tree site. As Lorie peered over her shoulder, she typed in the password, but instead of the cheerful "Welcome Back to the Family" sign, she was greeted by an error message.

ID or Password incorrect. Try again.

"Hm. Must have typed wrong," Zephyr mumbled.

Focusing more of her attention onto the keyboard this time, she made her excited fingers move slowly, checking each letter and number as she went.

ID or Password incorrect. Try again.

"What?"

"Are you sure you remembered it right?"

"Pretty sure," she said, pulling out her mom's note with the sign-in code. "Yeah, that's what I thought I typed in. OK, one more time."

ID or Password incorrect. Try again.

Zephyr pushed away from her desk and opened her door. Leaning out she called, "Mom? Hey, Mom?" Heaving a sigh at the silence, she walked to the top of the stairs and yelled again. No reply.

"Heck," she muttered, walking back into her room. "She must be back in the office where she can't hear me. I'll text her."

After a few taps on her phone, an answering *ping* sounded.

> Changed the password. You need to finish your social studies report first and then I will give it to you. No arguments. OAO

Zephyr showed the message to Lorie and rolled her eyes with a big sigh.

"OAO? Over and Out?"

"Yeah. In Mom language that means, 'Don't bother to reply, case closed.' *Argh!*"

Zephyr looked at the countdown on her phone's background. "I don't have a lot of time! And in a couple days, I'll be back in PE and I'll lose my extra library hour."

"Yeah, bummer. But I'll be glad when your tallness is back on the basketball court."

Zephyr glared at her friend.

"OK. Sorry," she said, gazing down at Scam who kept rolling to the side as he attempted the feline "playing the cello" position to clean himself. She looked back up at Zephyr. "He *is* acting a little strange, and I can understand how Miss Research could lose track of time, but this whole ghost thing and Sam being possessed by a cat spirit is really out there, ya know?"

"I know," agreed Zephyr, nodding. "If you were the one sitting here telling me about it, I'd think you must have dreamed it up too."

"But," continued Lorie, her eyebrows rising, "you said your grandma believed you. Maybe because she just doesn't want to upset you?"

"No, she really believes me." Zephyr inclined her head toward her friend. "You have to promise to keep this to yourself."

Lorie crossed her heart. "Believe me, I'm not telling anybody any of this."

"After Grandpa died, Grandma used to watch out the window on moon mist nights because she'd heard it was the kind of night when the spirits of the dead came around, and she'd always hoped she might see him. She says she *did* see strange movements in the mist, but she was always too afraid to go out in it."

"I can see that. Hmmm. Our grandmas actually have something in common. My granny is really big on the Day of the Dead stuff."

"What's that? Sounds like some kind of zombie movie."

"Not exactly. It comes from Mexico and happens every year on November first and second. The tradition is that dead relatives come back to visit then, so families will pack picnics and go party in the cemetery with music and everything."

"Sounds pretty bizarre."

"Look who's talking," Lorie responded, tucking in her chin and looking over invisible reading glasses.

"OK, OK. Listen, there's one thing that might convince you," said Zephyr, sinking back down on her bed. "Of course, it's not guaranteed, and it involves canoeing on Lake Drummond."

Lorie set her fist on her hip. "I'm in the canoeing club, remember? What is it?"

Zephyr bit her lip. Doing this would either totally convince her the ghost was real, or totally convince her it was all in Zephyr's head.

"Well, Kanti told me something else I didn't tell you yet."

"I'm all ears," Lorie replied, plopping back on the bed beside Zephyr and leaning toward her.

"She said I could have a coin that her husband hid in a tree stump along the shoreline of the lake. She said he put it there in honor of their love."

Lorie's eyes widened. "A coin? Like a three-hundred-year-old coin?"

Zephyr nodded. "But, as Grandma would say, it'd be like trying to find a needle in a haystack, I'm sure."

"True," Lorie agreed. "But it'd be kind of fun searching for it. Like a real treasure hunt. And if we find it, I promise I'll believe that what you say happened to you actually happened to you. I mean, I believe *you* believe what happened really happened, but—"

Zephyr placed her hand on Lorie's arm. "Hey, it's OK. I get it. Do you think you could go to my grandma's next Saturday? Not sure how we'll get there, but we'll figure it out."

Lorie opened the calendar on her phone. "Looks clear to me. And I know my parents won't mind."

"I'll give Grandma a call right now and see if we could come over if the weather's good."

Zephyr pulled up the contacts list on her phone and tapped on the name "Grandma June."

"Hello?" her familiar voice answered.

"Hi, Grandma!"

"Zephyr, honey! How are you doing? How's your poor ankle?"

"Oh, it's a whole lot better. Listen. I told Lorie everything about last weekend. Don't worry, though, she won't tell anybody." She glanced at Lorie who pulled an invisible zipper across her lips.

"That's fine. I know you can trust Lorie. She's a good friend."

"Yeah, she is. Oh, and I've learned some pretty interesting stuff about our family on Grandpa's side. I told our librarian I wanted to find out something about lost Native American children in the Great Dismal Swamp area and she showed me how to use an ancestry website that might give clues. But you'll never guess who else has been researching the Stone family."

"Who?" asked her grandmother, "Your Aunt Wanda? She's pretty big into family history."

"No. Somebody whose last name is...White!"

"What? You're kidding."

"Nope. I'll tell you more about it later after I do some more research, but here's the thing—we want to take a canoe out onto

Lake Drummond next weekend and see if we can find that coin Kanti told me about. Any ideas about how we could do that? Do you have a canoe stored somewhere?" Zephyr asked hopefully.

"No. After your Grandpa Charlie died, I sold ours. And you girls are too young to take a boat out on your own, anyway. I know Virginia law requires somebody over eighteen for that. I'd find us a canoe and go with you myself, but I'm hosting our local book club that day and I'll be busy preparing lunch and dealing with all that."

"Hang on, Grandma," said Zephyr, taking the phone from her ear. "Lorie, she says we're too young to take a canoe out by ourselves and she's going to be busy with a club meeting at her house."

Lorie poked out her lips and frowned but then suddenly brightened. "I know!" she said, raising her hand like she was trying to get her teacher's attention in school. "My sister owes me a favor. Michelle's going to be home on break from college next weekend. I bet I can get her to take us. She's on her school's rowing team and knows a lot about boats. Does your grandma have a canoe we could borrow?"

Zephyr shook her head no to the canoe question and put the phone back to her ear. "Lorie's older sister could take us. She's over eighteen and she knows boats."

"Perfect," said Grandma June. "I can get George Porter to loan you his canoe. He's a good family friend and I know he wouldn't mind pulling it down to the lake and launching it for you. And here's a bonus—George is a member of the Nansemond tribe. Maybe he'll have some insights."

"Great! Do you think Mom and Dad will think it's strange I want to go back to your house so soon?"

Grandma June laughed and Zephyr realized how it sounded. "Oh! I didn't mean it was strange for me to want to see you, just that...I kind of complained last time...before I spent the weekend...that you didn't have internet or cable. But—"

Grandma June chuckled again. "You don't have to explain, sweetie. I completely understand. But, yes, they might think it's unusual for you to want to come back so soon. Hmm. How about I tell them I could sure use your help with my book club luncheon?"

"That should work. I'll tell them Lorie wants to come, too, and her sister will drive us. They like Michelle a lot and always talk about how mature and levelheaded she is. I think it's because she goes to the University of Virginia like Dad did, and they want me to go there too. *If* my grades are good enough," added Zephyr. "Anyway, we could help you set up before we take out the canoe, so it wouldn't be like we were lying."

"Perfect."

"Thanks, Grandma. Love you!"

"Love you too, sweetie pie. See you later, alligator!"

"After 'while, crocodile!"

Zephyr tapped the end button and smiled at Lorie, whose forehead was furrowed into deep creases.

20

BACK TO THE SWAMP

"ZEPHYR STONE, I HOPE THAT CROCODILE TALK WAS JUST for fun."

Zephyr laughed. "There aren't any crocodiles in the Great Dismal Swamp. Not sure about alligators though..." she trailed off as she tried to recall the wildlife information from the Visitor Center.

"No way!" Lorie protested, fist on her hip. "I'd rather face a ghost than an alligator!"

"I'm sure we'll be safe. It's not like we'll be slogging through the Florida Everglades. It's Virginia. Plus, we'll be in a boat."

Lorie crossed her arms, unconvinced. "A very small boat."

"Honestly, Lorie. When was the last time you heard of an alligator attack in Virginia?"

"I don't follow the Virginia news."

"Hang on," said Zephyr, moving to her desk and clicking her computer keys. "I'll do a Google search."

Lorie came over and looked over Zephyr's shoulder.

"There. See?" Zephyr said, pointing to an article about the range of alligators. "It's been over a hundred years since gators have hung around the Virginia part of the Great Dismal Swamp. The farthest they come is North Carolina."

Lorie raised one skeptical eyebrow. "You think alligators can read maps?"

"Noooo. I think it's too cold for them up there."

"Yeah, but what about global warming?" Lorie pressed, squinting at the screen.

"Lorie," pronounced Zephyr, turning in her chair to look her friend in the eye. "Do you want to go on this treasure hunt or not? Should I find somebody else to go with me?"

"No. I'll go. I guess it *is* getting colder now. The gators probably went south for the winter."

They aren't like birds, Lorie, she thought to herself but opted not to mention it out loud. "Good thinking," Zephyr agreed instead. "I better get started on my homework so I can get on that social studies report."

"OK. I've got to get on mine, too," Lorie said, beginning to gather up her things. "And don't forget Ms. Grimstead's giving us a major historical vocabulary test tomorrow. I'll call Michelle tonight and tell her we're looking for a colonial *artifact*." She stopped and smiled broadly at Zephyr. "Aren't you proud of me for saying *artifact*? It's going to be on our test."

"Very cool. You might even say *esoteric*." Zephyr replied, cleaning up the crumbs from their chips.

"Eso-what?"

"It's one of my mom's vocabulary words. See how educational this is getting to be?"

Lorie scoffed and put her backpack strap over one shoulder. "Yeah, right. You're just trying to get my mind off alligators and ghosts."

"Maybe so," said Zephyr, raising one eyebrow with a grin. "Come on, let's see if Mom can give you a ride home."

"I really appreciate this," Zephyr said again as Lorie's sister pulled their car into Grandma June's driveway the next weekend.

"No problem," Michelle replied. "It'll be fun searching for historical artifacts, and I can use the canoe practice anyway. I mostly only get to row these days now that I'm on the crew team at school."

Grandma June opened her front door. "Hello, girls! I just happened to pass by the window when I saw a car drive up. I was hoping it was you all and not one of the club members arriving early! So good to see you again, Lorie," she said, walking down the porch steps and opening her arms for a hug. "And, Michelle!" she exclaimed as her arms encircled the two younger girls in a group hug. "It's been so long. You're a grown-up woman now!"

Lorie snickered as she stepped out of Grandma June's embrace. "Well she may be grown, but she didn't grow very far *up*."

Michelle flashed her dark eyes, which were level with her younger sister's. "Hey, I may be small, but I'm mighty!"

"That's right, *Hermia*. You tell her!" Grandma June cheered, and turning to Lorie, she continued, "Don't forget what Helena said—'And though she be but little, she is fierce!'"

"Hermia?" Zephyr questioned.

"Helena?" Lorie asked.

"Yes, Hermia and Helena," her grandma responded, reaching up to ruffle Zephyr's hair. "From Shakespeare's *A Midsummer Night's Dream*." She chuckled at the two seventh graders. "I guess you haven't read it yet. But I bet Michelle has."

"Yes, I have. And I did relate to Hermia. In fact, I'm planning to name my first boat after her."

"Ha," Lorie said. "And here I always thought it'd be called the *Lorie Anne* after your favorite sister."

"Come on in, y'all," Grandma June said laughing. "I just need you to set the table for me, then I'll call George to meet you down by the boat launch spot at the lake."

A few minutes later, the dining table was covered with an autumn-gold tablecloth and set with Grandma June's monogrammed pewter flatware and eight book-shaped plates.

"Wow," Lorie breathed. "I've never seen plates shaped like books before."

"Aren't they neat?" her grandma said, touching one proudly. "I like to tell the club members that the 'S' on the flatware actually stands for 'stories' when they're matched with these plates." They all stepped back to admire the table for a moment before Zephyr peeked at the time on her phone screen.

"Would you mind calling Mr. Porter, now?" she asked her grandma. "We can go on ahead and meet him at the lake."

"Good idea," said Grandma June as she opened a desk drawer and drew out two pieces of paper. "Here," she said, handing them to Michelle. "It's pretty straight forward getting to Lake Drummond, but this map will show you the whole area. And you'll need to fill out this permit and leave it on your dashboard so it's visible through your windshield. I picked one up for you this morning."

"Thanks, Mrs. Stone. Does Mr. Porter have two paddles, and life vests for all of us?"

"Yes, he's got everything ready for y'all. I'll call him now."

"Thanks for arranging this, Grandma," Zephyr said, stepping forward to give her a hug.

"My pleasure. Thank *you* all for helping me with the table," she answered smiling. "And good luck on your treasure hunt, girls" said Grandma June as the trio headed out the door. "Oh!" she called, leaning out of the doorway as the girls neared Michelle's car. "I almost forgot." She disappeared back into the house, then returned in a few moments with a large pair of binoculars. "Here, Zephyr. These might come in handy. They belonged to your Grandpa. I use them a lot when Doris and I go out duck watching."

"Great! Thanks, Grandma," Zephyr said, taking the binoculars from her and pecking her on the cheek.

"Now," said Grandma June. "Do you have water? And a compass?"

"Check and check, Mrs. Stone," Michelle replied. "I think we've got everything we need now. Have a good book club lunch. See ya!" she sang out as they got into the car and slammed the doors. "Here," she said, turning around in her seat to hand the map to Zephyr. "You've been here before. You can be the navigator."

Driving along the edge of the forest, Zephyr noticed Lorie staring out the window, eyes glued to the passing trees, marshes, and pools of water.

"See?" she said to her wide-eyed friend. "No alligators."

Michelle giggled. "But you should watch out for snapping turtles. They can be pretty brutal."

As they drew closer to the lake, the trees thinned out and the land opened up to wider marshy vistas. Once they got to the end of the road, Michelle pulled over to the side, a few yards back from the boat launch area. While she worked on filling out the permit, Zephyr and Lorie climbed out and walked onto the wooden boardwalk that led to an observation deck over the lake. The air was completely still as they looked out over the broad expanse of water that reflected the blue sky and white, puffy clouds above. The lake water changed to the color of amber tea where it lapped gently against the shoreline, which was littered with brown cypress tree needles and tumbled-down tree stumps. There weren't any other cars, which struck Zephyr as odd since it was such a beautiful Saturday.

Wonder if they know something we don't know?

A large black and white osprey soared overhead, its high-pitched whistle piercing the quiet. Zephyr looked up, holding her freckled hand above her eyes to shade them from the bright sun as she watched the graceful raptor fly out of sight. Lowering her gaze, she breathed in the fresh air, marveling at how peaceful and un-spooky it all was in the light of day. As they turned back toward the car to wait for Mr. Porter, an unearthly sound rose up behind them, and they stopped in their tracks, nearly toppling over each other as their toes stubbed on the uneven boards. It was a harsh, dry, rattling call, not quite human but not quite animal. Zephyr and Lorie stared at each other with wide eyes. The sound sent prickles through Zephyr's eardrums and all over her skin. To her, it seemed to be crying,

"*Help! Help! Help!*"

21

LAKE DRUMMOND TREASURE HUNT

Lorie grabbed Zephyr's upper arm in a painful grip. "Wh-what's that?"

A shadow swept over them as the wisp of a breeze fluttered across the tops of their heads. The girls instinctively ducked, and then, looking up, saw long, black, slender legs trailing behind a sleek white-feathered body. Its wings were silently flapping, and its serpentine neck was tucked inward.

"It's an egret!" Lorie proclaimed. "Where the heck did it come from?"

Zephyr shaded her eyes with her hand as she watched it fly across the marsh and disappear. *Yeah, I wonder...*

Lorie ran to her sister's car and stuck her head into the open window. "Did you see that? Did you see it coming?" she asked excitedly.

Michelle looked up from her phone. "See what?"

"Are you kidding me? You didn't see that egret dive-bombing us on the dock?"

Michelle set her phone on her lap and looked up at her sister. "No. I can't get any signal out here, so I was organizing my photos into albums. What happened? You get hit with some major bird poop out there?" she asked with a smirk.

Lorie shook her head. "Nooooo, we—"

She was interrupted by the rumbling of an old pickup truck towing a canoe-laden trailer.

"That must be Mr. Porter," Zephyr noted. "I hope so, anyway." As the truck came closer, she read its front license plate: GPRTR.

Yep. That's gotta stand for George Porter.

The faded, red Ford pulled to a stop and the driver poked his head out the window. "You girls belong to June Stone?"

Zephyr stepped forward. "Yes, sir. I'm her granddaughter, Zephyr, and these are my friends, Lorie and Michelle."

Lorie waved as Michelle stepped out of the car saying, "Thanks for letting us use your canoe, Mr. Porter. I promise we'll take good care of it."

The truck door creaked as Mr. Porter climbed out. He slammed the door shut with a hollow metallic clunk and then held out a leathery palm to shake each of their hands.

"I have no doubts you will," he said, keen blue eyes twinkling beneath the brim of his green John Deere baseball cap. "I've known June for many a year, and her husband longer than that, rest his soul. If she says you're trustworthy, then you are. End of story. All I need to know is about how long you think you'll be out so I can make sure to be here when you get back."

Michelle and Lorie looked to Zephyr who shrugged. "Um... two or three hours, maybe?" she guessed.

"Well then, I'll just mosey on back in a couple and bring a book along to read while I wait if you're not back yet. Got nowhere else to go. No rush." He ambled over to the trailer and began the process of unloading the canoe. The girls hurried over to help with what they could.

While Lorie and Michelle buckled on Mr. Porter's life

vests, Zephyr stepped closer to the old man. "Uh, Mr. Porter? Grandma June said you're a member of the Nansemond Tribe."

"That's right," he said, pushing up his cap brim. "Except we are the Nansemond Indian Nation."

"Oh, I..." stammered Zephyr, heat rising up to her face.

Mr. Porter returned Zephyr's embarrassment with a kind smile. "That's alright, dear. I expect I may be the first Nansemond you've met."

Zephyr nodded. "That's true, you are," she replied, feeling her flushed face begin to cool. "Mr. Porter, I was wondering if you might know anything about a little boy who got lost in the swamp back around 1705. I heard a story...somewhere...about a two-year-old boy who got lost in the Great Dismal Swamp. His mother was Nansemond and his father was a colonist. The little boy was just visiting here with his mother since he was part of the Nansemond that moved to the Nottoway. Does that make any sense or ring any bells?"

"Well," he said, removing his cap and scratching his head, "I can't say I've heard about a specific lost child. The swamp can be a dangerous place, you know. But I can give you some of our history."

Zephyr nodded as she reached for a vest.

"Back in 1638, the daughter of a Nansemond chief married an English man by the name of John Basse. Then around 1650, our people split into two groups. One side chose to take on more of the English ways, intermarrying with them and becoming baptized Christians. Those folks settled by the Great Dismal Swamp. The other group, though, wanted to remain separate from the English colonists and moved west to the Nottoway River near the Nottoway people. By the 1800s, the western group had pretty much melded in with the Nottoway and no longer existed as their own separate tribe. I descend from the ones who chose to live here, near the Great Dismal Swamp."

"Wow," breathed Zephyr. "Do you ever wonder what it might have been like to live in the Nottoway group?"

"Sometimes," he said. "But even though my people took on some of the colonial ways, we still have our own honored traditions. Lately the young people have taken a real interest in the old ways. As a matter of fact, we have a great pow wow every August with singing and drumming, and some members dance in full regalia. There's delicious food and crafts for sale and sometimes even wild bird exhibitions. Everyone's welcome to join us. You should come to the next one! It's a great way to learn more about the Nansemond Nation and have fun at the same time."

"Sounds really cool," said Zephyr, thinking she just might take him up on that offer. It all sounded really interesting. She refocused her thoughts on her questions. "Does the name Thomas Drake mean anything to you? He might have been the little boy's father."

Mr. Porter's brow creased in concentration. "Hm, nope. Can't say I've heard of any Drakes."

Zephyr sighed and nodded. *Of course it couldn't be that easy.*

After buckling on Mr. Porter's life vests, the girls helped him slide the canoe off the trailer.

"OK," Michelle said, taking command. "I'm the most experienced so I'll steer from the back and be the sternman. Lorie, you'll paddle up front as the bowman. And, Zephyr, you just sit in the middle and tell us where to go."

Lorie giggled and Zephyr blushed slightly. She could tell she'd been given the easiest of responsibilities.

"You know what I mean, Zeph, you're the only one who knows exactly what you two are looking for," Michelle reassured. "Lorie just told me you've read about old colonial arti-facts sometimes hidden in old stumps around the lake." Once the girls had dropped their bags and backpacks into the canoe, they helped Mr. Porter push it toward the water's edge. Then, one by one, they each climbed in and settled into their assigned positions. Once they were seated, Mr. Porter pushed the boat the rest of the way into the glassy water and waved them off.

"So," Michelle began, using her paddle on the lake floor to help push them out further. "Where to?"

Zephyr twisted her head from side to side as she weighed her options. She hadn't put a lot of thought into this past getting out on the water. "How about we go out toward the center a little way and let me get an overall look at the shoreline."

The sisters paddled the canoe smoothly across the lake, and although they engaged in their usual trade of sibling insults and sarcasm, Zephyr was impressed at how good of a team they made when they worked together.

"Let's stop here," Zephyr suggested. Both girls pulled their paddles up and the canoe slowed until it rotated in a small circle and stopped. With a perfect reflection in the lake, it looked as though they were floating in a powder-blue sky amid cotton candy clouds. Pulling out the binoculars, Zephyr scanned the shoreline for likely tree stumps. *If I were a bird-shaped tree stump holding a three-hundred-year-old coin, where would I be hiding?* "Geez. I don't know. How about we head for that clump of trees over there." She pointed at the shore. "Probably some old stumps mixed in with them."

Michelle used her paddle and aimed them for the shore toward the southern end of Lake Drummond. "You're the boss. I don't care where we go as long as I have this kind of scenery to enjoy," she exclaimed. Zephyr and Lorie glanced back to see her gesturing her arm at the trees mirrored all around the lake.

Lorie turned back ahead and quietly nodded her agreement, putting her own paddle back into the water.

As they moved toward Zephyr's choice of shoreline, the clumps of white clouds began to merge together until there was more white than blue reflecting in the still water. By the time they reached the stretch of old cypress trees, the blue had disappeared completely, and the white clouds were beginning to be tinged with gray. With no sunlight shining through to warm them, the girls suddenly felt chilled. Michelle reached for their packs and pulled out the sweatshirts they'd brought along, passing them forward.

"This is really strange. The weather changed so fast," said Michelle, tugging on her UVA Cavaliers sweatshirt and pulling the hood up over her short cropped hair.

"I'll check the weather report on my phone," Lorie offered, pulling it from her pocket.

"I don't think you'll get a signal out here," Zephyr cautioned. "Michelle couldn't even get one back at the car, remember?"

Lorie tapped at her phone screen. "You're right. Nothing. Nada."

"Well," Michelle said, "it's probably just a cold front coming through. I checked the forecast before we left and there wasn't anything about rain."

"That's good," Zephyr replied, crossing her arms and hugging them close to her middle. "Alright, so I heard a...legend...about a coin hidden in an old stump that's shaped like a big bird."

"You mean like Big Bird on *Sesame Street*?" asked Michelle.

Lorie looked back at Zephyr. "I swear I never told her about you and Big Bird," she whispered.

Zephyr lifted one doubtful eyebrow at her friend. "No," she

answered, turning to face Michelle. "I've heard that the coin is hidden inside a stump that's shaped like a large, flying bird. A real bird, not a Muppet bird."

"Got it," said Michelle, steering them closer to shore, as they had started to drift a bit.

Tall cypress trees dripping with veils of dusky gray Spanish moss clustered together in the shallow water. Their accompanying cypress knees sprouted around them, bringing Zephyr uncomfortable memories of her grandmother's dancing wood elves and her desperate search for Sam that night in the moon mist.

"See anything promising?" Michelle asked.

"Not yet," Zephyr said as Lorie shook her head no also. "How about we move to that section, over there," she suggested, pointing toward an area crowded with broken down trees.

Drawing close to the water's edge, Lorie and Michelle pulled in their paddles and let the canoe glide to a stop. Michelle sneezed, and as Zephyr turned around to offer a quick, "Bless you," her eyes widened instead at what she saw behind them.

"What is *that*?" she asked, pointing in shock.

[22]

PHANTOM TOMBSTONES

Both sisters swiveled in their seats as they watched a gray wall of thick mist swiftly slip across the water toward them.

"Fog!" said Michelle. "Wow, I've never seen a fog bank move in so fast!"

"What should we do?" cried Lorie.

"We better sit tight for right now. See what this fog is going to do. It could lift pretty fast, but we don't want to get caught out in the middle of the lake and then not be able to see the shore if it doesn't end up lifting," Michelle warned. "As long as we hang close to the shoreline, we can't get too lost. I mean, it's a big lake, but eventually we *should* be able to get back to our starting point if we hugged the edge of it."

Should. Geez, something's off here. It just doesn't feel right. But it won't do any good to say anything. Zephyr scanned their surroundings. All but the immediate area was blanketed in a thick fog. *This feels way too much like the moon mist.*

"Let me check my compass. It should at least help us to get our bearings," Michelle said, reaching back into her pack again.

She pulled out the compass and rotated it in the palm of her hand, frowning.

"What direction are you looking for? Can you find north?" Lorie asked, turning around in her seat.

Michelle held out the compass on the flat of her palm for them both to see. "I can't find *anything!*"

Lorie and Zephyr leaned toward Michelle and looked down at the compass. Its needle was spinning around like a crazy, runaway merry-go-round.

"Why's it doing that?" Lorie asked, alarmed.

Michelle's black eyebrows scrunched together. "Your guess is as good as mine," she murmured as she slipped the compass's braided neck strap over her head.

"What should we do now?" Zephyr asked.

Michelle looked around. "I'm not sure. But this fog doesn't show any signs of lifting, so let's just hug the shoreline and start moving. Lorie, push off and let's turn around the other way. Maybe that's the shortest way back...maybe."

Zephyr crossed her arms and slumped down. *Man. So much for finding the coin today.*

The sisters maneuvered the canoe around and began paddling back the way they hoped they'd come. To their left was the pine needle strewn sand where a ghostly mist was now shrouding the trees and stumps and cypress knees, and to their right, where they should've seen the expanse of the lake, was nothing but a smoky, gray wall.

"Hey! What's that?" Lorie called, pointing ahead.

Zephyr craned her neck around Lorie. Iron-gray rectangles of different sizes, some with rounded tops, some with angular edges, huddled together several yards away. "They l-look like tombstones," she stuttered.

"We didn't see them on our way in," Michelle moaned. "That's not a good sign."

You can say that, again. And not just because it means we're lost!

"Guys, this is getting really creepy. Do we have to keep going in this direction?" asked Lorie as she pulled in her paddle.

My thoughts, exactly!

"I know it's creepy, but an old graveyard can't hurt us," Michelle said in the calming tones of common sense. Zephyr was grateful she'd come along. "Let's just keep moving. We can't keep changing direction or we'll never get out of here."

Lorie put her paddle back into the lake and slowly drew it through the water. "Why do I have to be the one in front? I don't even like to be in front on roller coasters," she muttered.

Stroke by stroke, they drew closer to the graveyard. Despite how creepy the whole thing was, Zephyr found her curiosity piquing. However, just as they pulled within a few feet of it, a cloud of mist blew in front of the canoe, obscuring their sight of the graveyard entirely. The mist wafted by them in a matter of seconds as they continued to paddle, and soon enough, they were able to see again. But...there was nothing to see.

"It's gone!" Lorie gasped, placing the paddle across her lap.

"What do you mean?" Zephyr asked, leaning to her left around Lorie's back, convinced that she must be looking in the wrong direction.

"The graveyard! It just disappeared!"

Both of the younger girls turned to face Michelle. Mouth slightly open and forehead creased, she simply shook her head. "Alright. So it must *not* have been a graveyard. Must have just been a bunch of stumps, and now that we're closer, they don't look like tombstones anymore."

"I'm not so sure about that," Lorie said, skepticism coloring her reply.

"Me, either," Zephyr agreed.

"That's a *good* thing, guys. It means we're probably heading in the right direction after all. Keep paddling!" ordered Michelle.

"OK, OK. Keep your shirt on," Lorie grumbled. A few silent minutes passed as the girls continued forward, the only sound being the quiet dribble of water flowing over the paddles into the lake. "Look!" shouted Lorie, her voice flat against the sodden air.

"You've got to be kidding me," Michelle groaned.

"It looks just like the other—whatever they were—before they disappeared," Zephyr said. Looming several yards away was another group of tombstones, identical to the first ones.

"It's got to be an optical illusion or something," whispered Michelle under her breath. "Keep paddling, Lorie."

Zephyr grabbed the binoculars and looked through them. There was no mistaking them this time. "Those definitely aren't stumps," Zephyr confirmed, staring through the lenses. "I can even see markings on them. And, oh, God. I can read the name on one of them!"

"What's it say?" Lorie asked as they drew closer. "Wait. I can see them myself now." She gasped. "Zephyr! That one says 'Stone'!"

Just then, a swift cloud of mist swirled around them, blocking their view. When it cleared, the phantom graveyard was gone again. But this time, there was a difference. As they came close to the spot where the stones should have been, the quiet was broken by the sound of giggling. It was the same mocking laughter Zephyr had heard in the moon mist.

"What's so funny, Lorie?" Michelle asked.

Lorie whipped around. "That's not me! I thought it was one of you!" Zephyr and Michelle shook their heads as the giggling grew louder.

Michelle struck her paddle hard into the water. "Keep

paddling!" Bursts of maniacal laughter popped around them like soap bubbles as the girls plunged forward.

"I see another graveyard ahead!" Lorie warned, a hint of hysteria raising her pitch into a high soprano range.

"Ignore it!" Michelle shouted, paddling hard. Again, a thick cloud of mist rolled over them, obscuring their sight. When it didn't clear as quickly as it had before, Michelle ordered her sister to stop paddling. "I don't want to stop, but we can't see where we're going, and we sure as heck don't want to run into a stump or a rock in the water and then capsize," she explained.

Lorie pulled up her paddle and turned around facing Zephyr. "Do you hear that?"

Zephyr held her breath to listen and then shook her head. "I don't hear anything."

"Exactly," Lorie confirmed. "At least the freaky laughing stopped."

The girls exhaled a trio of deep, ragged sighs into the blinding mist. Zephyr turned around to Michelle. "Maybe try the compass again." Michelle held the compass down in front of her, frowning as she turned it 360 degrees around. "No good?" asked Zephyr.

"Nope. The needle just keeps going around in circles. Just like I'm trying to keep us from doing."

Zephyr looked up and scanned the shoreline. "Hey! Look over there!" Zephyr said, pointing at a grove of ghostly cypress trees. "Is that the egret?"

"It looks like *an* egret. Don't know if it's *the* egret that supposedly spooked you guys back at the dock, though," Michelle countered.

"Let's get closer," said Zephyr. *Too many egret sightings to be a coincidence, I think!* "It looks like its wings are spread out, so it will probably fly away as we get nearer, though." The fog blocked out all sound other than the sluicing of water over the paddles. Once more, Zephyr was reminded of the moon mist night when Kanti's spectral canoe slipped in on a stream of luminous vapor.

"If that's your egret, it's awfully tame," Michelle noted as each stroke brought them closer. "It's not moving a muscle." She was right, it wasn't moving. Its wings were still outstretched. Maybe it had its eye on a fish in the water?

As they moved within a few feet of the stationary bird, Lorie pulled in her paddle and looked back at the other girls. "And it's not going to move a muscle either."

"What do you mean?" asked Zephyr, confused.

"Because it isn't a bird— it's a tree stump."

[23]

A SHOCKING EXPERIENCE

"What? Really?" Zephyr asked, rising from her seat.

"Careful, Zephyr!" Michelle warned. "You'll tip us over."

"Sorry!" She hastily sat back down. "Can we get closer to it?"

"I think so," Michelle said. "Lorie, watch out for stumps in the water. We could tip over if we hit one too hard."

Lorie nodded as she carefully dipped her paddle. It was hard to tell where the filmy air ended, and the water began. Within a few careful strokes, their canoe bumped gently against the old stump. It had weathered to a streaky, pale, sun-bleached gray, and it did look like an egret or some other large wading bird crouched down, wings spread, ready to take flight.

"Can y'all pull us sideways to it?" Zephyr asked, leaning forward to see over Lorie's shoulder.

"Sure," said Michelle. "Lorie, push off of it gently and I'll paddle on the other side."

The girls worked together until Zephyr found herself sitting right next to the stump, close enough that she could touch it. Reaching out, she lightly grazed its rough surface. A mild, electric sensation coursed through her fingertips, into her hand, and went up through her arm. She jerked back.

"What's wrong? Get stuck by a splinter?" Michelle asked.

"No," Zephyr answered. "It's almost like it's electrified. Not strong enough to hurt, just enough to feel a kind of fluttering up my arm."

"That's strange," Michelle said, looking around the stump and scanning the surrounding area. "There's no way there could be any electricity out here." She tapped her paddle against the stump, then used it to bring her hand within touching distance. She took a deep breath and placed one fingertip on the wood, then two, then her whole palm. She exhaled in relief. "I don't feel anything."

"Let me try," Lorie said, paddling them backward until she could reach the stump. After placing her own fingers on it, she twisted around to face Zephyr. "Try it now, Zeph. I don't feel anything either."

Zephyr leaned forward and placed her hand on the stump again, feeling the same electrical surge as before. "I still feel it!"

"That's odd," Lorie commented, removing her hand and steadying the boat. "So, you want to look inside and see if the coin's in there?"

Zephyr nodded. "I'll have to stand up, though, so I can look down inside."

"OK," said Michelle. "We'll hold the canoe as steady as we can. Try to maintain your balance and don't lean over any further than you have to. I don't have any idea why you feel electricity and we don't, but you'll have to brace yourself against the stump for support. Can you do that? Or is it too uncomfortable?"

It's uncomfortable, alright, but the electric sensation is just a small part of it!

"I think I'll be alright," Zephyr replied, keeping her

thoughts to herself. She slowly rose from the center seat and placed her hands onto the stump for balance. She looked down into its depths but couldn't see anything. "It's too dark. I'll have to use my phone's flashlight."

Carefully, Zephyr reached into her pocket and pulled out her phone, tapped on the light app, and aimed it inside the stump. Glossy black bumps and ridges glimmered within the beam. "Better not be any snakes in here," she muttered, shuddering slightly at the idea. Moving her light around only revealed more nooks, crannies, and nestled clumps of dried cypress tree needles. Leaning down and focusing on the deepest area of the stump, Zephyr saw a shadow flit across the light. "Ach!" At the same moment that she realized it was just her own hair swinging into the light's path, she dropped her phone into the stump. "Heck!"

"What happened?" Lorie asked anxiously.

"Dropped my phone!" Zephyr looked inside the stump. "And the light went out!"

"Oh man," said Michelle. "That's a problem."

"Shoot. Now I'm going to have to reach in there and feel around till I find it."

Zephyr steadied herself, then crept her fingers along the inner sides of the stump until she reached the bottom. Something sharp among the smooth weathered lumps and edges poked her finger and she jumped back.

"Steady!" cried Michelle as the canoe sloshed from side to side.

"Sorry!" Zephyr apologized, inspecting her finger. "Something stuck me, but it's not bleeding. OK. I'm going in again," she said, reaching back inside.

Get a grip, girl. You know there's nothing in here to be afraid of...maybe...

Zephyr gently patted her fingers along the black surface.

Yes! Her fingertips touched the unmistakable rectangular shape and smooth, silicone cover of her cell phone. "Found it!" As soon as she gripped it, the flashlight popped back on.

"Huh. That's str—" Something glinted in the beam of light. Something small and flat with a rounded edge and, although grimy and dark, definitely metal. The electric sensation, to which Zephyr had almost grown accustomed, increased until her fingers buzzed with its vibration. Her quickening pulse thrummed in her ears as she closed her fingers around the disc and brought it up into the misty daylight.

Placing it in the outstretched palm of her trembling hand, she held it out in front of her. As she gazed at it, a phantom breeze blew across her face, softly billowing her hair, with the sound of a soft and breathy *haaaaaaaa.*

"Is that—" began Lorie.

"I th-think so," said Zephyr. She eased back down onto the canoe seat and peered at the circle of metal in her hand.

"Wow," breathed Lorie. "That looks like an old coin to me! What do you think, Michelle? Michelle?"

Lorie and Zephyr looked at the older girl who sat wide-eyed and immobile, staring at Zephyr.

"Did—did you see that, Lorie? Did you feel that, Zephyr?" she asked.

After what Zephyr had just experienced, Michelle would have to be more specific.

"See what?" Lorie asked.

"The breeze that just blew through. I mean, I couldn't feel anything. And nothing...nothing moved except for Zephyr's hair!"

"What are you talking about?" her sister questioned. "I didn't see anything like that! Although, I wasn't looking at her hair, I was looking at her hand."

"Exactly," said Michelle. "But I was looking at her face and

I saw her hair fly all around her head and I heard a strange sound like somebody—and it wasn't Zephyr—let out a long breath. Didn't you feel it, Zeph? Or hear it?"

Zephyr raised her eyes until they met Michelle's. "Yes. I did."

"What's going on here, you guys?" asked Michelle.

24

BIG WIGS AND TINY ELEPHANTS

LORIE LOOKED FROM ZEPHYR TO HER SISTER AND BACK again, her silent message clear to Zephyr: *do you want to tell her?*

"Not completely sure," Zephyr said, in response to both the asked and unasked questions. "But I think we should try to get back to the dock if we can."

"OK," Michelle agreed. "But let me see what you pulled out of the stump first."

Zephyr handed her the coin. Michelle pulled out her water bottle and poured a few drops on the coin's surface, using the hem of her sweatshirt to rub away some of the dirt. A few swipes revealed a dull, golden gleam. "Anybody have a magnifying glass?" she asked hopefully.

Zephyr reached into her backpack. "I do actually! It's attached to a little pocket knife my Uncle Tom gave me for Christmas."

"You had that at school?" asked Lorie, her eyes rounding wide.

"No, of course not. I know the rules against weapons on

school grounds. I just brought it along today in case it might come in handy."

"And it has! Hand it over," directed Michelle, reaching out toward Zephyr.

"It has a little light you can switch on, too," Zephyr added, pointing to it as she placed it into Michelle's waiting hand.

"Perfect," said Michelle. Inspecting it through the lit magnifying glass, she exhaled a whistle.

"What? What is it?" Lorie asked.

"Here. Take a look for yourselves," Michelle offered, handing the coin and magnifier to Zephyr.

Lorie leaned over Zephyr's shoulder as she aimed the glass at the coin.

"Looks like some ugly woman with curly hair. And"—Lorie squinted—"is that a tiny elephant?"

"That 'ugly woman' is probably the King of England in a wig. And that elephant stands for the country of Guinea where the gold came from. That's why the coin's called a guinea," Michelle said.

"Wow," Zephyr whispered.

"How come you know so much about old coins?" Lorie asked her sister, frowning.

"Because Mike's father collects them, and he's been telling me all about them."

"And you've been paying attention because you want to get on his good side."

"Exactly," said Michelle.

"Mike is Michelle's new boyfriend," Lorie explained to Zephyr.

"Got it," Zephyr said nodding.

"So is this coin worth like a million dollars or something?" Lorie asked, turning back to Michelle.

"Well, no, not that much, but I'd guess it may be worth a

couple thousand," Michelle said, still eyeing the coin in Zephyr's hand.

"Whoa," Lorie breathed. "Did you hear that, Zeph?"

Zephyr stared at the coin. For her, the coin's true worth was far beyond any monetary value. She turned and looked into Lorie's shining eyes. "Oh," said Lorie, as the real impact of finding the coin finally hit her. "Then this means..."

"...that you believe me?" Zephyr asked her friend hopefully.

Lorie swallowed and nodded as Zephyr zipped the coin inside an inner pocket of her backpack.

Turning back around, Lorie pointed forward. "Hey, look!"

A small, white halo of light was glowing in the distance through the mist, growing larger and brighter as it drew closer. *Kanti? Oh my gosh, is it her?* Zephyr felt, as much as she heard, the rhythmic wafting of air as a white egret swooped over their heads toward the approaching light. Just like the night she and Scam had been trying to find their way back to Grandma June's in the moon mist, the fog thinned with each beat of the bird's great wings. Through the lingering shreds of mist, they could see the outline of a small boat moving toward them. An aluminum skiff powered by a silent electric motor and bearing a *US Fish and Wildlife* emblem on its side materialized from the vanishing fog.

"Is that you, girls?" called a husky voice.

"Zephyr! Is that you, honey?" asked a higher pitched one.

"Ranger Doris!" Zephyr cried out, recognizing the woman leaning forward in the boat. "And Mr. Porter! Are we glad to see you!" Zephyr twisted around toward Michelle. "I met Ranger Doris at the Visitor Center last weekend. She's a friend of my grandma's."

"Hooray for friends with boats!" cheered Michelle.

"Oh, thank goodness," said the ranger as they pulled alongside the canoe. "This is such strange weather. It's perfectly clear at the Visitor Center."

"Yep," Mr. Porter agreed. "I drove back down to the landing, but I couldn't believe my eyes when I saw that the whole of Drummond was locked in with fog. Nowhere else, though, just over the water and its banks. I was worried you girls might get turned around out here, or that you might run into something and capsize, so I hightailed it to the Visitor Center to tell Doris."

"I know I looked at him like he was crazy when he told me," said Ranger Doris, looking at Mr. Porter with a grin, "but I also know he isn't one to exaggerate. The other rangers are off today, so I left Mr. White in charge while I got the boat."

"Mr. White? You mean the Mr. White you told Grandma and me about?" Zephyr asked.

"The very one. He volunteers regularly now, from noon until four on Fridays and Saturdays. I think that man knows more about the swamp than even I do!"

Mr. Porter looked around at the clearing skies and shook his head. "Welp, looks like all we did was clear the air for you. Mighty odd weather we're having. Now that it's lifted, you can see the dock from here." He pointed over his shoulder at the dock they could now see in the distance. "You want a tow, or do you want to paddle in, yourselves?"

The three girls exchanged glances and shrugged their shoulders. "I think we'll be fine, now that we have visibility again, Mr. Porter," Michelle answered. "You two can go on so Ranger Doris can get back to the Visitor Center, and we'll meet you back at the dock. We really, really appreciate you looking for us, though."

"Of course! No way, I was going to leave June's girl out in that fog. Or her lovely friends either," he added, tipping his cap.

"Okie dokie, then. I'll help Doris stow her boat and I'll be right back to meet y'all at the launch."

The girls waved and shouted in unison, "Thank you!" Ranger Doris's boat circled around and they watched as it headed toward the boat ramp. Lorie and Michelle put their paddles back into the water and the three of them began their own trek back. Twenty minutes later, they landed the canoe at the boat launch where Mr. Porter stood, offering his hand to each of them as they stepped out with their bags. After helping him secure the canoe back onto his trailer, the girls took turns giving him goodbye hugs, his face growing redder with each embrace.

Watching Mr. Porter's truck rattle away, Michelle asked, "You guys ready to head back to Mrs. Stone's house now?"

"Oh yeah," said Lorie. "Right, Zephyr? Zeph?"

Zephyr stared out across the lake. *That disappearing grave-yard had looked a lot like the one on the White Farm...*

25

THE FAMILY PLOT

"Zeph!" repeated Lorie.

"What?" She pulled herself from her thoughts. "Oh, yeah. I'm ready," she said. The three girls loaded their packs into the trunk of Michelle's car before climbing into their seats. Once Michelle heard Lorie and Zephyr buckle themselves into the back bench seat, she carefully drove forward, circling in front of the dock and heading back out toward the park's main entry road.

As they drove down Wildlife Drive, Zephyr whispered to Lorie. "Those gravestones out there looked like the ones I saw on Mr. White's land."

Lorie nodded. "And one of them had 'Stone' on it!" she reminded her, eyebrows inching higher.

"So," Zephyr said, thinking out loud. "Since Mr. White's going to be at the Visitor Center until four, I think I want to take a closer look at his cemetery before we go home to Colington Island."

"You do?" squeaked Lorie.

"Will you come with me?"

Lorie nodded up and down like a bobblehead doll. "But what about...you know..." she said, tilting her head at her sister in the driver's seat.

"You know I can hear you, don't you?" Michelle called back to them, catching their eyes in the rearview mirror. "So, I'm going to pull over on the side of the road now and we're not moving until you two tell me exactly what's going on." Michelle slowed the car to a halt on the side of the road beside a dark pool of water with cypress trees reflecting in its glassy depths. Zephyr searched Lorie's face for an answer.

"It's OK," Lorie assured her. "She's heard weirdo stuff from our family before."

"So, um," Zephyr began, looking up at Michelle. "Do you believe in ghosts?"

Michelle took off her seatbelt and turned to face Zephyr. "Maybe."

Unbuckling her own belt, Zephyr leaned forward and told Michelle her strange story. "And then I did genealogy research and found out there's some connection between the Whites and the Stones. Haven't had any luck yet with Thomas Drake, though."

Michelle sat silent, lost in thought.

"What do you think?" Lorie asked her sister.

"Well," Michelle finally said, "if I hadn't seen the coin, and if we hadn't shared that freak show on the lake today, I'd probably be searching for some kind of natural explanation. But this whole day has supernatural written all over it. You know who'd be all over this?" she asked, turning to her sister.

"Oh yeah," said Lorie, smiling. "Granny."

"Yeah." She turned back to Zephyr. "And you know what else I think? I think that Mr. White of yours is hiding something for sure."

"That's what I think, too. And that's why I want a closer look at his family graveyard," Zephyr explained.

"OK," said Michelle. "Let's go see what your grandma thinks about all this."

Over plates of chicken salad left over from the book club meeting, the girls took turns filling Grandma June in on the details of their adventure on Lake Drummond.

"Oh my, girls. You must have been so frightened out there." Grandma June's forehead crinkled with worried lines.

"Yeah. It was pretty scary," Zephyr admitted.

She brightened. "But finding the coin—that's amazing! May I see it?"

"Of course!" Zephyr grabbed her backpack and pulled out the coin as well as her tiny pocketknife with its attached magnifying glass.

Grandma June took the coin over to the light of the kitchen window and looked through the magnifier. "This is astounding. A true historical find, Zephyr. And beyond that..." she looked up at her granddaughter.

Zephyr nodded. "I know. Kanti. And Michelle knows everything that led up to this, Grandma, so we can speak freely in front of her."

"How does all this strike you, Michelle?" asked Grandma June.

"Well, like I told Zephyr, if I hadn't witnessed all the stuff today, I'd have thought she dreamed the whole moon mist business, but now it makes sense in a strange, supernatural kind of way."

"I agree," said Grandma June.

"So, here's the thing, Grandma. I want to go back and take a closer look at that graveyard on the White property. Ranger Doris said Mr. White would be volunteering at the Visitor Center today until four."

Grandma June looked up at the kitchen clock. "It's nearly three o'clock, now." She turned to Michelle. "How about I take you to the center and we can both keep an eye on Mr. White to be sure he doesn't leave early while Zephyr and Lorie check out the gravestones?"

"Sounds like a good plan," Michelle agreed.

"Does that work for you, Zephyr? Lorie?"

Lorie nodded and Zephyr answered, "I think that's a good idea. I don't want to get caught out there with him showing up like last time."

Grandma June opened the deep bottom drawer of her desk and rummaged around. Grasping two hand-sized, black objects, she turned around and announced, "Walkie-talkies. Cell service is too sporadic to trust out here, but good old walkie-talkies work just fine. It's old-school communication, but it's trustworthy. Your grandpa and I used them a lot, and these carry a long distance," she said as she handed one to Zephyr.

Zephyr turned it around in her hands. She loved that it was something her grandpa had once used.

Lorie leaned over her shoulder. "Cool."

"They're very simple to operate," said Grandma June, showing Zephyr which button to push to talk. "You just have to wait until the person speaking to you stops talking before you say anything, otherwise, it cuts off their sentence. You two keep one and we'll keep one. This way, when Mr. White leaves for home, we can let you know it's time to get the heck out of Dodge if you haven't already."

Lorie turned confused eyes toward Zephyr. "Dodge? I thought we were going next door?"

Zephyr laughed. "We are. That was just one of Grandpa's favorite sayings. It goes back to some old TV show."

"*Gun Smoke*," Michelle confirmed.

Lorie looked at her sister. "And how did *you* know that? Oh, wait, does your new boyfriend's dad say that too?"

"Nooo, but his grandpa does."

"Man, you *have* been paying attention. You must really like this guy."

"Maybe," Michelle said smiling.

"Time to get moving," Grandma June urged as she reached for her jacket hanging on a hook by the kitchen door. "Zephyr, take this with you, just in case," she said, handing her granddaughter a small flashlight. "It gets dark fast inside the woods, as you well know. And you might want to take along a bottle of water."

"I don't think we'll need water, Grandma. It's not hot and we aren't going to be gone that long."

"Not for you. For the gravestones."

Zephyr and Lorie cocked their heads. "The gravestones?" said Zephyr.

"Yes. Etchings on old stone are often worn with age, but applying water to them can help bring out the letters. It's something I learned when your grandpa and I took an archaeology trip to Greece, back in our college days."

Wow. I never knew they went to Greece. And on an archaeology dig!

"That's a good idea," said Lorie. "Could we use a spray bottle?"

"Exactly! Good thinking, Lorie. That's just how it's done," Grandma June praised. "I have a small one in the laundry room that I use with my dry iron."

Michelle folded her arms and gave her sister an approving smile. "Every now and then, Sis, every now and then."

As Grandma June and Michelle headed for the front door, Zephyr held up her hand. "Wait!" she said. The pair turned around as Zephyr ran and pulled her grandma into a close hug. "Thank you so much, Grandma."

"Hey," she said, gently pushing Zephyr out at arm's length. "We're in this together! Good luck, sweetie. We'll meet you back here in an hour." As soon as Grandma June and Michelle closed the door, Zephyr and Lorie pulled on their jackets. Zephyr filled the spray bottle with water from the sink before tucking it into one of her jacket pockets. She dropped the walkie-talkie into the other and then handed Lorie the flashlight.

"You hang on to this for us."

Zephyr led the way out the kitchen door and over to the tall trees lining the back of the yard. When they reached the darkened deer path, Zephyr stopped and turned to place her hands on Lorie's shoulders. "You ready?"

Lorie set her fists on her hips. "Let's do this!"

[26]
THE SECRET CEMETERY

"Follow me," Zephyr said stepping in front of Lorie and into the shadows of the forest.

As soon as they moved out of the golden autumn sunlight and into the twilight world of the towering trees, the earthy smell of peat and decaying leaves filled Zephyr's nostrils, bringing with it the memory of her last visit. Slipping her hand into her jacket pocket, she felt the comforting weight of her grandparents' walkie-talkie in her palm. *At least I won't have Scam tugging at his leash this time. Less chance for me to end up sprawled in the dirt.* She reached up and pushed aside a low-hanging vine of bright-red leaves.

"That's not poison ivy, is it?" asked Lorie, hand poised in the air beside the dangling vine.

"No, it's Virginia Creeper. Not poisonous. See," she pulled the vine and held it out for Lorie to have a closer look. "It's got five leaves. Poison ivy leaves come in threes." Zephyr let go of the vine and turned back around to continue down the path.

"Oh, well that's better. We'll just get tangled up in Virginia Creepy vines. Kind of appropriate."

"Creeper not creepy," Zephyr said, enunciating the difference. "Because it creeps up the tree, sort of like what we're doing— creeping along this trail."

"Yeah, I guess we're just a couple of Carolina Creepers creeping down a creepy Virginia trail."

"That's it," Zephyr said, smiling.

The afternoon shadows deepened as they worked their way along the path. Zephyr kept her eyes aimed toward the ground, watching for signs of ankle-grabbing vines and toe-tripping roots that might be concealed beneath the fallen leaves. A rustle in the undergrowth beside the trail brought both of the girls to a sudden halt. With their eyes wide and pulses racing, the image of a pair of scared rabbits, frozen in place, flashed through Zephyr's mind.

"What was that?" rasped Lorie.

Zephyr rotated her head in slow motion, facing the direction from which they'd heard the sound.

"Oh!" Zephyr whispered in relief. "Don't move. But look over there," she said, pointing her chin. A few feet away, a white-tailed doe and her speckled fawn stood, unmoving, locked in place like lawn statues as they kept cautious eyes on the two girls.

"Awwww, look at them! They're beautiful!" Lorie cooed.

"Grandma did say this was a deer path. I guess we have them to thank for making it for us. Let's move away slowly so we don't scare them off."

"Thank you, deer. Bye, deer," Lorie whispered as they crept away.

A few feet later, Zephyr stopped and held up her hand.

"What now?" Lorie asked.

"It's the log I twisted my ankle on," Zephyr said, gingerly placing her foot on its damp surface. "Watch it. It's slippery."

161

"Bad log. Shame on you, log," scolded Lorie as she climbed over its slick, dark chocolate colored bark.

Several yards further in, Zephyr pointed to a rough-barked cedar tree. "And that's where I had the vision, or residual haunting or whatever, of those two men I told you about."

Lorie picked up her pace. "Let's keep moving. I'm not in the mood to meet Dumb and Dumber out here this afternoon, especially since your grandma mentioned it was a residual haunting from a trauma that happened. No thanks."

Gradually, the filtered rays of sunlight grew brighter as the girls neared the trail's boundary.

"Aren't you proud of me?" Lorie asked Zephyr's back, her tone shining with confidence. "I never once mentioned snakes, or gators, or snappy turtles this whole time."

"Yes, I—"

"Arghhh!" cried Lorie.

"What?" Zephyr shouted, spinning around.

"Giant spider web! Get it off me!" pleaded Lorie.

Zephyr laughed. "It's not a spider web," she said, pulling a veil of Spanish moss off her friend's face and holding it out for her to see.

"It sure felt like it!"

"Come on, Bilbo. This isn't Mirkwood from *The Lord of the Rings*," Zephyr joked. She gazed up at the shaggy trees. Their crooked branches, dripping with ghostly gray moss, reached out like giant arms. Woody vines, thick as a man's arm, twisted around their trunks like enormous hairy snakes and sprouted flame-red leaves in the tell-tale three-leafed pattern of poison ivy. *Although it sure does look like Middle-earth in here.*

A few moments later, the remaining trees framed a window of warm, yellow light.

"Are we there yet?" Lorie asked, hopefully.

"Yes," said Zephyr, leaning forward and poking her head

into the sunshine of Mr. White's cornfield. Looking left and right, she said, "Coast's clear." She motioned for Lorie to follow her. "When I was here before, Scam pulled me through one of the rows of cornstalks. But I think if we just walk down this row right in front of us, we should come out to the clearing."

"Whatever you say," whispered Lorie, scanning the wall of dry, brittle cornstalks.

Bing bong!

Both girls jumped.

"Is that your countdown thingy?"

Zephyr breathed a sigh of relief and nodded. "I forgot to turn off the sound." Fishing it from her pocket, she glanced at the counter and muted the phone.

7 weeks + 5 days

Deep within the chattering stalks, Zephyr turned around to face Lorie. "You OK? You've been really quiet since we left the woods."

"Yeah, I'm OK. This is just bringing back some not-so-happy memories of getting lost in a Halloween corn maze when I was little."

"You mean *last year* when our class went on that field trip to the pumpkin farm and the farmer had to send in his bloodhound to find you?" Zephyr laughed.

"Was that just last year? Really? Seems a lot longer than that. Guess my brain pushed it back so I don't live in constant humiliation and—fear—every time I see a cornfield."

"This would make a pretty good maze, actually," Zephyr said thoughtfully, pressing forward.

"Yeah, it would," Lorie grumbled in agreement.

As the girls rounded a curve, the shuddering stalks opened up onto the green circle of land harboring the White graveyard.

Just like before. Except there's no egret sitting on the fence this time, and Scam isn't yanking my arm out of its socket.

"You know," said Lorie, squinting at the picket fence. "If you hadn't told me what's behind that fence, I might have just figured there was some kind of garden behind it. Must have been pretty freaky finding graves instead of vegetables."

"Yeah. It was. Come on. Let's check this out before I lose my nerve, or before Mr. White shows up like he did last time I was here...or both," said Zephyr as she gripped the walkie-talkie in her pocket. The girls linked arms as they walked toward the shoulder-high fence. A pair of glossy black crows flew ahead of them and landed on the pickets, each taking a post on either side of the entrance.

"You know what they call a group of crows?" asked Zephyr.

"What? You mean like a flock or something?"

"It's called a *murder* of crows."

"Oh, gee thanks, Miss Fountain of Knowledge. Could have lived without that little tidbit of information right now."

The crows croaked a head-bobbing greeting as the girls turned the corner of the fence and faced the enclosed graves.

"Could this get any creepier?" Lorie muttered as she clutched Zephyr's arm.

The fence sheltered about a dozen tombstones. Some were still standing sturdily upright, but others, especially those in the back, were tilted sideways, leaning forward toward the ground, or leaning backward toward the sky. Zephyr read one of the markers in the front row:

*Sacred
To the Memory of
Christopher White.
Who was born Nov 5th, 1815
And died Oct 7th, 1872.*

Aged 56 years 11 months, 2 days.
Precious in the sight of the Lord
is the death of His saints.

"They certainly were specific," Lorie noted, leaning down toward the gray stone.

"That's for sure," said Zephyr scanning the other tombstones. "These all look like people from the White family. Let's go further in and see if there's one with Stone written on it like we saw at the lake."

"Um, I think I should stay up front here and watch for Mr. White or his cat," said Lorie, inching backward.

"OK. That's fine," Zephyr replied, patting Lorie's shoulder. "Why don't you take pictures of the tombstones up here while I check out the ones in the back? We can study them later, when we have more time at home. You never know what might give us a clue."

"I like that plan," said Lorie, pulling out her phone and aiming it at Christopher White's stone.

Zephyr picked her way among the markers while trying not to step on the graves. The tombstones seemed to huddle together as if drawing comfort from one another. Several marked the passing of children, some only having lived a few days. *So sad.* At the far corner of the graveyard, Zephyr saw several markers that were too worn with time to read. Stepping closer, she could just make out a large "S" on the tallest of the group.

"Hey! This might be it! Unless it's just the beginning of one of those 'Sacred to the memory' ones."

Lorie looked up from her phone camera. "Use the spray bottle. And take a picture of it. We can up the focus and contrast later if we need to see it better."

Zephyr pulled the bottle from her pocket and sprayed a

light mist over the stone. Like magic, the letters became clearer.

"It says Stone, alright." She opened her camera app and clicked several shots. After spraying more water on the marker, she leaned closer, resting her hand on its top for balance. As soon as she touched it, electricity coursed through her fingers, just like it had with the tree stump on the lake. She jerked backward.

"You alright?" asked Lorie, inching closer to her friend.

"Yes. I just felt an electric charge like I did on the lake." *Weird.*

"So weird," said Lorie.

"My thoughts exactly," Zephyr agreed, keeping her hands to herself but closely inspecting the etched letters. "It says 'Moses Stone. Died April 4th, 1757.' That's all I can make out."

"Huh. I wonder—"A sudden rattling broke off Lorie's words. "Is that the wind?" she asked, whirling around to face the cornstalks.

"I don't think so," said Zephyr, standing up and staring beyond Lorie. They both watched as, several yards inside the cornfield, a cluster of brown stalks bowed and swung from side to side. The chaotic dance moved like a wave toward the edge of the field, racing toward the green grass and the graveyard where they stood. In two impressive leaps, Lorie jumped to Zephyr's side. "Is it Mr. White or his cat?"

"I don't think so," repeated Zephyr. "Grandma would have warned us if he'd left the Visitor Center. And Hamish is big, but not big enough to do this!"

The girls clung to each other as the swirl of clattering cornstalks reached the edge of the grass behind a small black cloud, rotating in place like a mini tornado.

[27]

THE BLACK TORNADO

"WHAT THE HECK IS THAT?" LORIE GASPED, CLINGING TO her friend.

Zephyr shook her head. "No idea!"

The two crows flew off, abandoning their stations, croaking and cawing as the twirling cloud lifted and blew into the graveyard, blocking the girls' escape.

"What should we do now?" cried Lorie, her hair flying and tangling about her head.

"Lie down flat, I think. That's what I heard you should do in a tornado. But this isn't like any tornado I've ever heard about."

Just as the girls got down on their knees, the small twister pushed forward toward their corner. They scurried to the other side of the graveyard and knelt down, wrapping their arms around each other. A high-pitched whistle arose from the cloud as it rotated even faster. Then, through its darkness, a form began to take shape.

"Look!" said Zephyr, "There's a woman inside it!"

"What? I don't see anybody!"

A woman wearing a white, ruffled cap and long, walnut-brown dress spun in ever-slowing circles as the cloud dissipated around her. The high-pitched whistle melded into high-pitched crying as the woman came to a standstill in front of Moses Stone's grave.

"Don't you see her now? She's dressed like those guides in Colonial Williamsburg, and she's crying," Zephyr whispered into Lorie's ear.

Lorie shook her head and squinted. "No. I just see the cloud, but it stopped spinning. It's just hovering in place, and it sounds like Granny's whistling teakettle."

The woman dropped to her knees, placing her white hands on either side of the tombstone. "It was right! It was right! It was right!" she cried.

"Can't you hear her talking?" asked Zephyr.

"No," said Lorie. "But the whistling is breaking up. More like a sputtering. Like the teakettle's running out of water. What do you hear her saying?"

"She's holding on to that tombstone and crying, 'It was right,' over and over again."

The colonial woman turned her head slowly toward the girls and fixed Zephyr in a piercing gray-eyed gaze. Pointing a boney finger at her, she said, "You can see me!"

Zephyr nodded. "Yes, m-ma'm. I can see you."

"And you can hear me!"

"Y-yes," stammered Zephyr, her body trembling like she'd been dunked in ice water.

"Is she talking to you?" said Lorie, gripping her tighter around the waist.

Zephyr nodded.

The woman rose and turned toward the huddling girls. "It was right! It was right! It was right!" she screamed, head thrown back facing the sky, arms stiff at her sides, hands curled into trembling fists.

"The black cloud has red streaks in it now!" Lorie whispered urgently. "Like lightning!"

The woman slowly lowered her chin until she locked eyes with Zephyr again. "Do you judge me? Have you come to judge me?" she asked, her voice dropping to a guttural growl.

"No. No, ma'am," said Zephyr.

"What's she saying?" whispered Lorie.

"She thinks I'm here to judge her."

"You do!" screamed the woman. "You do judge me!" She pointed a quivering finger at Zephyr. "Judge not, that ye be not judged!"

The woman raised her hands above her head and spun in a circle, crying, "It was right! It was right! It was right!" Her dark skirts whirled around her until she was, once more, enveloped inside the spectral storm cloud.

"I can't see her anymore," yelled Zephyr above the sound of the whistling wind. She clutched her hair in both hands as it swirled around her face like leaping flames.

The black tornado lifted several feet from the ground and sped toward the crouching girls. "Get out! Get out! Get out!" it screamed.

Zephyr grabbed Lorie's hand and pulled her through the opening of the picket fence, stumbling to their hands and knees just outside the graveyard. The whirling black cloud spun out beside them and disappeared back into the dying cornfield.

"Wh-what just happened, Zephyr?"

Zephyr shook her head. *I have no words for that.*

A crackling rose from her pocket. "Zephyr! Zephyr! Can you hear me?"

"It's Grandma!" said Zephyr, fishing out the walkie-talkie.

She pressed the "Talk" button. "Yes, I can hear you! You won't believe wh—"

Grandma June cut her off. "Are you still at the graveyard?"

"Yes! But—"

"You've got to get out of there! Now!" ordered her grandmother. "Mr. White left early and he's heading home. He said something about letting Hamish out for a run in the cornfields before it gets too dark."

"OK!" said Zephyr. "We're leaving right now."

"Good. We'll see you at home!"

Zephyr dropped the walkie-talkie back into her pocket. "Come on. We're out of here!"

"Right behind you," said Lorie, jumping up.

As soon as they entered the wooded deer path, a dark curtain of deep shade dropped around them, blocking out the sun. "Our phone lights won't be bright enough. Flashlight!" Zephyr demanded.

Lorie pulled the slender metal cylinder from her pocket and slapped it into Zephyr's outstretched hand. "Wait," said Zephyr. "If I carry it in front, you won't be able to see what's under your feet. We can't afford to have you falling out here."

"Give it back, I know what to do," Lorie said. She turned it on and twisted a ring encircling the neck of the flashlight. "My dad has one like this. See? I can make the light spread wider. Not as bright as it is with a tighter beam, but bright enough. I can carry it and aim it so we can both see the ground."

"You're brilliant!" said Zephyr.

"OK, my brilliant butt wants to get out of here, so let's get the heck out of Dodge!" said Lorie.

The girls sprinted along the path, dodging roots and vines. They brushed aside swaths of Spanish moss that looked even more like giant spider webs as shadows swung in the flashlight's bouncing beam. Drawing near to the end of the trail, a steady white light greeted theirs.

"Grandma!" cried Zephyr. "You won't believe what happened back there!"

Grandma June placed her arm around Zephyr's waist. "Come on in and tell us all about it." She turned toward Michelle, who was hugging her little sister. "I know you have to get back home soon, but I'll pack you some sandwiches to take along while the girls tell us what happened."

As Michelle helped Grandma June prepare a box supper, Zephyr and Lorie sipped cups of hot cocoa and recounted everything they'd seen and heard. The girls finished telling their different versions of the strange experience just as Grandma June snapped the lids on the plastic containers of their dinner. She sat down beside Zephyr and took both her hands in hers.

"Sweetheart. I have something important to say to you."

Zephyr's pulse quickened at her grandma's serious expression. "Yes?"

Grandma June glanced up at Michelle and Lorie. "You girls have all been through a lot together today, so I know I can speak freely and you will understand."

Zephyr and the two sisters nodded with focused, wide eyes. A blanket of anticipatory silence settled over the room.

Bang! Bang! Bang!

All four jumped and Zephyr's pulse thumped wildly within her throat. "What's that?" she cried, her mind still reeling from her recent supernatural encounters.

"You mean *who's* that," Grandma June corrected as she rose from her seat and looked into the living room at the glass-paneled front door. Taking a step closer, she said, "Judging by the tall, thin silhouette behind the door curtain, I'd say it's Mr. White."

"What! Oh no, Grandma! What if he saw us?"

"You girls stay in here. I'll see what he wants."

Lorie took Zephyr's hand as the girls scooted away from the door's viewing range. They heard the turning of the knob and the sweep of the door as Grandma June pulled it open.

"Mr. White! What a surprise! What brings you over on this lovely evening?"

"Um...I just wanted to be sure the girls were alright after their...adventure on the lake. Doris told me all about the fog."

"Oh, they're just fine, thanks."

Silence.

Why don't they say something?

Mr. White cleared his throat. "Is Zephyr available?"

Lorie and Zephyr both gasped and Michelle placed her hands over their mouths.

"Oh, I'm afraid not. She's getting a shower before they head home. I'd invite you in for a cup of tea, but I'm busy getting them a box supper together for their trip."

"I see."

More silence.

"OK," continued Mr. White. "Well, since you mentioned this afternoon that Zephyr's quite a reader, I thought perhaps she might like a new book. I brought this one for her. She may know the story, but this is Nathaniel Hawthorne's 1850s version."

The door creaked.

"That's so nice of you, Mr. White! I'll see that she takes good care of it, and we'll get it back to you soon."

"Oh, no bother. It's from my collection of old books. I'd rather she kept it. As a matter of fact, I insist upon it."

"Well, thanks again. I'm sure she'll be very interested in reading it."

"Be sure you give it to her before she leaves."

"Of course. Have a good evening!"

The door swept shut, and the girls exhaled their bated breath together. Grandma June stepped into the kitchen with a small book in her hand.

"Wh-what do you think that was all about, Grandma?"

"Well, the title of this book he wanted you to have speaks volumes," she said, handing it to Zephyr.

With trembling hands, Zephyr took the book and laid it on the table beside her mug of cocoa. *Pandora's Box*. She squinted up at her grandma. "Isn't that the Greek myth about the girl who wasn't supposed to open a box, but she was so curious she did anyway and ended up letting out a bunch of awful stuff into the world?"

"Yep," Michelle confirmed, picking it up and glancing at the artwork on the front.

"This doesn't seem like just a gift, Zephyr," said Grandma June, frowning. "It seems like a warning."

Zephyr looked up at her grandma in alarm.

"Do you think he knows we were in his cemetery?" asked Lorie as her sister set the antique book down on the center of the round kitchen table.

"I'm not sure," said Grandma June. "But he knows Zephyr's continuing to show interest in the Great Dismal Swamp, and he may have figured out that our properties connect."

"I knew there was something fishy about him," grumbled Lorie.

"Well, be that as it may," said Grandma June as she resumed her place at the table and held her hands out to Zephyr. "I still have something to say before you all pile back in the car and leave."

Zephyr swallowed the lump rising in her throat and took her grandma's hands.

Grandma June closed her eyes for a moment, then opened them and looked deeply into Zephyr's. "There's a reason Kanti's spirit sought you out, why you experienced the residual haunting, and a reason you could see and hear that poor woman in the graveyard, even when Lorie couldn't. I believe you have a gift, a very special gift," said her grandma, squeezing Zephyr's hands in a gentle grip. "It seems that you're able to cross over the line that normally separates the living from the dead. It's as though your encounter with Kanti has opened some portal between your soul and the souls of those who've passed on."

"And...and you think this is some kind of gift?" asked Zephyr, looking into her grandma's loving eyes.

"Yes, I do," she whispered.

Can I give it back?

[28]
PANDORA'S BOX

"ARE YOU SURE YOU DON'T WANT TO COME WITH ME ON the field trip to the Library of Virginia tomorrow?" Zephyr asked Lorie one last time as they shared a seat on the homeward bound school bus.

"Sounds totally exciting," said Lorie, yawning dramatically. "But I think I'll pass. You go and have a good time. I'll just stay home, sleep in late, and finish working on my Halloween costume. Maybe meet Meghan and Hannah for an afternoon show at Kill Devil Hills Movies and grab a slice of extra cheesy at Colington Pizza. You know, really boring stuff like that."

Zephyr shot her a tucked in smile. "Alright. I get it. But Mrs. Creadle thinks I might actually find some clues about our family's connection to the Whites and maybe about Native American children lost in the Great Dismal Swamp also. I could even learn something about Thomas Drake!"

Lorie nodded, still unimpressed. "Knock yourself out, kiddo."

Zephyr glanced behind her to see if anyone was eavesdropping on their conversation. She saw Luke Barnes looking her way, but he dropped his gaze as soon as they made eye contact. Ignoring the little flutter in her stomach, she turned back to Lorie and leaned in close to her. "Listen," she whispered. "I know it won't be as exciting as the canoe trip or the graveyard, but I may get some answers."

Lorie shuddered. "Believe me, I'm not looking for more of that kind of excitement any time soon. I really do hope you find something. I'm just not personally very good at the research thing. When I have to do internet searches for homework, I've been known to keel over at the keyboard." Lorie rubbed her forehead.

Zephyr chuckled. "OK. I actually like to do research, you know."

"I know," said Lorie. "That's one of the truly weird—I mean, *wonderful*, things about you."

Zephyr laughed and shoved against Lorie's shoulder.

"Garcia's Getaway," announced Mrs. Tillett, stopping the bus and opening the door.

"See ya, Zeph. Don't do anything too wild and crazy at the library."

"I'll try to contain myself."

Lorie stopped at the top of the bus steps and turned back to Zephyr. "See you later, alligator."

"After 'while, crocodile."

As Lorie stepped off the bus, Zephyr heard a girl in the back of the bus snicker and say, "Dorks."

Zephyr grinned. *If she only knew.* A couple stops later, Zephyr stepped off the bus to the sound of wind chimes tinkling from her backpack. She smiled at the ringtone she'd assigned Grandma June and fished out her phone.

"Hi, Grandma!" she answered, holding the phone in one hand and throwing her pack over her shoulder with the other.

"Hi, sweetheart! Are you home from school yet? I was afraid you might still be on the bus."

"Just got off and heading for the door. You doing OK?"

"Oh sure. It's a baking day for me and you know how much I love to bake, but I just wanted to tell you about something that happened at the Visitor Center today."

Zephyr stopped short, a few feet from her front steps. "Is it about you-know-what?"

"I believe it is. Can you talk now?"

"Hang on. Let me go in and see if Mom and Dad are in their office." Zephyr opened the door and tiptoed into the living room. "All quiet in here," she whispered. "I think Scam must be with them, too. I'll go on up to my room."

Zephyr padded up the stairs and closed her door. "OK. So, what about the Visitor Center?" she asked, dropping her backpack by her desk and climbing onto her bed.

"Well I went by there to talk to Doris today, and I saw that Mr. White was on volunteer duty."

Just the sound of his name sent goosebumps creeping across Zephyr's skin. "Did he talk to you?"

"Oh, yes. He was very interested in how you were doing, and he kept going on about how he'd seen black bears out in his cornfields the other morning, and how dangerous it would be if anyone were to accidentally wander onto his land. He said to be sure and tell you about the bears because he was certain you'd find it of interest."

"Uh huh." Zephyr rolled her eyes at his obvious ploy.

"He wanted to know when you might be coming back for a visit. I tell you, if I didn't think I knew the real reason for his interest in you, his behavior would make me extremely uncomfortable."

And you're not uncomfortable now?

177

"I mean, of course, it still makes me uncomfortable," her grandma stammered, "...but for other reasons...I mean..."

"I know what you mean, Grandma. What did you tell him?"

"I said you and your parents were coming for Thanksgiving, but that I didn't think you'd be visiting before then."

"Good."

"He doesn't need to know you're getting dropped off here on your way home from the Library of Virginia tomorrow. And he sure doesn't need to know you're coming back with Lorie the day after Halloween while your parents are away at your mom's college reunion. I said I didn't *think* you were visiting sooner."

"Exactly." *Thank goodness Grandma's in this with me!*

"I really appreciate you giving me a hand pulling boxes down from the attic tomorrow, by the way. There are a lot of things up there I want to include in the community yard sale and I just can't manage them all by myself."

"No problem, and we're all happy you're driving me home after. Mom's fixing her special Brunswick stew for dinner tomorrow night." Zephyr's mouth watered just thinking about the stew. It was one of her favorites.

"Sounds yummy. And I'm really looking forward to staying over there with you all for the weekend. It will be so much fun!"

"Sure will. Dad's going to make one of his famous Saturday pancake breakfasts in your honor. He says it's an early reward for letting me stay with you while they're at that reunion."

Her grandma laughed. "You're all the reward I need, sweetheart. But, about the November first visit—don't you think you should try to reconnect with that cemetery ghost and find out what she knows? I have a gut feeling she can shed some light on our little mystery if she's approached right. And I bet Lorie would go along to support you."

We're talking about a ghost, not the nosey neighbor lady down the street, Grandma!

"I don't know, Grandma. The thought of seeing her again really scares me, and trying to talk with her sounds way off the charts."

"Of course, it does," sympathized her grandma. "But I'm convinced you have a gift, sweetheart, and you might even help her spirit find some peace, just by listening to her."

"I guess," murmured Zephyr.

She looked up at her wall calendar and lifted the page to view November. A big red circle surrounded the next full moon, the Beaver Moon, only three and a half weeks after Halloween. *Time is running out to save my Sam!*

Zephyr exhaled a ragged breath. "And...she didn't hurt us last time. Just scared the living cra—I mean, *daylights* out of us."

Grandma June chuckled. "Anyway, back to Mr. White. He also asked what you thought of the book he gave you."

"Geez. I haven't even touched it. Just looking at the cover weirds me out." Zephyr shivered with a sudden chill. She'd stuck the book in her backpack before leaving her grandma's and, once she'd gotten home, had immediately tucked it between two taller ones on her bookshelf so she wouldn't have to see it. Having the book in her room at all felt invasive, like Mr. White himself had crept into her personal space.

"I figured as much. I told him you were very appreciative because you always enjoyed reading about the ancient Greek myths and legends."

"Well that was partly true, anyway."

"Oh, by the way," said Grandma June, dropping her voice to a conspiratorial whisper, despite the fact that, unlike Zephyr, she was alone in her house. "I haven't said anything to them about it, but I was wondering if you had told your mom and dad about finding the gold coin?"

"Yeah actually, I did," replied Zephyr, then matching her grandmother's whisper, added, "I didn't tell them we got lost in the fog, but I did tell them I found it when I was looking inside an old stump."

"I bet they were surprised!" Grandma June responded, delight brightening her pitch.

"Yep. Dad's going to get it appraised. He said it could be the start of my college fund, but only if I wanted to give it up."

"I imagine you'd rather hold onto it, wouldn't you?"

"You betcha."

"Well, I've got to go, honey. I have some sweet potato pecan bread in the oven for Doris and it's ready to come out. Just know how much I love you, and remember, you're much braver than you think you are."

Yeah, right. I'm glad you think so. Wish I did! Zephyr sighed but kept her self-doubts to herself. "Love you too, Grandma."

"Hope you can finally get some information on Thomas Drake."

"Yeah. That would be great."

"And," Zephyr heard a slight hesitation in her grandmother's voice, "maybe you'll learn something that will help you with the cemetery ghost."

"Maybe so." Zephyr's stomach clenched into a knot.

"Have fun, sweetie. See you tomorrow. Bye!"

"Bye."

Zephyr heaved another sigh as she placed the phone on her desk and looked at her bookshelf. There it was, crammed between *Anne of Green Gables* and *Wonder.* "Alright, Pandora, let's see what's in that box," she whispered as she pulled the book from the shelf.

She laid it on her desk and thumbed through its yellowing pages. The illustrations were really quite beautiful. Despite herself, her natural curiosity and love of books took over as she read the great author's version of the ancient story. Turning the page to find out what happened next, Zephyr found something else, something that jarred her back into the real world.

Tucked between the pages was a small white envelope addressed to *Pandora*, the name crossed over with a single line of black ink. Beneath it was another name; *Zephyr*. With trembling fingers, she fumbled with the envelope and pulled out a sheet of neatly handwritten paper.

DEAR ZEPHYR,

I ENJOYED MEETING YOU WHEN YOU ACCOMPANIED YOUR GRANDMOTHER (AND HER DELICIOUS APPLE PIE) TO MY HOUSE. IT IS ALWAYS A JOY TO MEET ANOTHER YOUNG, BRIGHT MIND SUCH AS YOURS. EVEN THOUGH OUR VISIT WAS BRIEF, I SEE A GREAT FUTURE FOR YOU, POSSIBLY EVEN AT RADFORD UNIVERSITY! I COULD TELL RIGHT AWAY THAT YOURS IS AN INQUIRING MIND, AND ONE THAT CAN LEAD YOU TO MANY PLACES AND IN MANY DIRECTIONS. THAT KIND OF CURIOSITY, ALTHOUGH EXCITING, MUST BE CHANNELED IN APPROPRIATE DIRECTIONS. TO THAT END, I PRESENT YOU WITH THIS BOOK. CONSIDER IT A CAUTIONARY TALE AND AN INVESTMENT IN YOUR FUTURE.

BEST REGARDS,
ROGER WHITE

Even though she knew her quest was for a purpose higher than just idle curiosity, she felt the heat of embarrassment creep over her face, as though she'd been caught with her hand in the cookie jar. Folding the letter back into the envelope, she closed it inside *Pandora's Box* and returned it to her bookshelf.

Bing bong!

It was her daily countdown alert.

5 weeks + 0 days

[29]

NOT SO PLAIN VANILLA

THE NEXT AFTERNOON WHEN THE SCHOOL ACTIVITY VAN dropped her off at Grandma June's house on the way back from Richmond, Zephyr bolted up the front steps and into the living room.

"I'm back!"

Zephyr's grandma stepped in from the kitchen, smiling. "How was it? Did you learn anything helpful?"

"I sure did! And it's a really cool place, not dark and stuffy like I thought it'd be. They even have a café and a gift shop. But the best thing is they have this incredible collection of records, and even though we're too young to handle them by ourselves, Mrs. Creadle and the library staff helped us look up all kinds of things. There were even copies of pages from old family Bibles where people wrote down their personal histories."

"I'd love to go there myself sometime," Grandma June said wistfully. "And Richmond's a great city to explore. I once—"

Zephyr interrupted her grandma before she got them both off topic. "Sorry. But I need to tell you about what I found in one of the Bibles."

"Oh that's fine, honey. Tell me!"

"So I found a copy of records from an old Stone family Bible. I think a really distant cousin must have brought it in a long time ago. The family history listings stretched from my great-great-great-grandpa, Elijah Stone, all the way back to the early 1700s." Zephyr paused. "All the way back to...*Moses Stone!*"

"What? You're kidding!"

"Not kidding. It listed his father as James Edward Stone and his mother as Anna *White* Stone!" As soon as she said the name out loud, Zephyr felt all the blood rush from her head as the vision of the howling woman in the dark colonial dress filled her mind and struck deep in her heart.

"Wow. This whole thing's hitting a lot closer to home than I thought it ever would," whispered Grandma June.

"It sure is," said Zephyr, her initial excitement turning inside out into something cold and strange. *There's got to be another way to figure this out so I don't have to talk to that graveyard ghost again. I'm afraid since she can see me that she might be able to actually do something to hurt me if she gets mad enough. She might even follow me home!* A warming thought bloomed to the surface, though, and her mood buoyed slightly. "I spent a lot of the time searching for Thomas Drake and came up empty, but I have something that could make talking with the scary cemetery woman unnecessary."

Her grandma cocked her head to one side.

"The button! I've got it here, in my bag. It's got to be the connection to that 'vanilla' haunting. If I can follow Clem and Hiram further in, I bet they can show me what happened to Ahanu, and then I can tell Kanti, and then I can get Sam back! I could get it all settled without having to go back to the cemetery!"

"Hmmm, I don't know, Zephyr."

184

"Why not? You said so yourself—it was a residual haunting, so they can't do anything to me." *Like the cemetery ghost might be able to!*

"But it would make us later for dinner with your mom and dad."

And that's more important than saving my dog? Really, Grandma?

Zephyr shook her head and frowned. "Thirty minutes late, tops. I'll set my phone alarm, and if I'm not done in half an hour, I'll stop when I hear it go off." Zephyr took her grandma's hand. "Please, Grandma. I need to do this, for Sam." Zephyr felt tears pooling in her eyes at the thought of her beloved dog adrift in a ghostly canoe, lost to her forever if she didn't have an answer for Kanti by Thanksgiving.

Grandma June sighed and looked out the window. "Well, alright. But you better do it now before it gets any later. I'll stand right at the entrance to the trail and wait for you. I'd go in with you, but I'm afraid it might interfere with whatever combination you had that called the vision into being the first time. Even if nothing happens, though, you come on out after thirty minutes, anyway. Promise?" she asked, squeezing Zephyr's hand.

"Promise!" Zephyr agreed with a big smile. "Thank you so much, Grandma! And then I'll help you get those boxes down from the attic super fast. The stew will keep until we get there. Mom already said not to worry about getting home any particular time and to just give her a call when we're leaving."

"OK. You've convinced me, I guess. Let's go."

Leaving Grandma June stationed at the trailhead, Zephyr located the tree she'd leaned against after her first escape from

Mr. White's cemetery and pressed her back against it. Pulling the button from her pocket, she gripped it tightly and whispered, "Clem? Hiram?"

She opened her eyes and looked around. Listening intently, she only heard the sounds of the forest; the knocking of a woodpecker's beak against a hollow tree trunk, the far-off belching call of a bullfrog, the whispery soughing of the breeze through the pines. *How is it different this time? What was I doing before that made them appear?*

Closing her eyes again, Zephyr searched her memory. *I was leaning on this tree because I'd just run away from Mr. White. I was scared I'd get caught. I was sad about Sam...* Zephyr groaned to herself in frustration. *Come on! I only have a little time left! If I don't figure this out, I'm going to lose Sam forever. He'll be caught in that other world for eternity. I'm so scared he'll think I've abandoned him! Oh, Sam.* Zephyr felt her chest rising and falling with shallow breaths as tears squeezed out from her tightly shut eyes.

And then, she heard them.

"I'm athinkin' he's gone thisaway."

"Maybe. This swamp's full of hidey-holes."

Zephyr sniffed in her tears and opened her eyes. *Oh, thank goodness!* Just as before, when the two men stepped in front of Zephyr, the dark woods lightened, like theater lights coming on at the end of a movie. Except this was like she was *inside* the movie!

"Did ye bring a map?"

"Why would I bring a map, Clem?"

"Cuz I didn't, Hiram!"

Remembering what should happen next, Zephyr tucked the button into her pocket and scooted away from the tree just as Clem slumped down against it. Sure enough, the button popped off his pants when he hit the ground. "I can't think of ever'thing, ye know," the man grumbled.

"Well, ye sure got that right, anyways. I'd settle fer ye rememberin' somethin' just ever now and then," Hiram replied, leaning on his long rifle. "We ain't gonna get no reward if'n we don't keep lookin, ye know."

It was like seeing the rerun of an old TV show as Zephyr watched the two men's repeat performance. After Clem hauled himself to his feet and they started back on the trail, Zephyr found it easier to keep up with them without Scam along to slow her down. With every step forward into the deepening forest, she felt her own world slip further and further behind. A nearly electric shiver flooded over her and she stumbled from its force.

Come on. Get a grip. This may be your only chance to get Sam back!

Her dog's sweet face and sad whimper filled her mind and heart as she pushed onward behind the apparitions. She followed right on their heels, not wanting to risk losing sight of them in the gloom of the swampy wilderness.

Without warning, Hiram stopped and dropped to a low crouch. Zephyr fell forward right into the ghost's back. "Ach!"

The sensation of sticky spiderwebby filaments draped over her face and arms. Zephyr jumped back, pulling at the invisible threads. *Ectoplasm? Like the green slimy stuff left by ghosts in the old* Ghostbusters *movies?* She gasped as the fibers flexed into her open mouth. Coughing and spitting, she felt a wave of panic surging up from her stomach.

"Mommy!" she cried, then shook her head at that unexpected regression into early childhood.

"Hesh! I think I hear somthin' from over thereaways," Hiram hissed, pointing to his right.

Zephyr clamped her trembling hand over her mouth. *He can't hear me...can he?*

"Hesh, yerself," whispered Clem in response. "I ain't the one thrashin' 'round like a hunert-pound sow."

Hiram motioned for Clem to get down, so Clem knelt beside him.

What do they hear? A bear? An alligator?

[30]
THOMAS DRAKE

Straining to block out the sound of her own thumping heartbeat, Zephyr heard the ebb and flow of soft conversation behind a heavy curtain of Spanish moss.

Hiram pressed his forefinger to his lips and Clem did the same. Sliding his hands into the dangling moss, Hiram pulled it aside and leaned his head out for a peek. Nodding, he sat back on his heels and held the moss for Clem to peek through.

"I bet he's there with that bunch," Clem whispered as he pulled his head back.

"Good chance of it. And ye know, his ma might even be there too, and ye know what that would mean."

His ma? Kanti? Thomas is looking for her, too?

"Oh, yeah. T'would be more'n twice the reward!"

"Shh! Keep yer voice down. Don't want to let on we're here till we be ready. Now, check yer rifle."

As Clem worked on his gun, a wrinkled piece of paper slipped out of his patched-up pocket and floated to the ground at Zephyr's feet. She stooped down to pick it up, thinking maybe it would be like the coin, but her fingers slipped right through it. *Of course I can't touch it. This all just seems so real.* Bending down, she read words that slid into her brain and turned the warm blood flowing through her veins to ice.

50 Dollar Reward

For my slave girl, Sukie, runaway from the Subscriber's plantation, Saturday night. About twenty years old. Slim build. About five feet high of light complexion. Missing little finger of right hand. May have her son with her. About three years old, copper complexion and blue eyes. Will pay 25 Dollars for the child. May be hiding somewhere in The Great Dismal Swamp. The above reward will be given for the apprehension and delivery of said slaves to Drakewood Plantation or to a local jailer.

Thomas Drake
August 27, 1853

What! No! "No, No, No, No!" Zephyr moaned. "This can't be! They're bounty hunters looking for runaway slaves in 1853? No!" The memory of Ranger Doris reading to her and her grandma about The Great Dismal Swamp being part of the Underground Railroad and a home for escaped slaves swept over her. "I can't believe it! All that time I spent searching for Thomas Drake and now I find out he's a nineteenth-century slave owner? And these two are hunting down his slaves?"

Anger swallowed up Zephyr's frustration as she watched Clem and Hiram burst through the Spanish moss, guns pointed at a pair of African American women who were bent over cooking pots on a low fire.

"No!" Zephyr yelled at the men. "I thought you were good, but you're not! You're terrible!"

The women screamed and ran toward a half-circle of small huts. Heads popped out from open doors and windows and then quickly retreated inside. Three men strode forward, two with their own rifles pointing toward the bounty hunters. In the distance, Zephyr heard hollow clacking like a stick beating a log, followed by an even more distant repeating of the sound. *Some kind of warning signal maybe? Was that what I heard in the moon mist?*

"What you want? You got no business here," said the tallest of the three.

"All we want is the little boy. You know the one I mean," said Hiram.

"But we want the girl, too, Hiram!" Clem hissed in his ear.

"Shedup. I know what I'm doin'. Git the boy, an' his ma will follow."

"We got no child here," said one of the men, aiming his gun at Hiram. "Move on an' we won't kill you."

An ugly laugh burbled up from Hiram's throat. "I don't think so. My partner's got his gun trained on that shack right over there, an' he's gonna shoot straight through its sorry, ramshackle side if'n ye don't give up the boy right now."

Clem turned confused eyes toward his companion. Hiram poked him with his elbow and nodded at the closest of the huts. "Point it there!"

Clem nodded and aimed his rifle as instructed.

Zephyr's breath lodged painfully in her throat.

"I'm gonna give ye till the count of three, an' if'n the boy don't come out," shouted Hiram, "ye can say goodbye to whoever be in that shack—ONE!"

"No!" screamed Zephyr, horrified at the scene unfolding before her.

"TWO!"

Zephyr felt a tightly wound coil of rage threaten to explode within her.

"THREE!"

The blast of four firing rifles split the muggy air as Zephyr lunged at Clem. She hit the spongy earth, sailing straight through the ghost's residual presence, sprawling hard onto the ground. A light flashed white behind her eyes before she felt herself plunge into the darkness of unconsciousness.

A distant chime echoed in the back of Zephyr's brain.

Ting! Ting! Ting! Ting!

She rolled onto her side and felt the soft tickle of moss against her cheek. *What? Where am I?* Blurry green and black smudges swam before her eyes as she opened them.

Ting! Ting! Ting! Ting!

Zephyr raised up on one elbow and shook her head. *My phone alarm!*

Everything came rushing back into her mind like a hot gust of wind and she nearly fainted again. *Got to get up. Got to find Grandma.*

Struggling to her feet, she pulled out her phone to turn it off, and when she did, the old brass button fell out of her pocket and onto the leaf-littered ground. Zephyr scooped it up and flung it with all her might, deep into the surrounding thicket. "Argh!" She pushed her way back to the deer path, amazed at how close the trail was. It was actually only a few feet away from where she'd fainted.

"Zephyr? Zephyr? I'm coming in, ready or not!" called Grandma June.

When Zephyr saw her grandma hurrying toward her, she burst into tears and slumped to the ground.

"Honey! What happened?" Grandma June threw her arms around her.

"Oh Grandma," sobbed Zephyr. "It was awful! And it didn't help me find Ahanu and I couldn't help those poor people!"

"What people?" asked Grandma June, picking bits of dead leaves and moss from Zephyr's hair.

"The slaves!" cried Zephyr, tears streaming from her eyes as she looked into her grandmother's worried face. "The ones hiding in the swamp. I had it all wrong. Those two men weren't looking for Ahanu after all. They were from a whole different century. They were bounty hunters looking for runaway slaves in 1853. And the Thomas Drake they mentioned wasn't Kanti's Thomas. It was some plantation slave owner! Oh, Grandma. I tried to stop them, but I couldn't!"

Grandma June gently rocked Zephyr from side to side. "Come on, honey. We'll talk about it inside. I was afraid something like this might happen."

Zephyr's thoughts reeled in a swirl of confusion and disappointment as they made their way back to her grandmother's house. Curled up on the couch with her knees tucked close to her body, she filled her grandma in on everything that had happened since she started following the two men.

"I can't believe how much time I wasted on those two. And knowing what kind of men they were makes it even worse. I felt so helpless, Grandma. And I don't even know what happened. I fainted before I saw."

"Oh, sweetheart," said Grandma June, setting a cup of hot honeyed tea on the table beside her granddaughter. "Your heart and mind were both in the right place. I thought it was a good lead, too, you know. All the pieces seemed to fit in the right places. I mean—the swamp, those men searching for what they called a little 'mixed-blood boy,' a man named Thomas looking for him. It just turned out to be a case of 'right pew, wrong church,' as my mother used to say."

"But those poor people, Grandma." Zephyr shook her head.

"I've been thinking about that, Zephyr," said Grandma June, leaning forward in her chair, "and I have a theory. It seems the residual playback of the events was dependent upon the combination of that button and the place in which you found it. That was Clem's button, you said. That means it was Clem's emotional trauma that imprinted itself there. I have a feeling it was the bounty hunters who may have lost their lives that day, not the runaway slaves."

Zephyr nodded. "Does it make me a bad person to hope it was them who died?" she asked.

Grandma June shook her head. "No. It makes you human. It makes you a human who feels anger when she encounters the inhumanity like those two exhibited."

Zephyr shuddered. "I don't want to wish anyone dead. Not really, you know."

"I know, honey. But whatever happened to those two men, they brought it on themselves. It was their choice to risk their lives for a few dollars." They were both quiet for a few minutes as Grandma June's theory settled into Zephyr's mind and heart. "So listen," her grandma continued. "How about we forget the boxes. I can get Mr. Porter to help me later this week."

Zephyr uncoiled herself from the couch. "No. Let's go ahead and do it now. I think it will help me to do something constructive."

Grandma June smiled. "That's my girl."

[31]

HALLOWEEN

"How do I look?" Lorie asked, rotating slowly in front of Zephyr's mirror.

Zephyr inspected her friend's red, gold, and black Spider-Woman costume. "Fantastic. How about me?" she said, tugging at the neckline of her emerald-green leotard and straightening the silk ivy leaves encircling her tights. "Skinny watermelon?"

Lorie took her friend by the shoulders and spun her around, looking Zephyr in the eye. "You look good, girl."

"If you say so," said Zephyr.

"I do. Now," said Lorie, picking up her trick-or-treat bag, "let's go hunt down some major candy. I heard Mrs. Phelps is handing out full-size bars. And not that icky, knockoff brand stuff, either. The real stuff. Come on, I can hear a Snickers bar calling my name."

Zephyr's mom, wearing a long black dress and a tall, pointed witch's hat, stood at the bottom of the stairs, aiming her phone camera at them as they descended.

"Wave, girls! I'm getting this on video. Your last trick-or-treat night! *Batman* better watch out for this dynamite duo. You both look fabulous!"

"Mo-om. Really?" Zephyr moaned, but then grinned in spite of herself.

Scam trotted into the living room and looked up the stairs.

"Oh my gosh," said Lorie. "Is he wearing a cat costume?"

"Uh huh. Mom thought it would be cute," said Zephyr, shaking her head as Scam rubbed his black felt cat ears against her mother's leg. As her mom leaned down to scratch Scam's head, Zephyr lowered her voice and whispered into Lorie's ear, "I really do think Mom is psychic and just doesn't know it."

Lorie nodded as she waved and smiled at the phone's lens.

Mom followed them out the front door, keeping the camera pointed their way. "Have a good time at Katie's after-party! Stick together and be home by ten thirty! Call if you need a ride!"

Zephyr gave a thumbs-up as she and Lorie walked down the driveway, which was lined with glowing jack-o'-lanterns.

"See ya!" said the scarecrow leaning against a pine tree.

"Bye, Dad."

"Bye, Mr. Stone," said Lorie, giggling. "Your parents sure get into Halloween."

"They do," Zephyr agreed with affection.

As Poison Ivy and Spider-Woman reached the street, a group of tiny ghosts, fairy princesses, and mini-zombies charged up the driveway. A few seconds later, a chorus of squeals echoed through the night.

"They met the scarecrow," said Zephyr, laughing. "At least he didn't dress up as a clown this year."

"Oh, my gosh. I almost peed my pants last year when he popped up from behind your bushes. There's nothing scarier than a clown on Halloween."

Zephyr looked up at the lopsided ivory moon hanging in

the deep purple sky. *At least there isn't any fog tonight. A Halloween moon mist would be kind of spooky-cool, though.*

"Hey! Look over there," Lorie called, pointing down the street. "That witch and angel look familiar. Let's check 'em out."

The girls jogged toward the pair, who stood head and shoulders above a throng of little minions and monsters milling around a two-story brick house. When they reached them, Zephyr tapped the witch on the shoulder and Lorie tugged the back of the angel's long white gown. Both whirled around, the witch's black arched eyebrows raised high above her purple-shadowed eyes, and the angel's brow creased in a frown. Both broke into smiles of recognition.

"It's you guys!" said the angel, a sprinkle of silver glitter shimmering across her coffee-brown cheeks. "I thought it was Eric and John again. They've been bugging us all night."

"Yeah," said the witch, nodding her head of frizzy blond hair. She took a step back and swept her eyes up and down Zephyr and Lorie. "You two look awesome!"

"Thanks!" said Zephyr, inspecting the two girls. "Hannah, you've got a real witchy thing going on there."

"And who would have thought Meghan could look so angelic?" said Lorie.

"Watch it," said Meghan. "I'd slap you but it might make my halo slip off!"

"Got much, yet?" asked Zephyr. "We had a late start because Mom made us eat a big Halloween dinner before we could get dressed. You know, worms with bloody guts, mouse brains, and dead man's fingers."

"Eeew!" squealed Hannah.

"Actually," Lorie countered, "it was really good, even if it was just spaghetti and meatballs with raw cauliflower and carrot sticks."

"So," Zephyr said, gesturing toward the crowd of kids jostling their way to the front porch. "What's all that about? This isn't Mrs. Phelps's house. I don't even know who lives here now, since the Millers moved out last month."

"Me either," said Meghan. "And they're not even giving out candy."

"Then what's got all these kids pumped?" asked Lorie, watching a *Star Wars* stormtrooper shove his way past a pink unicorn.

"Word on the street is they own some kind of import business," Hannah explained. "Maybe they're giving away something from their stock."

"Wow. Sounds good. Let's get in line while they still have some," said Zephyr. The four girls waited their turn until the last group of kids ahead of them jumped down the porch steps.

"Trick-or-treat!" they all chimed together.

"Oh, just look at you!" said the short, middle-aged woman holding a box of little plastic action figures. "What a pretty angel. Here, dear, take your pick," she said, smiling at Meghan. "And look at this mysterious witch!" she said, holding the box out to Hannah next. "Oh, and I'd recognize Spider-Woman, anywhere!" she said, beaming and offering it to Lorie once Hannah had made her selection.

"Thanks!" said Lorie, sifting through the figures. "These are pretty awesome."

"You're quite welcome, dear."

As Lorie moved aside with her prize, Zephyr stepped forward and reached her green painted hand into the box. "And who," said the woman, raising her eyes from Zephyr's red polished nails up to her green ivied torso to her tousled red hair, which was several inches higher than the woman's own cap of dyed strawberry-blonde curls, "do you think you are, young lady?" she asked, snatching the box away from Zephyr's reach.

"I-I'm Poison Ivy...ma'am."

"Well," sniffed the woman, moving the box to her hip. "You're obviously too old to be out here trick-or-treating. You should be ashamed of yourself, taking treats away from the little ones. There's an age limit, you know," she said, frowning.

"But I'm only twelve," Zephyr protested, her face flushing red as her hair.

"That's right!" Lorie said moving back beside her friend. "She's in seventh grade with us at school. She's just really tall, that's all."

The witch and angel stepped back up on the porch. "It's true!" Hannah agreed as Meghan nodded, her halo bobbing up and down.

"Hmm, if you say so," the woman said, bringing the box back in front of her and holding it out toward Zephyr.

"Um, no thanks," muttered Zephyr, turning around and rushing down the steps into the front yard.

"You should carry some kind of ID next time!" the woman called after her.

"There won't be a next time," seethed Lorie. "This is our last year!"

"Well, it's not my fault your friend is so tall," the woman sniffed.

"It's not hers, either!" Meghan yelled over her shoulder before pushing past a pint-sized ghost to reach Zephyr.

"Don't mind her," Lorie reassured, sliding her arm around Zephyr's waist. "What does she know?"

"Not much, apparently," said Hannah. "Like we'd have some kind of ID to carry around proving our age."

Zephyr felt tears prickling her nose. *Everybody's staring at me!* "Maybe I should just go home and help Mom hand out candy. I can meet you at Katie's at eight."

"No way!" said Lorie. "You can't let some old lady ruin your last trick-or-treat night. You're sticking with us."

"Come on," said Meghan. "Let's get over to Mrs. Phelps before she runs out of the good stuff and starts handing out pennies."

"Good plan," Lorie said, checking her watch. "It's seven o'clock. We've got an hour before trick-or-treating ends and the party begins."

Zephyr heaved a sigh. "Alright. But, I swear, if anybody else tells me I'm too old—"

"We'll knock them out!" Lorie declared.

"Halo, or no halo!" said Meghan.

"OK. You win," Zephyr said, smiling.

"Great," said Lorie. "Now get your green butt moving before Mrs. Phelps pulls out her piggy bank!"

THE ADDAMS FAMILY

EIGHT O'CLOCK ARRIVED WITH THE DOUSING OF JACK-O'-lanterns and the switching off of porch lights, the universal signal of "No more treats!" Free of marauding trick-or-treaters, island neighbors tucked themselves in for the night as a crowd of costumed seventh graders descended on the home of the county sheriff.

"Wow! Look at the decorations!" Zephyr said as the girls crunched down the Brown's long gravel driveway lined with burning tiki torches.

Poison Ivy, Spider-Woman, the witch, and the angel gazed wide-eyed at the dozens of gauzy white ghosts floating from tree limbs, the tombstones leaning at haphazard angles that were lit with little pumpkin-shaped solar lights, and the ragged man-sized scarecrows with leering jack-o'-lantern heads propped up by sticks.

"I wonder if Sheriff Brown got your dad to come over here," Lorie mused, looking up at a red plaid flannel-shirted scarecrow.

"I hope not," said Zephyr.

"I think your dad's pretty cool," said Meghan.

"That's 'cause he's not *your* dad," said Zephyr.

"True," Meghan agreed. "Even cool parents need to stay home on Halloween night."

A yodeling wail bellowed from the Brown's fenced-in backyard.

"What's that?" cried Meghan.

"Sounds like a banshee!" said Hannah in alarm.

Zephyr sighed. "Sounds more like Katie's beagle. I forgot she had one...too."

Lorie slipped her arm around Zephyr's waist. "Hang in there, Zeph," she whispered as Meghan and Hannah picked up their pace and took the lead.

The girls stopped at the bottom of the front steps. Screams, demonic laughter, and spooky organ music rose from behind the shrubbery. A fog machine pumped white mist across the porch floor, and they all looked up to see giant spider webs dangling from the rafters. Zephyr pushed a web aside as she led the girls up the steps. *Creepy laughter, thick fog; I wonder if Lorie's having the same flashbacks I am?* Zephyr turned around and raised her eyebrows at her friend. Lorie's eyes widened and Zephyr nodded, knowing they were on the same wavelength.

The front door, draped in cottony webs, displayed a sign written in squiggly letters: NO ENTRY AFTER 8:45. Zephyr turned the doorknob and pushed, but it didn't budge.

"Look," said Hannah, pointing at another sign beside a large brass disk. "Ring gong for entry," she read.

"Oh! Let me," cried Lorie, grabbing the long, wooden-handled mallet.

"Go for it!" Zephyr encouraged her friend.

"Stand back, everybody," Lorie warned the girls and several other kids now crowding the porch.

Gripping the mallet in both hands, Lorie slammed its

rubber head against the gong. A deep-throated *bonng* bellowed from the brass disc. As Lorie set the mallet back in its place, the front door cracked open.

"You rang?" said a deep, bass voice.

"We're here for the party!" said Meghan.

"Yeah!" yelled the excited chorus of kids around them. "Let us in!"

"Not so fast," said the voice as the door slowly swung open to reveal a giant, tuxedoed man with a huge head looking just like—

"*Lurch!* It's Lurch from *The Addams Family!*" Lorie said excitedly.

It's Sheriff Brown making sure no older kids crash the seventh graders' party.

Mrs. Brown, wearing heavy eye makeup, a waist-length black wig, and long tight dress, stood beside her husband. "Welcome to the Addams Mansion! I am Morticia Addams and you've already met our butler, Lurch. Have fun but behave yourselves. We'd hate to have Lurch kick you out."

"Hmmmm," rumbled Lurch, nodding solemnly.

Lurch stepped aside as the trick-or-treaters pressed into the foyer. A muffled bass rhythm vibrated against the closed inner door that led to the living room. As the kids passed by Lurch's appraising gaze, Mrs. Addams opened the door and invited them in.

All of the Brown's furniture had been pushed against the walls, and the open space thronged with kids dancing, laughing, and filling their faces with the snacks that were piled high on refreshment tables stationed around the room. Ghosts and bats suspended by invisible string swung above their heads, and orange twinkle lights glittered along the walls.

"Boy, they sure know how to throw a party!" Zephyr commented, heading for a table holding a glass bowl filled with orange punch. Silver candleholders with flickering electric candles glimmered on either side of the punch bowl. Zephyr picked up the plastic ladle and a cup and leaned over the tall bowl to dip out some punch. She promptly burst into laughter.

"What? What's so funny?" Lorie asked, coming up behind her.

"Yeah, what?" said Meghan, adjusting her crooked halo as she and Hannah sidled up to the table.

"Look!" Zephyr pointed into the bowl. Green ice in the shape of a large hand floated on top of the orange liquid and blue eyeballs bobbed along the surface. "Here. Hold up your cups and I'll dip some for you," said Zephyr.

"I'll take mine without the eyeballs," said Lorie, giggling.

Forty-five minutes passed while Zephyr and her friends talked and laughed with their classmates, every now and then breaking into spontaneous dancing depending on the song that played. At nine o'clock, Lurch carried the gong into the room and struck it nine times. A pale-faced girl with long black braids and wearing a knee-length black dress, black tights, and shoes stood beside him.

Wednesday Addams (a.k.a. Katie Brown) announced, "It's time for the first game! I'll pick two teams. I'm looking for opposites based on your costumes. When I call your name, get in line over there in the order I call you." She pointed to a spot on the side of the room.

"Then what?" yelled a vampire.

"You'll just have to wait and see!" Wednesday said, grinning and placing her hands on her narrow hips. "Everybody stand against the walls."

"How come she gets to decide who's on the teams?" Meghan grumbled.

"Because it's her party, goofus," whispered Hannah.

Katie walked into the center of the room and began calling

out names by Halloween character. "You, wizard, stand over here," she said, pointing to a place on the floor. Folding her arms, she scanned the room until she spied Hannah. "You, witch! Come stand behind the wizard."

"Wish me luck!" said Hannah, stepping toward a boy dressed in a long, purple robe and tall wizard's hat. Zephyr watched as two more pairs were called to the center of the room. Then—

"Batman!" Katie called out and a tall boy dressed as the dark knight stepped to the line.

"Poison Ivy!" cried Katie.

Though she knew it was probably coming, the sudden focus of everyone's attention rooted Zephyr in place.

"That's you, silly," Lorie said, giving her a gentle shove.

Ugh. I hate being stared at! With a quickening pulse and sweating palms, Zephyr ducked her head and slumped to her spot behind Batman. She avoided making eye contact, unsure who was behind the black mask, and looked pleadingly toward Lorie. Her friend gave her a bright smile and a thumbs-up.

"OK! That's team one. Now, for team two!"

"Spider-Man!" Katie called, and Zephyr smiled.

Which could only mean she'd have to next call—

"Spider-Woman!"

Lorie skipped into place.

About midway through her pairings for the second team, Katie called out, "Devil!"

Gotta be Meghan next.

"You! Angel!"

Meghan adjusted her halo, squared her winged shoulders, and walked to her spot behind the red-horned boy.

Once Katie had filled out the second team, she announced, "Now! This game only needs one piece of equipment for each side, and here it is," she said, holding her hands out to Lurch.

Sheriff Brown reached into his pants pockets and pulled out two oranges. A mixture of laughter, boys shouting, "Oh yeah," and random girls asking, "What?" swept over the party.

I hope this isn't what I think it is.

"The rules are pretty simple," she continued. "I'll give an orange to the first person in each line—the wizard and Spider-Man—and then they will pass it to the person behind them and so on until the orange reaches the end of the line. The last person to get the orange passes it back to the person in front of them and it moves back up the line. Whichever team gets the orange back to their starting person first, wins."

Wait for it...

"But the thing is," continued a smirking Wednesday Addams, "The orange is going to be tucked under your chin, and you can't use your hands or any other part of your body to pass it on. If you drop it, you have to pick it back up, put it under your chin, and try again."

I knew it. Public humiliation guaranteed.

[33]

BATMAN AND POISON IVY EXCHANGE PRODUCE

Hoots and whistles erupted throughout the room. Zephyr caught a glimpse of Lorie, who was clapping and laughing. *At least one of us is having a good time.*

Batman turned and faced her. Leaning toward her ear, his familiar voice said, "At least we're about the same height. That should make it easier."

Oh no. Batman is Luke Barnes!

Zephyr stared at him, speechless, as his eyes swept down to her feet. *Here it comes. Watermelon? String Bean? Cucumber?*

"How's your ankle?" he asked, scanning back up to her eyes.

What? My ankle? He wants to know how my ankle's doing? "Um, it's fine now."

"Good," he said, turning to face the back of the cheerleader in front of him. Zephyr noticed the girl's blond ponytail stood in stark contrast to her rapidly reddening neck. *At least I'm not the only one dreading this!*

Once Spider-Man and the wizard stood facing their opposites, chins clamped tightly around their oranges, Katie announced, "When Lurch strikes the gong, you start!"

Silence fell across the room as Lurch stood gripping the gong. His long arm pulled back and then swung forward, striking it with an echoing *bonng*. The room went wild with high-pitched shrieks and squeals. The witch and wizard neck wrestled for a few moments until the witch was able to clamp onto the orange and turn to face a yellow-toothed rat. In the other line, Spider-Woman Lorie struggled to keep her orange from dropping to the floor as it migrated down the chest of a ratty-shirted zombie.

Zephyr eyed the kids contorting their bodies as they fought to gain control over their oranges. The ones with the longer necks seemed to have it easier. *At least I've got that going for me.*

"Go! Go! Go! Go!" chanted the spectators.

An orange rolled under Zephyr's feet and she skittered out of its way as the devil plowed his way into her line to retrieve it.

"Hurry up!" demanded Meghan in a less than angelic tone of voice.

Zephyr's attention returned to her own team as she watched Luke bend his tall, black-suited torso down toward a much shorter cheerleader, enveloping her throat with his. *Ick. They look like they're making out.* Zephyr's face flushed nearly as red as her hair as she watched the two work the orange from one person's chin to the other. Then the moment she was dreading arrived. Luke turned toward her, orange secured beneath his chin and dark brown eyes locked on hers. *OK. Here goes.*

Zephyr tilted her head at the opposite angle of Luke's and stepped closer to him. Batman closed the short gap between them and pressed the orange into the hollow of Poison Ivy's throat. The pressure of his chest against hers startled Zephyr and she jerked her chin up just enough to set the round fruit rolling down her chest. Batman's bat ears grazed Poison Ivy's shoulder as he sought control over the orange.

No, no, no!

Zephyr stood frozen, her arms straight by her sides and hands clenched into tight fists as she willed Luke to just let it drop to the floor and start over. Just like the uncooperative citrus though, Luke refused to give up. *Stubborn!* Whistles and catcalls swirled around them as it appeared to everyone else that Batman had his face planted directly in Poison Ivy's chest. Just as the orange touched the edge of her ivy-leaved leotard neckline, Zephyr felt the pesky sphere reverse direction and begin rolling back up toward her chin. *Thank you!* As soon as she felt the orange tickle the base of her throat, she raised her hands out to her sides and clamped her chin around the fruit.

"Hurry, Zeph!" Hannah squealed along with other members of their team.

Darting her eyes to the side, Zephyr saw a furry werewolf in an unholy hands-free embrace with an angel, Meghan's halo in imminent danger of slipping off her head completely.

OK. Get a grip. The only thing worse will be if I make our team lose!

Zephyr inhaled and looked into Luke's eyes. One deep brown eye winked at her through the slits in his mask, threatening her grip on the orange as her heartbeat suddenly pulsed in her throat and her stomach did a quick flip-flop. *Focus!* Tilting her head, she pressed the citrus under Luke's chin. Taking firm hold of the fruit, he lifted it away from Zephyr and reversed direction to send it back to the cheerleader. What had before seemed like hours now sped by in seconds. The orange moved more swiftly back through the line, thanks to some of the seventh graders having figured out a winning technique while watching others struggle or succeed.

"Go witch! Go witch!" Zephyr joined her teammates urging Hannah to pass the orange to the wizard, his mustache tickling her witchy nose.

"Spi-dey! Spi-dey!" chanted the other team as Lorie cranked her head sharply toward her shoulder and pushed the orange into Spider-Man's throat. Her forceful maneuver triggered a choking cough in the web-slinger, though, and Zephyr watched the orange drop between their feet just as the wizard gripped the orange under his chin and raised his arms in triumph.

Cheers exploded from Zephyr's team and their friends around the room. Exuberance took over and the wizard and the witch fell into a spontaneous embrace, followed by the cat and the rat, the football player and the cheerleader, and, before she could even think about it, Batman and Poison Ivy. *What am I doing!* Zephyr pushed herself out of Luke's arms, heat flowing up from her throat. As she stepped back, she noticed Batman's own throat was a shade pinker, too. *Probably from the orange.*

"Um, good job, Zephyr," he said.

"You too, Luke. Uh, see ya," she said, turning on her heel and heading for the chips and cookie table. Lorie, Meghan, and Hannah all converged on the table at the same time.

"That was fun!" Lorie said. Zephyr smiled. Her friend didn't seem to mind at all that her team lost. "So," she continued, "did you figure out who Batman is?"

Zephyr looked down at Lorie's bright face. "Yep. Luke Barnes."

"What? Oh no! Did he say anything mean to you?" Lorie asked, scowling. Meghan and Hannah leaned in closer.

"Actually, no."

"Really?" said Lorie, suspicion shading her voice. "That's strange," she said, scanning the room.

"Yeah. Pretty strange," Zephyr said as she dipped a corn

chip in a bowl of salsa that was decorated with plastic spiders clinging along its edge.

After the eat-the-swinging-donut-without-your-hands game, Lurch struck his gong one final time. "Go straight home," he growled. The four friends made their way outside and walked down the driveway, exchanging hugs before Meghan and Hannah headed in one direction and Zephyr and Lorie set off together in the other.

"I'm so glad I can stay over tonight. It makes Halloween even more fun," Lorie said, linking her arm through Zephyr's.

"Me too," Zephyr agreed, looking up at the moon floating among ragged, silver clouds. "And I'm so glad you're staying at Grandma June's with me tomorrow. Are you sure you're still up for going to the White graveyard with me again?"

Spider-Woman's shoulders visibly quivered. "Well..." she whispered, then gave her head a little shake. Setting down her bag of candy on the sidewalk, she planted her yellow-booted feet firmly on the pavement and crossed her arms in front of her chest. "Hey, what are superhero friends for?"

"You're the best," Zephyr said gratefully and gave her a hug.

"I know," Lorie said, giggling as she hugged her back. Picking up her bag, Lorie declared, "Onward! As our friend, Buzz Lightyear, says, 'to infinity and beyond!' I just wish we didn't have to pass a graveyard on the way back to your house. Isn't there another way we can go?"

Zephyr shook her head. "No. You know it's the only road leading to ours."

"Yeah. I know. I was just hoping you'd discovered a shortcut I didn't know about."

"Come on," encouraged Zephyr as she draped her arm around Lorie's shoulders.

As the girls approached the island cemetery bordering the

dark road, Zephyr saw something flit through the tombstones and settle beside a tall memorial at the front corner. "Did you see that?" she asked.

"See what?"

Zephyr pointed to the stone several yards ahead of them.

Lorie squinted. "I see a light. Is somebody holding a flash-light by that memorial?"

Zephyr stopped and stared as a figure materialized beside the gravestone. A man wearing tall fisherman's boots and a yellow rain slicker looked down at the grave. He stood in a soft circle of light, but Zephyr couldn't see where the light was coming from.

"Do you know that man?" Zephyr asked.

Lorie leaned forward and shook her head. "What man, Zeph?"

[34]

KNIGHT IN SHINING ARMOR

"Are you telling me you don't see that man over there wearing a yellow raincoat and knee-high, white rubber boots that those commercial fishermen wear at the docks?" Zephyr asked.

"No, I just see the memorial lit up. Maybe it's got those little solar lights that come on at night. I've seen them on other graves lately..." Lorie said, trailing off without commenting further on the fact that her friend could see things that she couldn't see...again. Zephyr watched the gray-haired fisherman raise his bowed head and turn to face them, his dark eyes locking onto hers. "But I do see a big ol' scarecrow walking down the street toward us," said Lorie with relief coloring her voice. She pressed her elbow into her friend's side, breaking Zephyr's stare with the man by the memorial.

"Dad!" Zephyr called out. "What are you doing here?"

"Just thought I'd escort the two most beautiful girls on Colington Island back home," he said, shambling toward them. "Figured I'd come across you along the route home from Katie's."

"That really wasn't necessary," said Zephyr.

"Your mom and I knew you'd say that, so that's why we didn't bring it up," he said chuckling. Zephyr would never admit it out loud, but her dad's presence dropped like a comfortable blanket over her shoulders.

"Whatever," she replied and glanced back at the fisherman who...was no longer there.

Things are getting stranger all the time. Zephyr shuddered.

"Are you cold, pumpkin?" her dad asked, noticing her shiver. "Want my jacket?" he offered, unzipping the old coat sewn with more colorful patches than original fabric.

"Uh, no," said Zephyr, "I'm fine."

"If you say so," said Dad. "How about you, Lorie? Want to wear it? I'm told it's the height of Halloween fashion this year. Rated number one by scarecrows everywhere. As a matter of fact, I saw this very jacket on the front cover of *Scarecrow Fashion Weekly* just the other day."

Lorie giggled. "No thanks, Mr. Stone."

"Suit yourself," he said, stationing himself between the girls.

"Um, Dad? Could you maybe walk behind us?" Zephyr asked as a group of their seventh grade classmates shuffled by them and waved.

He laughed. "What? Embarrassed by your old man?"

"No. It just makes me feel like a baby, that's all."

Dad gave her a quick one-armed squeeze around her waist. "That's because you are our baby," he said softly, "and we wouldn't want anything to ever happen to you, or to Lorie either."

"Awwww," cooed Lorie.

"But, no, I can't walk behind you. What do you think Sheriff Brown would think if he saw some big, old guy in a costume walking behind you this late at night?"

"Stalker!" said Lorie.

"Exactly," said Mr. Stone.

"OK, OK, you win. Let's just get home before *The Witching Hour* movie starts." *And before anybody else shows up unannounced and unseen by anyone else but me.*

"So how was the party?" asked Dad as he ambled down the street between them.

"It was a lot of fun," Zephyr responded. It really had been a good time. *Even with everyone watching me walk across the room to join our team. Even after I discovered that Luke was Batman. Maybe...*she swallowed hard...*especially after that.*

"Yeah," Lorie agreed. "We got split into two teams and played that pass-the-orange-under-your-chin game. Zephyr's team won! It was pretty hilarious, actually."

"Ha! I remember playing that game, myself! Who were your passing partners? Were they good at it?"

"Mine dropped the orange at the last minute. A kid named Billy dressed up like Spider-Man. Zephyr had Batman."

"Well, that was appropriate. Did you know Batman?"

"Luke Barnes," Zephyr muttered under her breath.

"Who?"

"Luke Barnes!" announced Lorie.

"Really? The Luke Barnes who likes to tease you so much?" Her father looked down at her. He was one of the few people who still towered over her.

"Yeah."

"But he's been weirdly nice to her lately. I personally think it's a plot to catch her off guard," Lorie said.

"What do you think, Zephyr?" asked Dad.

Shrugging her shoulders, she focused on the pavement passing beneath her green slippers.

"So, when did Luke start acting 'weirdly nice'?"

"Um, about the time I sprained my ankle."

"I thought so!" said Dad.

Zephyr stopped and squinted at him. "What do you mean?"

"Being a boy myself, I have the inside scoop."

Lorie giggled.

"You know," said Dad, "it's never OK for anyone to hurt another person or be really mean to them, and you should let parents or teachers know if that happens. But, as you may have guessed, sometimes boys tease the girls they like the most, even when they don't know it themselves yet. We—I mean *they*—like to get the girls' attention, see their reaction, even if the boys themselves look pretty silly doing it."

Huh. That made sense when it was worded like that. And Dad still likes to tease Mom, even now!

"So," Lorie began as they all started walking again. "How come he's nice all of a sudden? Does that mean he doesn't like her anymore?"

Dad's floppy straw hat bobbed side to side as he shook his head. "No. Something pushed him to the next level. And I'd guess it was Zephyr's injury. Brought out the knight in shining armor side of him, like Sir Galahad from the days of King Arthur and the Knights of the Round Table."

"Huh," said Lorie, thinking it over. She turned to look at Zephyr. "So maybe he'll be a knight in shining armor at next year's party. You going to be a damsel in distress again?" Zephyr shot Lorie a sharp look. Lorie laughed. "Just messing with you, Zeph. You're the least distressed damsel kind of girl I know. Just don't go slipping off any more logs anytime soon. No telling what Luke might do!"

Thirty minutes later, the pajama-clad girls and Scam were settled on Zephyr's bed with a big bowl of buttered popcorn and an array of Halloween candy culled from their stash. Lorie and Zephyr took turns tossing popcorn to Scam.

"We can't give him too much," Zephyr warned. "I think he's putting on weight."

Lorie nodded. "I'll pick out the little ones just for him. Besides, he's spending more time batting them around than eating them anyway."

Zephyr looked at Scam tapping his paw at a piece of popcorn, and sighed. *Sam wouldn't waste time playing with his food.* "So," she began, "you really didn't see that guy in rubber boots and rain slicker at the graveyard?"

Lorie shook her head as she unwrapped a mini chocolate bar. "Nope," she said, thoughtfully munching the candy. Swallowing, she raised her eyes to Zephyr's. "You think it was a ghost, don't you?"

Zephyr nodded, her eyes growing wide.

Cocking her head, Lorie said, "Maybe it's that ghost communication thing your grandma was talking about?"

Zephyr sighed. "Yeah, I think it must be. But it sure creeps me out when I see people nobody else sees. Makes me afraid I'm losing my mind."

"Yeah, I'd worry about the same thing if I were you," said Lorie.

Zephyr frowned and pulled in her lips. *Geesh. Maybe I am losing it.*

"Except," Lorie continued, "every time you see somebody I don't see, I do see something strange—like the freaky, black tornado at the White graveyard, and, tonight, I saw that light at the memorial. It's like the rest of us can see weird stuff happening, but you can see what's—actually, *who's*—causing it to happen. That's why us normal..."

Zephyr raised her eyebrows.

"I mean us *less gifted* people try to come up with a natural explanation for what we see, whereas you see the real reason and it's actually *super*natural."

Lorie's logic makes sense. "But why's it started all of a sudden?"

Lorie shrugged her shoulders. "Dunno. But I think it's pretty cool."

"That's 'cause you're not the one attracting all the otherworldly attention," Zephyr grumbled, popping a kernel of candy corn into her mouth and stirring her fingers through her trick-or-treat bag. "Hey, what's this?" she asked, pulling out a small, orange drawstring pouch. "I don't remember getting it."

[35]

THE WITCHING HOUR

"Did you get one?" asked Zephyr, holding up the little orange velvet sack.

Lorie rummaged around in her own bag. "Nope. Guess you must be the special one."

"Huh. There's a tag attached to it; *Zephyr, Hope you have a most fortunate night. Happy Halloween!*"

"Weird that it has your name on it. That's very specific for a random kid showing up to a door in costume. I wonder when you got it. Does it say who it's from?"

"I don't think so. Just some kind of little mark. Let me look at it under the desk lamp."

Zephyr twisted around and held the tag beneath the light. "It looks like...like..."

"What? What does it look like? Let me see," Lorie said, leaning toward the lamp. "A Batman mask! Is this from who I think it's from?"

Zephyr shrugged her shoulders, trying to show a lack of interest while the prospect of Luke giving her something actually made her kind of nervous. Good nervous or bad nervous, she wasn't quite sure which.

"Well go ahead and open it. Hope a snake doesn't pop out! I'm not totally convinced of your dad's theory."

"It would have to be a pretty small snake," observed Zephyr as she held the bag in the palm of her hand. She felt her pulse speeding up as she fumbled with the drawstring bow.

"You want me to open it for you?" Lorie asked, teasing her flustered friend.

"No. I've got it now," said Zephyr, releasing the string and opening the mouth of the bag.

"So far, so good," Lorie noted. "Nothing jumped out at you."

Zephyr turned the bag upside down and a fortune cookie, like the ones they got from the local Chinese restaurant, dropped onto the bedspread.

"*Fortun*ate, huh? Well at least Luke gets points for cleverness," mumbled Lorie.

"If it *is* from Luke," said Zephyr.

Lorie shot her a who-do-you-think-you're-kidding look. "Go ahead and see what's inside. Let's see how fortunate you really are."

Zephyr cracked open the crisp, almond-scented cookie like an eggshell and pulled out the white strip of paper tucked inside.

"Well? What does it say?"

Zephyr read the tiny print aloud. "A ship in harbor is safe, but that is not what ships are built for."

"Huh. So who's the ship, here? You or Luke?"

"I opened it, so I guess I must be the ship." *And tomorrow this ship's pulling out of safe harbor, for sure.* "But hey, you could be the ship too, since you agreed to go with me back to the White cemetery tomorrow when I try to call up the scary ghost woman. I know Grandma thinks I have some special ability to communicate with the..." A chill snaked up Zephyr's back. "...dead...and that ghost could possibly be one of my ancestors. She might even give us info we need to help Kanti and Sam. It's like a real Halloween haunted forest come to life! At least it won't still be Halloween."

"Nope, not Halloween. Day of the Dead," said Lorie, reaching into the popcorn bowl.

"Oh my gosh, I forgot that!" Zephyr gasped, her eyes growing as wide as bright green saucers.

"That means we should take bread and flowers to the grave-yard," Lorie said matter-of-factly.

"Really? Bread and flowers? How come?"

"Granny says spirits like them, but not just any flowers or bread. The flowers have to be marigolds, especially the giant orange or yellow ones. Their bright color and strong scent are supposed to help guide the family spirits to their living rela-tives. And the bread's special too. It's kind of sweet and has a skull and crossbones design on the top. Your grandma have any marigolds?"

"She might...I think I've heard her say that their smell keeps the bugs away, so maybe she'll have some in her garden."

"We can swing by my house on the way out tomorrow and I'll pick some marigolds, just in case, and grab one of the extra loaves Granny left in our freezer."

Zephyr shook her head. She wasn't convinced smelly flowers and baked goods would make that much difference.

"Hey, look," Lorie said, turning toward the television hanging on Zephyr's wall. It's Witch Hazel and her minions. She's about to tell us what movie they're going to show."

A tall, long-haired woman with black lipstick and

eyeshadow, dressed in a clingy, floor-length, low-cut, purple dress and black lace veil stirred a steaming cauldron as her crazed-looking underlings tossed in fake spiders, rats, and snakes. "Hmmm," she said. "What is brewing tonight? It's All Hallows' Eve, you know. Ahhh," she exhaled. "Look into my magic cauldron and you shall see...if you're brave enough!" She cackled and her assistants giggled along with her as the camera zoomed in on the swirling steam.

Sheesh. I could do without the freaky laughing.

Crooked black letters slithered up from the cauldron, spelling out the title of the night's movie: *Thirteen Ghosts.* Zephyr sighed. *Well, that's perfect. Just what I need,* more *ghosts.* Despite the movie's high fright factor, Zephyr found her eyes shutting on their own accord about halfway through. The combination of physical and emotional exhaustion, and the after-effects of sugar/carb overload, pulled her into a heavy-headed stupor as she fought to stay awake. Looking through drowsy eyes at Lorie and Scam, she saw they'd both given in to the inevitable. Her friend was flopped over sideways on the edge of the bed, and Scam was curled into a cat-beagle ball on the rug. Zephyr glanced at her clock; 12:15 a.m.

OK. Time to go to bed.

Picking up the stray candy wrappers, Zephyr dropped them into the empty popcorn bowl before setting it on her desk. She pulled open a drawer and tucked the orange velvet sack and its tag inside. Glancing at Lorie to be sure she was really asleep, she slipped the paper fortune into the front pocket of her overnight bag, already packed for their upcoming weekend with Grandma June. *Thanks, Luke. I needed that.* Aiming the remote at the TV, she clicked off the image of people running madly away from something. *Must be one of those thirteen ghosts.*

She yawned and clicked off her bedside lamp, leaving the room bathed in a sterling, silver light that flowed through her window. Pulling back the curtain, she saw a bright spotlight of a moon glittering over the dark canal. And there, wings spread wide, stood a tall, snowy-white egret. The strange beauty caught Zephyr's breath for a moment, and when she exhaled against the cool glass, the crystalline scene softened into a white mist. *I've created my own moon mist.*

"Goodnight, egret. Goodnight, moon. Goodnight, Lorie," she said, crawling into bed between her comatose friend and the wall. "Goodnight, Sam, wherever you are," she whispered as she drifted into sleep.

Ding-Ding-Ding-Ding!

Zephyr's bedside alarm clock startled her awake just as Lorie rolled off the mattress and tumbled onto the floor, scaring a sleeping Scam into a yodeling yowl.

"What! What's going on? Where am I?" Lorie asked blearily, flailing her arms.

Zephyr slid across the mattress and leaned over to look down at her friend. Lorie's tangled hair covered her eyes as Scam licked his paws in feline concentration. "Good morning, Lorie."

Parting her hair away from her face, Lorie looked up, blinking like a startled owl. "Geez. Morning, already?"

"Already."

"How'd I get down here," she asked, leaning back on her elbows and looking around.

"It was a short trip," Zephyr replied as she got out of bed and offered her a hand.

Lorie grabbed Zephyr's wrist and hauled herself up off the floor.

"Come on," said Zephyr, heading for her closet. "Let's get dressed so we have time to stop at your house for marigolds and dead bread on our way to Grandma June's."

[36]
DAY OF THE DEAD

"Thanks again, Mom," Zephyr's dad said as he hugged Grandma June in her driveway. "We really appreciate you letting the girls and Sam stay over." Handing her Scam's leash, he looked down and shook his head as the dog rubbed against her legs. Grandma June chuckled as she leaned down to pat his head. "You know I love it!" she replied, beaming.

"And Lorie brought you these beautiful marigolds and her grandma's homemade bread," Zephyr's mom said, retrieving the bright yellow bouquet and aluminum foil-wrapped loaf from the back seat.

"Oh, how lovely!" said Grandma June.

"We'll tell you more about them later," Zephyr whispered as she hugged her grandma hello.

Grandma June raised her eyebrows and stepped back with a small nod and a smile.

"We'll be back late Sunday afternoon," her mom said. "And then it will only be about three weeks until we're back for Thanksgiving."

"Can't wait!" said Grandma June.

"Bye!" called Zephyr and Lorie, waving as her parents' car backed out of the driveway.

"We'll say 'hello' to the scary ghost woman for you," said Zephyr, just loud enough for Lorie and Grandma June to hear.

Lorie giggled.

"Come inside, girls," said her grandma. "We need to talk."

Grandma June set out plates of pumpkin walnut bread and glasses of cold milk on the kitchen table. "First of all, what did you want to tell me about the flowers and the bread?"

"Oh," said Zephyr, spreading cream cheese on her slice. "Did you know today is called the Day of the Dead?"

Her grandma nodded as she nibbled her pumpkin bread.

"Well," continued Zephyr, "Lorie's family celebrates the Day of the Dead, especially her granny."

"Right," said Lorie, "and Granny always bakes this special bread each year as an offering to share with our dead relatives who might come...visit."

"*Pan de Muerto*," said Zephyr's grandma knowledgeably.

"Exactly!" Lorie cheered, holding up her palm to high five Grandma June.

"How'd you know what it's called?" Zephyr asked.

"I've always wanted to be in Mexico on the Day of the Dead," her grandma answered. "So I've researched it. And that's why I know these gorgeous flowers are called *cempasúchil*, and that they're also going to the White cemetery with us."

"Us?" said Zephyr.

"Us," Grandma June stated firmly. "But not you, this time," she said, scratching behind Scam's ears. "Now that we know there's a restless, unpredictable spirit and you, my dear, will attempt to call her up to get answers, I want to be there to support you. And, besides, I'm really curious!"

"You know what they say about curiosity," Zephyr mumbled.

"Yes, well, curiosity won't kill this old cat. My name's not Pandora, and if there's even the slightest hint of danger, I'm not going to let you girls go in alone!"

"Thanks, Grandma," Zephyr said, rising and hugging her.

"Speaking of cats," said Lorie, glancing at Scam. "Aren't we afraid Mr. White's big cat might join us?"

"Hamish?" Zephyr asked. "I wouldn't worry about him unless Mr. White comes looking for him."

"All the more reason to have me along as an extra lookout," Grandma June added.

"So when should we do this?" asked Zephyr. "Is Mr. White at the Visitor Center today?"

"No. They decided to end Saturday hours for the season, but I overheard him tell Doris that he and Hamish always eat dinner early at four thirty. Something about it being a holdover from his teaching days when he had to fit it in between his last afternoon class and his evening class."

"So you think we should go when he and his cat are busy eating dinner?" asked Lorie, setting down her empty milk glass.

"Yes," Grandma June answered. "I think it's probably the safest time to go and not worry about him showing up to pay his respects to his ancestors."

"Gee. I never thought of it that way, before," Zephyr said. "I guess those *are* his dead relatives in that graveyard."

"Indeed they are, and if your research from the Library of Virginia is correct, it means there's a link between the White family and the Stone family."

"And since the scary ghost woman was dressed in colonial style clothes, she might know something about the Native American ghost lady's child," Lorie pointed out.

"That's right," said Grandma June. "Zephyr's job will be to

call up the woman's ghost, offer her reassurance, then ask her about Kanti's child. Hopefully, kind words from someone who can see and communicate with her might be enough to calm her down and allow her to move on. And if she can also give information about the lost child, Zephyr may be able to help soothe two souls." Looking down at the cat-beagle, she added, "Well four, actually."

Zephyr shook her head. *This is asking an awful lot.* "I don't know, Grandma. I have no idea what I'm doing. I mean, last night when we were walking home from our friend Katie's party, I saw a man in the cemetery, but Lorie couldn't see him. Another ghost! He just appeared from nowhere. I'm pretty scared about all of this," she admitted, tears swimming in her eyes.

Grandma June reached over and placed her arm around Zephyr's shoulders. "I'd be surprised if you weren't at least a little bit scared, sweetie. This is uncharted territory for all of us. But I do know you've been given a gift, and we're never given gifts without good reason. Granted, yours isn't the ordinary kind, like opera singing or painting, but that's all the more reason to embrace it. The gift to know, for certain, that our souls outlive our bodies, to communicate with spirits caught in ghostly limbo. Other gifts pale in comparison to yours." She sat back and placed her hand over Zephyr's. "You are very special, sweetheart."

I think I'd rather be a little less special right now.

"And, besides," Lorie added, standing and folding her arms, "we've got your back."

"Thanks, Spider-Woman. I may need your superpowers today," Zephyr said, smiling at her loyal friend.

"Gee, Zeph. You know this gift of yours is like having a real superpower! What should we call you? What do they call people who communicate with the dead?"

"Mediums?" Zephyr suggested.

"Yeah. We could call you Medium Woman!" said Lorie.

Zephyr laughed nervously. "That's impressive."

"No," said Grandma June. "Not Medium Woman—*Ghost Charmer.*"

"Ghost Charmer!" exclaimed Lorie. "I like that!"

"Better than Medium Woman, anyway," said Zephyr. "But, seriously, Grandma, what do I do? How do I 'call her up' or whatever?"

"You've already seen for yourself that spirits are attracted to you. I believe your innate gifts will present themselves and you will know what to do and what to say. Just listen to your inner voice."

Yeah, well, right now my inner voice is saying RUN!

Grandma June continued, "Ever since your first spirit encounter, I've been doing research. Wait here a minute," she said, pushing back her chair and walking to her desk. Lorie and Zephyr watched as Grandma June opened a drawer and pulled out a small black sack, gathered at the top by a gold ribbon. "This is for you, Zephyr. It will help protect you and aid in your work," she said, placing the pouch in her granddaughter's hand.

Zephyr untied the ribbon and reached inside. Feeling a metal chain, she looked up at Grandma June.

"Go ahead, honey. Take it out."

Pulling the silver chain from its satin bag, Zephyr's eyes widened at the oval pendant hanging from it. As she held it up to the light, she saw dozens of thin black needles intersecting within a crystal-clear stone.

"It's tourmalinated quartz," said her grandma. "The black threads of tourmaline are said to have protective qualities that absorb negative energy into themselves and away from you, kind of like the tradition of a dream catcher. And the clear quartz is thought by some to aid communication with the spirit world."

Zephyr would have to add crystology to the growing list of Grandma June's surprising interests. "It's beautiful, Grandma."

"Wow," whispered Lorie. "It's like magic!"

"Well," said Grandma June, considering Lorie's statement. "I don't know about that, but it can't hurt! And the most important thing about it is that all my hopes, prayers, and love for you go with it," she said, taking the chain from Zephyr's hand and placing it around her granddaughter's neck.

"Thank you, Grandma. It will be like having you with me whenever I wear it."

"That's the spirit!" said Grandma June. They all made eye contact then and burst into laughter when they all realized her unintended pun.

Bing Bong.

Zephyr pulled out her phone, glanced at the screen, and shuddered.

"What is it?" her grandma asked.

Zephyr held it up for Lorie and Grandma June to see.

∃ weeks + ५ days

At 4:15, Grandma June took a brown, wicker basket from her pantry. "This should hold both the bread and the flowers, I think."

Pressing the crystal against her heart, Zephyr glanced at the clock. *Am I ready for this?*

"I'll carry the basket until we get there," her grandma offered as Lorie placed the sunny marigolds and the round loaf of bread inside. "You girls can each carry one of those little flashlights," she added, pointing to a pair on the shelf. "We'll need them until we get through the woods. After that, there

231

should be enough sunlight left to light our way. Better wear our jackets. Getting chilly out there."

"Hang on just a second," said Zephyr before running to the bedroom. Unzipping her overnight case, she pulled out the fortune cookie message and tucked it inside her jeans pocket. *Time for this ship to set sail.*

Basket and flashlights in hand, jackets zipped, and Zephyr's pendant warm against her thumping heart, Grandma June opened the backdoor and led the way to the deer path.

Ready or not, here we come.

37

THE GHOST CHARMER

ZEPHYR AND LORIE AIMED THEIR FLASHLIGHT BEAMS ON the ground ahead as Grandma June carried the basket of offerings between them. Having her grandma with her gave Zephyr some courage but...

When we get to the graveyard it's totally going to be the Zephyr Show. What if the ghost doesn't show up? Or what if it does something really scary? I hope Grandma has a strong heart. Zephyr glanced over her shoulder at her grandma trudging behind her. *Of course she has a strong heart. Mine, though, I'm not so sure about.*

The trip through the woods seemed shorter than before. *We're there already? Couldn't we slow all this down a little?* Zephyr clicked off her light and tucked it inside her coat pocket. She heard an answering click as Lorie did the same with hers. Feeling her grandma's warm, reassuring hand on her back, she leaned forward into the lowering sunlight and looked around.

"Well that's new," she said, pointing toward the cornfield.

Directly in front of the deer path were two hand-lettered

signs. One stated, No Trespassing, and the other warned, Bears in Field.

"Hmm," said Grandma June. "Mr. White must have found this deer path."

Lorie stepped beside Zephyr and eyed the signs. "Do you think there really are b-bears in there?"

Grandma June shook her head. "I've asked around since he first told me about the bears and nobody else has had bears in their fields. I think it's just his way of discouraging us. We'll just keep our eyes out for signs like paw prints, flattened stalks, and scat, just in case."

"Scat? Like, if we see any, we *scat*?" Zephyr asked.

"No, scat as in bear poop."

"Oh," Zephyr replied, looking at Lorie's wide eyes and open mouth. "Well, I'm sure you're right about the signs, Grandma." *Yeah, like I'm sure about any of this!* "OK then, let's go. But we better keep our voices down, just in case," she whispered.

The rattling cornfield had grown even more ragged than it was before, and the crumbling stalks and leaves brushed against them as they passed through. Every step they took snapped and crackled in the still air. *So much for stealth mode.* The white picket fence sprung up into view way before Zephyr was ready for it. *Geez. Here we go. Don't see any creepy crows this time. That's good, anyway.* The trio walked in silence across the soft grass. *At least there aren't any added sound effects here to draw attention to ourselves. Until the screaming, black tornado appears, that is.*

Grandma June set the basket down at the entrance and bent down to look at the tombstones. "This is amazing. All these years, I never knew this was here."

"So, Lorie," Zephyr said, turning to her friend. "What do

we do with the bread and flowers? Is there some kind of cere-mony? Do we say a prayer, or something?"

"Well, I know Granny usually sends up prayers for our dead relatives—praying that they're doing well and hoping that they'll stop by and enjoy the *Pan de Muerto* with us. At home she makes a little altar with bread and flowers and candles. In the cemetery, she usually just sits by the family graves and places the flowers and stuff there."

"OK," said Zephyr. "So I guess we should put the flowers where the ghost was focusing her attention then; by the grave of Moses Stone." *My great-great-great-great-whatever-grandfather!*

Lorie picked up the flowers and stood looking toward the back corner of the graveyard. "Go ahead," urged Zephyr, taking her friend's elbow. "I'm right with you, but you know more about the flower and bread stuff."

"I'm coming, too," whispered Grandma June. "We should stick together."

Lorie nodded. "O-OK. Bring the basket with the bread so we can share it."

Stepping carefully around the graves, they approached the marker for Moses Stone. Lorie separated the flowers and placed them around the front of the headstone and down the sides where they imagined the eighteenth-century coffin must lay beneath the earth. "That looks pretty," Zephyr said. "Now what?"

"Now," said Lorie, taking the round, golden-brown loaf of bread in her hands. "I guess I should say a prayer before we start eating the bread."

"OK. Go for it," Zephyr said as Grandma June nodded and smiled encouragement.

Lorie squeezed her eyes shut and held the bread up to the sky. "I hope the scary ghost woman is feeling well today...and I hope the yellow flowers will guide her here...and I hope she likes my granny's bread because...it's really good...Amen." She opened her eyes and lowered the bread as Zephyr and Grandma June looked on, heads tilted to the side and eyebrows climbing to their hairlines.

"Well, that should do it," said Zephyr.

"I hope that was alright," said Lorie, her lips quivering. "I-I've never had to say the prayer before..."

"Yes, dear, that was very nice," said Grandma June, placing her arm around Lorie's shoulders. "I'm certain your efforts will make it easier for Zephyr to connect with the scar-*unfortunate* spirit. Now, let's try some of your grandmother's delicious bread."

Lorie broke the loaf into thirds and handed them out. She took a small piece of her portion and set it on the ground in front of the gravestone.

Zephyr raised one eyebrow. *I bet those crows come back for this!* After sampling her piece, she nodded and turned toward Lorie. "Hey, this is good."

"Yes. I'd love the recipe," Grandma June said in agreement.

I don't know which is stranger; eating bread in a graveyard hoping a ghost shows up, or discussing recipes like we're at a potluck supper.

A sudden breeze blew through the cornfields and swept over them as they huddled around the grave of Moses Stone. *Is the tornado lady coming already?* Grandma June turned questioning eyes to Zephyr's. Lorie continued to quietly munch her bread, seemingly unconcerned.

"The-the wind is picking up," Zephyr observed.

"That's normal," said Lorie.

Zephyr took Lorie by the shoulders to face her. "What do you mean, normal?"

Lorie swallowed her bread and explained, "Granny says when the wind blows, which it usually does after we start eating the bread, it's blowing the spirits home. Gives them a kind of tailwind."

Zephyr shook her head at Lorie's matter-of-fact explanation.

"I think this would be a good time for you to get started, Zephyr," whispered her grandma.

"Now?"

"Now," her grandma confirmed.

Heaving a ragged sigh, Zephyr stepped away from Moses Stone and stood at the entrance to the graveyard. Looking back, she said, "I think you two should stand over there in the other back corner. It might get kind of stormy on this side."

Zephyr unzipped the top of her jacket and reached in to clutch the quartz pendant. Then, closing her eyes, she focused on her breathing just like she'd done on the night of the moon mist when she'd fought to keep her hysteria at bay. The slower and deeper she breathed, the more relaxed she became, and with no conscious decision to do so, she found herself visualizing warm golden light entering her body with each inhalation. She saw, and actually felt, the soft comforting glow. She released the pendant and raised her arms to her sides, willing the light to envelope everything around her, especially her grandma and Lorie.

A gentle vibration tingled the soles of Zephyr's feet and rose steadily until it completely encased her entire body in a softly humming cocoon. She felt the sensation of being lifted into the air but, opening her eyes, she saw her feet still planted solidly on the ground. *Something's happening to me and I'm not controlling it. Not consciously controlling it anyway. But it seems OK. I think I'm going to be OK. Let's try calling up this spirit now.*

Zephyr closed her eyes. "I do not know your name," she said in a clear, steady voice that she barely recognized as her own. "But I know you are drawn to this place, and I know you are full of pain and deep sadness. Please. Please come to me now and talk with me. I am here to listen. Not to judge. And I believe I can help you if you will let me." *Wow. Where did all that come from?*

As soon as Zephyr's thoughts intruded into her mind, she felt the vibration falter and the light grow weaker. *Stop thinking! Just go with it!* A few deep breaths later, she felt the warming sensations return. "Come to me now," she continued. "Speak to me. I wish to know why you seek this place. Do you mourn Moses Stone? Do you ask his understanding? Come, now. I mean you no harm, dear lady."

As the sound of rushing cornstalks grew in front of her, she became conscious of a low whimper rising from behind—Lorie. She opened her eyes and gazed at the cornfield as the wave of swirling stalks flowed toward them. Fighting the urge to turn around and reassure Lorie, she envisioned the golden light folding itself around her friend and calming her down. Somehow, she knew that her grandma was OK and would lend her own strength to Lorie.

Just as before, a small black tornado spun itself to the edge of the cornfield, then lifted off the ground and flew toward Zephyr. This time, Zephyr did not move, even though the teakettle screaming filled her ears and threatened to blow her over with its intensity. Her heart raced, but Zephyr stood firm. "Thank you for coming to me," she said.

The black, spinning cloud slowed its rotation and the woman's somber form materialized through the thinning vapor. For several moments, the spirit stood still, her head bent down, her arms stiff at her sides, bone-white fists clenching and releasing.

Zephyr heard her grandma whisper, "Oh my God."

38

THE PHARAOH'S DAUGHTER

ZEPHYR CLOSED HER EYES AS SHE RAISED HER HANDS toward the ghost, trying to spread the golden veil of light over the apparition, but feeling it blocked several feet away. Opening her eyes, she saw the ghost's gray-eyed stare boring into hers. The woman raised her thin hand and pointed at Zephyr. "Let me pass! Let me pass!"

"Tell me your name," said Zephyr.

A shrill keening, as much animal as it was human, filled the air. "You judge me!" she screamed.

Zephyr shook her head. "No. I do not judge you. I judge no one."

The woman grabbed her white-capped head in both hands and wailed, "It was right! It was right! It was right!"

"What was right? Can you tell me?" asked Zephyr, gently.

"You will judge me," she growled. "Let me pass."

"Do you wish to visit the grave of Moses Stone?"

The woman's eyes flickered. "Yes," she hissed.

"I also came to visit his grave. We brought him flowers."

The woman pointed her chin toward the back of the graveyard.

"Who are they?" she whispered.

"One is my friend and one is my grandmother. They also wanted to honor him."

The gray eyes turned back to Zephyr. There seemed to be less madness lighting them. "Who are you?" the woman asked.

"My name is Zephyr."

The woman twisted her head to one side. "What be your family name?"

"Stone."

The somber woman collapsed to the ground, sobbing.

Zephyr pressed on. "Moses Stone stands in the line of my grandfathers. I am part of his family. And, you? Are you his family too?"

The woman rose to her knees and clasped her folded arms close to her body. Rocking from side to side she moaned, "Yes... no...yes...no..."

"Tell me what you mean. I may be able to help you."

The woman sunk back on her heels and laid her hands in her lap. "I found him in the forest. He was but a wee little one, barely stumbling around, and the poor thing was all alone." The whisper of a smile played at her thin lips. "His curls were deepest brown and his skin, the color of cinnamon. And his eyes," she said, her smile growing stronger. "His eyes were the brightest blue you ever saw, a pure reflection of the summer sky."

Zephyr fought to maintain her calm as the pieces to the mystery started coming together. "You mean you found...Moses?"

The woman nodded and looked up with pleading eyes. "But, you see, he was dressed in Indian garb. I'd heard of a man who had gone to live with an Indian woman, but then later sailed back to England by himself. Never knew his name." Lowering her head, she whispered, "Never wished to know his name." Returning her eyes to Zephyr, she continued, "I named the child Moses since, just like the Pharaoh's daughter in the Bible, I had found him abandoned in the wild. And, like the Pharaoh's daughter hid the Hebrew blanket, I hid his Indian dress."

"And-and you did not try to find his mother?"

"No! You judge me! You judge me!"

How could this woman keep a child away from his family? Who was she to decide her ways were better than his mother's? With dawning awareness, Zephyr was flooded with the understanding that this was a part of her own ancestry that had been suppressed. *I have Native American ancestors! I would have never known that if it weren't for my dog running off into a swamp!* Struggling to keep her growing anger in check as her feelings enveloped her, Zephyr felt her control and connection with the ghost begin to unravel.

Taking a deep breath, she held up her hands. "No. I do not judge you. I just want to hear your story. I believe you need to have your side of it told."

The woman clasped her hands together. "We were childless. Ten years of marriage and five tiny coffins. My babies never thrived. One lived for a year before he was taken by the pox. My precious twin girls were born too soon and so very, very tiny—they only breathed for three days. And my other two baby boys were..." She folded her arms against her stomach and bent low. "...stillborn. My dear, sweet babes," she sobbed.

Zephyr felt tears well in her own eyes, although she wasn't sure who the tears were for. "So you took the child to raise as your own?"

"I knew God had given the child to me—to save him from being brought up as a nonbeliever in the Lord and to save me from having a childless home. I brought him to our cottage in secret and bade my husband take him to my sister's house for a fortnight. Then he was to bring him back to our village and say that Moses was the orphan of my husband's cousin who perished afar in a fire." The woman leaned toward Zephyr. "He would say his cousin's wife was from Spain and that was why the child's skin was a darker hue. This way the boy would never be called Indian; there would be no connection with those people if his mother did ever come looking for him."

Zephyr's heart ached for Kanti. She'd never stood a chance of finding him.

"You see," the woman continued, clutching her hands to her heart. "I prayed to God for a child of our own, and just like the Pharaoh's daughter, one was provided; my little Moses. And since my husband's cousin was a Stone—"

The fictional cousin, you mean.

"—then the child could have the Stone family name with no lawful impediment. We could take him in as our own, and he would, in all ways, be our son, even in name."

Zephyr fought to keep the psychic connection flowing as she digested all she was hearing. Kanti was Moses' actual mother. *One of my own ancestral grandmothers!* Pressing her hand against the quartz pendant, she felt its smooth comfort against her chest. She had to take the next step and ask, "Did you never wonder how the child's mother must have felt?"

"Ooooooh," she groaned, bending low and sobbing.

Now we're getting to the heart of it. Legal names and cover-ups were one thing, but this woman felt a mother's love. The deepest part of that love understood and mourned the other mother's loss, no matter how much she'd thought Ahanu had been a gift from God.

"I did!" she cried. "I did think of her, but I could not let my new baby leave my side. One day I faltered and had thought of a way to let the Indian woman know that he was alive and thriving, a way to ease her possible despair, but then..." she moaned from the depths of her soul. "I soon heard a story about an Indian woman who'd died in the swamp while seeking her lost son. She'd been bitten by a snake while searching, and once her people finally found her, she lived only one more day."

Oh, Kanti.

Zephyr didn't know what to say, or even think. Closing her eyes, she willed herself to let that "other side" of her take over, as the pitiful spirit lay crumpled on the ground. "What is your name?" she asked, a note of authority coloring her voice.

The woman looked up. "My name is Anna. Anna White Stone."

"And your husband?" Zephyr asked. "Was he James Edward Stone."

She nodded silently, a deep line creasing her white brow.

"Anna," said Zephyr, stepping forward. "You should have returned the lost child to his mother, a mother who loved him dearly. And even after you learned of her death, you could have returned him to his family, to his own people. You knew there were Nansemond living near you who could have helped." Anna's trembling hands covered her face as she bent over. Zephyr shook her head, watching this spirit, wracked with pain, trapped in her own warring feelings of guilt and love. "But," Zephyr continued, "I believe, in your heart, you thought he was meant to become your child. You could have left him to wander on his own and possibly die, but because you took him into your home and kept him safe, I am alive today, over three hundred years into his future."

Anna raised her head, the tight band around her mouth loosening from its grip of pain and distrust into a growing softness.

Zephyr continued. "I am the result of the love of two

different women. One who gave birth to a child and gave her life in search of him, and one who raised the child with all the love she had to give. I will speak to Kanti, his first mother and I will let her know that her son was kept safe. That he grew to manhood and became the father of many generations, leading to my own. Anna—Kanti is a gentle soul and I believe she will forgive you if you ask it of her."

Anna rose eagerly to her feet and nodded, her face transformed from its mask of pain to one of vulnerability and kindness. "Yes. Please ask her forgiveness for me. I never wished to hurt her. I only meant to keep my—our—child safe."

Zephyr smiled. "I will, Anna. You may leave now. I'm sure you have better places to be than this cold cemetery."

Anna murmured a quiet, "Thank you" and then turned in an ever-speeding circle. But this time, rather than the terrifying, black tornado taking her shape, a sparkling veil swept over her instead, transforming her dull brown dress to a glistening silver. As she spun, she rose into a shimmering cloud, not back through the dying cornfield, but straight up into the late autumn sky, the lowering sun sparking gold within it. When the luminous cloud vanished from sight, Zephyr lowered her eyes. And there, across the open space, at the edge of the quaking cornstalks, knelt a man in the green grass, one hand covering his mouth as he stared into the sky.

"Mr. White?"

39

STRANGE RELATIONS

Zephyr glanced over her shoulder and saw Lorie and Grandma June, clinging to each other, mouths open and eyes wide. "Look! It's Mr. White!" she said, pointing toward the cornfield.

Lorie and Grandma June rushed to Zephyr's side just as Hamish emerged from the cornstalks and curled himself against Mr. White's legs. Zephyr took a tentative step forward and Mr. White lowered his gaze to her.

"Are-are you alright?" he asked.

"Yes," Zephyr answered. "We're fine, Mr. White. What about you?"

With an effort, he rose to his feet while Hamish rubbed his broad face on his master's unsteady legs. "I think I'm OK, now. Do you think she's g-gone for good?" Zephyr nodded, a thousand questions running through her mind. She stayed silent and waited instead. Mr. White lowered his tight shoulders. "I owe you an explanation."

You've got that right!

As if he had just noticed them, Hamish trotted over to

Zephyr and leaned heavily against her for a moment before
sidling over to Lorie and Grandma June to rub the side of his
face against their legs.

Mr. White drew in a long breath and sighed. "You see,
there's always been a story in our family concerning my ancestral grandmother. Supposedly, she took in a half-Indian orphan
that her sister had sent to her. She kept the child secret until
her brother-in-law took him back to live with them. It's been
told, down through the generations, that the little boy was given
their family name, *Stone*, and raised as their own kin. It was
always whispered about. A family secret. I never paid it much
mind or gave it much credence until..." Mr. White shuddered.
"Until I moved here and encountered that entity inhabiting the
family cemetery."

Lorie and Grandma June stepped forward to stand on
either side of Zephyr, placing their arms around her waist. She
hadn't realized how weak in the knees she was until she felt
their comforting support. "Thank you," she whispered, slipping
her own arms around their waists.

Mr. White closed his eyes and hugged his arms around his
middle. "One night, during a bright full moon, I was in the
backyard with Hamish when I heard a moaning across the
cornfield. I traced the sorrowful sound to the cemetery and
saw..." Mr. White opened his eyes and stared at the back corner
of the graveyard. "...I saw a black cloud hovering over the grave
of Moses Stone. And I heard a woman weeping, weeping like
her heart was breaking. But there was no one there. Just that
dark cloud. I asked if anyone was there, and the cloud began to
spin and scream, and flashes of red lightning slashed through it.
I grabbed Hamish and ran back to the house, but I could hear
the awful sound chasing us through the cornfield the entire way
back."

Zephyr felt Lorie and Grandma June's arms tighten as they leaned closer to her.

"Did you know what—or who—it was?" Zephyr asked.

Mr. White shook his head. "I wasn't sure, but I felt in the depths of my soul that it had something to do with that old family story."

"Do you know why Moses Stone was buried here in the White family graveyard?" Zephyr asked.

"No. That wasn't part of our family lore. Could have been any number of reasons. He might have lived nearby."

Like, right next door?

"Or this may have been part of his land at one time. But, you see, I couldn't let you know about the graveyard. It wasn't so much about the family secret as it was about your safety. Until I had a better handle on what was going on out here, I didn't want you, or anyone else, coming in contact with it."

That makes sense, I guess. "Could you hear what she said to me?"

"No," said Mr. White. "I could only hear your side of it. I was eating my supper when I heard the screaming. I tried to ignore it, but it pierced my heart and I had to come out here. Then, I saw you standing in front of it, so calm and unafraid. I could only drop to my knees and listen...and pray." Mr. White stepped closer and held his hand toward Zephyr. "I was so amazed at how brave and in control you were."

Well that makes two of us.

Mr. White continued, "I heard you say your name, and then, hearing the rest, I gathered what she was saying to you. So, in a way, I guess we're distant cousins of a sort."

"Of a sort," said Zephyr.

Grandma June slipped her arm from around Zephyr and took a step forward, smiling. "There are all kinds of family. It isn't just blood that links people together. The Whites and Stones share a deep history."

"Indeed, we do," he agreed.

"Do you have Thanksgiving plans, Mr. White?" she asked.

"Please, call me Roger. But, no, not really. I have no children, and my brother and his family live out in California, so I usually just eat with the students who don't go home for the holiday."

"Well, Roger, unless you're planning to drive to Radford, how about joining us at my house this year?"

"Will there be pumpkin pie?" he asked.

"The best," said Zephyr.

"Then I'd be happy to join you," he said, a smile as warm as the golden sunlight breaking across his face.

Zephyr's dad stretched his hands above his head, then lowered them and rubbed his middle as he yawned. "Well, that was probably the most delicious Thanksgiving dinner I ever ate."

"You say that every year," Grandma June said, chuckling.

"That's because I cannot tell a lie," he said. "And it was fun having Roger join us."

"It really was," agreed Zephyr's mom. "He had so many interesting stories to tell."

Zephyr and her grandmother shared a smile. *And she doesn't know the half of it.*

Her dad looked at his watch. "It's getting on toward ten thirty. I think it's time to put this belly to bed." He walked to the living room window and pulled the drapes aside. "The fog's rolled in, big time. Strange how white it is. Must be that full moon?"

Zephyr turned wide eyes toward her grandmother. *Another moon mist?*

"Yes," said Grandma June, answering both her son's spoken question and her granddaughter's unspoken one. "Must be the full Beaver Moon shining through it."

"Kind of pretty," her mom said, twisting around in her chair to see out the window. "Pretty in an eerie sort of way."

"Indeed, it is," Grandma June agreed and then walked over to her son for a goodnight hug.

Zephyr's mom rose and joined in the embrace, then turned around to Zephyr with an inviting smile.

"OK," said Zephyr. "Group hug!"

As they released their arms and wished each other "Goodnight," Grandma June asked Zephyr if she could help her in the kitchen for just a moment before she went to bed. Once her parents were secured behind their bedroom door, Zephyr looked into her grandmother's eyes and nodded. "It's time, isn't it?"

"Yes, sweetheart," she said, smiling gently. "It's the perfect time. There's even a moon mist to help things along. Are you wearing the pendant?"

Zephyr placed her hand over her heart. "Always."

"Good."

"Will you come with Scam and me?" Zephyr asked her hopefully.

"Of course, I will, if you want me to."

Zephyr nodded.

"Well, then," said Grandma June. "Let's meet here at midnight and we'll go out back. I think you only need to stand near the tree line. I have a feeling Kanti will respond to your call right away."

Zephyr hugged her and then went to her dad's old bedroom. Her parents were settled in her aunt's girlhood room since she wouldn't need it until Christmas when she flew in from Colorado. Zephyr pulled out her Nintendo Switch to try and pass the time but found it impossible to focus. The closer it came to midnight, the faster she felt her pulse race. *How will Kanti take the news? Will she be even sadder? Will she be angry? And Sam. Oh please, please, please make this work!* Zephyr pulled her phone from her jeans pocket and gazed down at the countdown app. The image of Sam tugged at her heart like a magnet.

0 weeks + 0 days

Time was out. It was now or never. As the digital numbers on her phone lit 12:00, Zephyr looked over at the snoring Scam curled up against her bed pillow. *Must be true what they say about the natural melatonin in turkey, and he's so stuffed with it, he'd probably sleep till noon if I didn't wake him up.* A tiny part of Zephyr wished she could just sleep in blissful ignorance of restless spirits and moon mists and ghost charming.

Remember—you're gifted! Right. I just wish I was as sure about my new abilities as Grandma seems to be.

"Come on, Scam," she whispered as she gently shook him into wakefulness. "Let's get you back to Kanti." The cat-beagle blinked his large brown eyes, then slowly got to his feet before jumping off the bed. "That's a good boy," urged Zephyr. He glanced up at her and then commenced his four-legged "yoga" stretches; first bowing down with his front paws reaching forward, then coming to a stand, and stretching back each hind leg in turn. He finished up with a full body shake. Zephyr shook her head and smiled down at him. "Ready now?" Scam wagged his tail in response. "I'll take that as a yes."

Peeking out her doorway, Zephyr looked across the hall and saw no light shining beneath her parents' door. Soft buzzing snores vibrated from the other side and she knew they were both deeply asleep. When she tiptoed into the kitchen with Scam at her heels, she saw her grandma leaning against the sink and staring out into the misty night, lost in thought. Zephyr's heart fluttered. *She must be thinking of Grandpa.*

She placed her arm around Grandma June's waist. "Are you sure you want to go out there with me? I'll be alright by myself this time."

Her grandmother turned toward her, a tear quivering in one eye. "Of *course* I want to go with you!" she whispered. "This isn't about me, or your grandpa. It's about Kanti. But I guess, in a way, it is about Grandpa too. It's about his family, after all; your family—our family."

Zephyr nodded and gave Grandma June a squeeze. After attaching the leash to Scam's collar, she looked up and said, "Alright, then. Ready?"

"Ready."

Opening the door into the shimmering veil of mist, Zephyr felt a rush of memories wash over her as she staggered forward.

[40]
KANTI

"ARE YOU OK, SWEETHEART?" ASKED GRANDMA JUNE.

"Yeah," whispered Zephyr. "It just kind of hit me all at once, that's all. But I have to remember it's different this time."

"That's exactly right. You're in charge now."

If you say so.

Scam walked with uncharacteristic calm as Zephyr and her grandma held hands, swimming through the milky air toward the direction of the forest. Zephyr looked down at him as he strolled a couple feet ahead on his leash. *He seems right at home out here in the moon mist. Maybe he's been a ghost for so long, this otherworldly atmosphere feels comforting to him. Maybe he knows he's going back to where he belongs. At least I hope that's where he's going.* After several yards, her grandma stopped.

"I think this is close enough. What do you think?" she asked Zephyr.

She nodded. "I think probably so."

"I'm going to step back a little. I don't want to interfere. But remember, I'm right here behind you, sweetie." Grandma June gave her a quick hug and moved silently behind her into the mist. Scam sat down and leaned against Zephyr's leg. She dropped his leash, feeling certain he'd stick close to her. Shutting her eyes, she repeated the breathing ritual she'd performed in the White cemetery.

As her pulse slowed, she opened her eyes and spoke. "Kanti. Kanti, please come to me. I have much to tell you." In her mind's eye, she envisioned the white canoe drifting toward her and Kanti's gentle face drawing nearer. She closed her eyes and called silently. *Kanti. Kanti. Please come to me now. Sam, I'm here, boy!*

Zephyr visualized the green glow of Kanti's lantern as it shone through the whiteness. She heard a sudden, soft inhalation behind her as her grandma gasped. Opening her eyes, Zephyr saw a point of green light gleaming from within a white, luminous halo. *She's here.* As the light came closer, Zephyr heard the rhythmic dipping of the paddle into the spectral waters and saw the bow of the canoe slide into view. Just as before, the canoe floated not on water, but on a cloud of mist, creating its own aqueous passageway. Zephyr watched the paddle dip and lift, and then Kanti's lovely face shone through the white glowing mist. Zephyr strained to see Sam.

"Zephyr. You came back," Kanti said, smiling, though her eyes remained sad. "And I see you've brought Cat."

Zephyr looked down at Scam who now stood at attention, a soft glow surrounding his body.

"Of course! Where's Sam? Is he alright?"

At the sound of his name, Sam's shimmering head popped up from behind Kanti, his whimper melting Zephyr's heart.

"He is fine. Sam is a good dog," she smiled and reached around to pat his glimmering back.

"I know." Zephyr's voice trembled. "C-can they—"

"Did you find the coin?" Kanti broke in. "Did you find..."

Zephyr bit her lip. *Get a grip. Stay in control.* "Yes, Kanti, I found the coin in the stump, just like you said. It's beautiful, thank you. And I've come with news—news about your little boy, Ahanu."

Kanti's dark eyes grew wide, sparkling through the swirling vapor. "Tell me! Have you found him? Is he safe? Can I see him?" she begged, placing the paddle across her lap.

Closing her eyes, Zephyr inhaled deeply and called on that new side of herself to guide her through this. *Grandma believes in my new abilities. It's time I believed in them myself.* Stepping closer to Kanti, she looked into her pleading eyes. "Kanti, Ahanu is safe. And I am certain you will be able to see him again, but you must listen carefully. What I have to tell you may be hard for you to understand, although I think if you listen with your heart, it will become clear to you."

"Please tell me," Kanti begged, her hands griping the paddle as she leaned forward.

Zephyr nodded as she pressed her hand against the comforting warmth of her pendant. "As you told me, Ahanu wandered away while you were sleeping. A colonial woman found him in the woods and took him home with her."

Kanti's eyes further widened and her lips parted, a mixture of confusion and surprise flooding her face.

"Her name was Anna and she was a kind woman, but you see, she gave birth five times and all of her dear babies died while they were still very young."

Pain shot through Kanti's face as she shook her head. "How terrible for her."

"Yes, it was terrible. So as soon as she saw Ahanu, she fell in love with him and wanted to protect him and keep him safe from the harms of the world that she'd seen befall her own children."

Kanti nodded. "I am glad of that. But..." her voice trailed off.

But why didn't she try to find his mother? Zephyr pushed forward. "Anna's heart was so broken by losing her own babies that I don't believe she was thinking very clearly anymore, and I don't think her husband had the heart to deny her what she longed for most in the whole world—a child of their own to love and care for."

Kanti's smooth brow creased in concentration. It was obvious she was desperately trying to understand. "So...she kept my child?"

"Yes, she did. She wanted to let you know he was safe and in good health, and I think she may have even considered returning him to you, but something stopped her before she had the chance."

"What was it?" Kanti asked breathlessly, folding her hands close against her chest.

Zephyr pursed her lips. *How do you tell someone they were killed?* "Anna found out that a Nansemond woman had been searching deep in the swamp for her lost child, but before she could reach her, the woman was bitten by a snake...and..."

Kanti lowered her hands, and spoke just above a whisper, "...and died."

Zephyr exhaled. "Yes, she...*you*...died."

Tears shimmered in Kanti's eyes and trickled down her pale cheeks, matching the tears slipping down Zephyr's face. "I'm so sorry, Kanti."

Kanti wiped the back of her hand across her eyes and sat up straighter. A line creased her forehead as she shook her head. "But this Anna did not return Ahanu to our family? Not even to my cousin who lived nearby?"

"No," breathed Zephyr. "She absolutely should have, and I know she realizes that now. She knows that it was wrong to keep him away from his people. Her soul was bound to the earth, to a lonely graveyard, with the torment of that guilt."

Kanti's deep sigh shuddered through the mist and Zephyr watched as her sweet Sam leaned in against her with comfort. "And did she take good care of my child?" Kanti asked.

Zephyr sniffed back her own tears. "Yes, she did. She brought him up as though he were her own. She did not know what you called him, so she named him Moses, and she and her husband gave him their last name—Stone."

Kanti nodded. "And did he have a happy life?"

"I am sure he did, Kanti. He grew up and married and had children of his own. And those children had children, and so on down the years until I was born over three hundred years later. My family name is Stone, and Moses—your Ahanu—is one of my ancestral grandfathers."

Kanti's mouth hung agape. "Then, you mean, you are one of the children of my future? You are my daughter of tomorrow?"

Zephyr nodded as new tears sprung from her eyes at this beautiful description of their relationship. Kanti rose and stepped from her canoe, reaching her hands toward Zephyr. "Come closer to me, child. Do not be afraid."

Zephyr looked back at Grandma June. "She's getting out of the canoe and she wants me to come closer. She's telling me to not be afraid. Do you...do you think it's OK?"

"Go to her, Zephyr," urged Grandma June. "I can't see her, but I can feel her presence somehow, and I'm sure you have nothing to fear. It feels right."

Zephyr nodded and took a deep breath. *It feels right to me, too.* She heard Sam's soft whimper as she walked forward, watching the spirit's diaphanous form grow as solid as her own while she held out her hands to Zephyr. *But how is this happening? How can I touch a ghost?*

As if reading her thoughts or her confused expression, Kanti explained, "When I meet a kindred spirit like you, I can will myself to push into your world so you can see me, and if I draw all my strength together, I can even make myself whole and firm again for a short while. It tires me, but I can manage it if it's important enough to me. And...you are that important to me, Zephyr."

Zephyr stepped closer and took the spirit hands into hers. She expected them to be cold, but they were as warm as Kanti's smile.

"You are so very beautiful, my Zephyr." She released her hand and stroked Zephyr's hair. "It is like the rising of the sun," she said, gazing at the silky red locks slipping through her fingers. "To me, you are the dawn, or *Wapun* in my language."

Zephyr found it hard to pull any words from her throat, but she knew she had one more thing she must say. "I have something to ask of you."

Kanti remained close but took a small step back. "Yes?"

"Anna asked me if you could please forgive her for not returning Ahanu to you or your people."

Kanti lowered her head and closed her eyes, dropping her hands to her sides. It seemed a lifetime before she raised her head and looked into Zephyr's eyes, then shook her head slowly from side to side.

Oh no. I was afraid this might happen.

"What she did was wrong," Kanti explained. "She kept Ahanu away from me and away from his family. Because of her, he never knew the ways of our people."

Zephyr bit her bottom lip. *Is she too hurt? Will she leave? Will she take Sam with her?*

"I cannot forgive a woman...who took my child into her heart and into her home and gave him the love I would have given him if I could have." Kanti raised her chin and continued in a firm voice. "But that is because there is nothing to forgive. She was wrong to keep him, but she did what she thought was best for him and I am grateful to her for that."

Kanti opened her arms and Zephyr pressed herself into her embrace. "Thank you, Kanti," she whispered.

"No, my Wapun," Kanti said, pulling herself away and holding Zephyr's hands. "It is for me to thank you. And now," she said, smiling and releasing her hands, "it is time for me to go." Looking down, her smile broadened. "Come, Cat!"

In a dizzying flash, Zephyr watched as the cat's spirit sprang from Sam's body and into the white canoe. Zephyr gasped as her beagle's body collapsed to the cold ground. "Sam!" she cried and dropped to the damp earth beside his lifeless form. Clutching his limp body, Zephyr rocked him and wept.

"Oh no," she heard Grandma June whisper behind her.

A raucous bellow split the quiet air and Zephyr looked up just in time to see Sam's glittering spirit leap out of the canoe through the milky moon mist and into his body. "Sam!" she cried again but, this time, with joyful tears spilling from her eyes as her dog, whole again with his spirit intact, jumped to his feet and hugged his front paws around her neck. Her dear Sam wasted no time in covering her face with warm, sloppy kisses.

Kanti's light laughter sparkled around them as she stepped back into her canoe. Cat rubbed his face against her arm as she raised her hand in farewell. Dipping her paddle into the current of mist, the canoe floated backward. "Live well and live long, Wapun. You are as brave as you are beautiful, and your heart's love will guide you until we see each other again."

Zephyr stood and lifted her hand in a silent goodbye, and although she couldn't begin to find the words to express her love and gratitude, she knew that Kanti, this woman whose DNA coursed through her own blood, understood completely. Family love was timeless, with ties that bind across generations, connecting those separated too soon and even those who might never meet in person. As soon as Kanti disappeared into the mist, the air began to clear, and in her place, stood a great white egret. Sam leaned heavily against Zephyr's leg as Grandma June stepped forward, placing her arm around her granddaughter's waist. Together, they watched as the luminous bird sprang into the air and flew across the ivory glow of the full moon.

"What a Thanksgiving, huh?" whispered her grandma. "We have a lot to be thankful for."

"Yes we do." Zephyr sent up a silent prayer of thanks for her grandma and for all the grandmas who had come before her. She gave thanks for the love that held families together. And she even gave thanks, at least a little bit, for the strange gift she'd been given.

[41]
OPEN FOR BUSINESS

A FEW DAYS BEFORE CHRISTMAS, ZEPHYR LAY SPRAWLED on the living room couch, enjoying the first full day of winter break away from school. Her parents were in their office finalizing a marketing campaign they wanted to complete before the end of the year, and she'd just gotten off the phone with Lorie. They'd planned to meet up for lunch at Lorie's house to do some last-minute Christmas shopping with Mrs. Garcia.

Thumbing through the new wall calendar that Grandma June had given her as an early present, Zephyr stopped at August's page and smiled. With her new pen that had come with the calendar, she circled Saturday the 18th and wrote "Nansemond Pow Wow" inside the white square. Zephyr sighed with contentment and scratched Sam's head as he nestled close beside her.

Life is good.

She aimed the TV remote at the screen on the wall opposite the couch and clicked through the choices of Christmas movies to watch. *Elf, It's a Wonderful Life, The Nightmare Before Christmas*...the list went on.

"Ahem," a male voice cleared his throat behind her.

Sam looked up and thumped his tail on the seat cushion.

Zephyr leaned up on one elbow and twisted around to look over the back of the couch. "Yes, Da—" She scrambled to her feet as her heart jumped into her throat.

A man she'd never seen before, dressed in what looked to be very old-fashioned army gear, stood in the archway leading to their dining room, glowing as though lit from the inside out. He took a step backward and held up one hand. "Excuse me. I'm sorry to disturb you. But we were told you could help us."

"H-help you?" she stammered, sidling back towards the hallway leading to her parents' office.

The man removed his bowl-shaped helmet and nodded. "Yes ma'am."

"Who are you?" asked Zephyr. *I should ask* what *are you, but judging by your shimmer, I know you've got to be another ghost!*

"Private First Class Ronald Barnes," he said, squaring his shoulders and saluting.

Barnes? Like Luke *Barnes?*

The soldier lowered his hand and continued, "I'm kind of home on leave from the war, you see." A wave of confusion flooded his young features. *He looks as confused as I am!* Somehow, that actually made her feel better. "But...but," he seemed to search for words. "All I know for sure is that we understand you can help us."

"*Us?*" repeated Zephyr.

"Yes," he said and stepped to one side, gesturing with his gloved hand.

Zephyr's jaw dropped as a line of luminous, semi-transparent people, dressed in all kinds of clothes from different periods in history, suddenly appeared, encircling the living room walls, weaving around and *through* the furniture.

Whoa. Zephyr staggered back to the couch and held onto it for balance as Sam continued to sit, gazing at Private Barnes and quietly thumping his tail against the seat cushion.

Scanning the anxious, ghostly faces, Zephyr's heart skipped a few beats. Could they *all* be lost souls asking for her help? *Am I even up to this?* Returning her gaze to the young soldier, she realized that he actually bore some resemblance to Luke. *Could...could they be related?* Private Barnes lowered his head for a moment as if giving her time to think, but when he looked back up at her, a tear glittered at the corner of his eye, and Zephyr knew her answer. She knew she had to try. Shrugging her shoulders in resignation, she took a deep breath of determination, remembering Grandma June's belief that gifts were given for a reason.

OK then. Take a number. Like it or not, it looks like Zephyr Stone, Ghost Charmer, is open for business!

ACKNOWLEDGMENTS

With this, my first traditionally published novel, I feel a bit like an actor clutching her first Oscar—staring out at the audience with a deer-in-the-headlights gaze—struggling to remember and acknowledge all the people to whom she wishes to thank, and worried she will leave someone out. So, with that caveat firmly in place, I will attempt to make my "acceptance speech."

My acknowledgements begin with my family. Thank you, to Oleta and G. C. Wood who, although no longer in my physical world, remain ever close in heart and spirit. I feel their encouragement and their love of the written word in my very bones. To my dear brother Terry, and irrepressible sister-in-law Betty Wood, who served as knowledgeable Beta readers. To my loving daughters Emily and Bevan, and their beloved husbands John Sutton and Gillen Elder, respectively. To my cherished grandchildren, Ava and Gabriella Sutton, and Colin Elder, who inspire me to write for young readers. To a lifetime of encouragement from my extended family, here and in the here-after. And, of course, to Bill, my darling husband of eight timeless years to whom this book is dedicated, and to the broader family he has ushered into my life.

So many friends have supported my writer's dream over the years and I am grateful to all of them but, in this limited space, I will name those who have served as my Beta readers and critique partners. To the talented and loyal members of my local writers' group, Wordsmiths of the Inner Banks, (in alphabetical order) Bill Ahearn, Chris Barber, Vernon Fueston, Mary Montgomery, and Michael Soper. To my friend and favorite "library lady," Claudia Resta, and to the Middle Grade students she brought under her wing to serve as my youngest Beta readers, Annelise Gummere, Carolyn Ayers, and Morgan Godwin.

To my remarkable hometown library and home away from home, Shepard-Pruden Memorial of Edenton, North Carolina. Head librarian, Jennifer Finlay, and her dedicated staff welcome readers with open arms and open hearts, kindred spirits all.

To Nikki Bass, a member of the Nansemond Indian Nation, who graciously read the passages related to the Nansemond, and offered her invaluable knowledge and insight.

To the Great Dismal Swamp National Wildlife Refuge and its enlightening visitor center, which helped inspire and inform the writing of this book.

To Blue Ink Press and its impressive team of professionals, who have worked diligently to help bring my book to life, with special acknowledgement to the tenacious, but kind, Christa Leonhart for her first round of meticulous editing. Thank you all for my warm welcome and for seeing Zephyr's potential. She lives in the world because of you!

Last but not least, I am grateful to all the young readers and to the adults who encourage them to spend time in the world of books. Thank you for including Zephyr and her friends in that special place in your lives.

Kate

ABOUT THE AUTHOR

Kathryn Louise Wood was born in Washington, North Carolina with deep ancestral roots in her home state stretching back to the 17th century. She received her BS in Education from Old Dominion University in Norfolk, Virginia and, as a life-long learner and wearer of multiple hats, has worked as a teacher, social worker, television re-enactment actress, nationally certified massage therapist, writer, and award-winning photographic artist. She and her husband live in the lovely, historic town of Edenton, NC, sharing their quirky, little 1890s cottage with their dogs, and the memories of loved ones with whom they have shared their lives.

CPSIA information can be obtained
at www.ICGtesting.com
Printed in the USA
FSHW010308210321
79698FS

9 781948 449090